BETWEEN THE SHEETS

BETWEEN THE SHEETS

REDONDO AND ROSE NEIGHBORS IN CRIME
BOOK 2

BONNIE HARDY

"I don't like to call it revenge.
Returning the favor sounds nicer."

Unknown Origin

VIVIENNE ROSE

Vivienne Rose

"Take a look at him." Rex Redondo pointed. "He's just a toddler and really good on that tricycle." A young boy pedaled down the middle of the street, his chubby legs pumping.

Rex's hand gripped her shoulder. "Oh oh!" The small boy's bike leaned to the left as he narrowly missed running down the orange cone. Several had been placed in the street, serving as an obstacle course.

An older man stood nearby on the grass. "Keep going, Josh. Look out for the next one!" He waved at Rex and Viv, a look of pride in his wide smile. "Isn't he great? Just like Ross Chastain," the man shouted.

"Who's that?" Viv called out.

"You know," the man explained, "like the NASCAR driver. My grandson. He's something else."

The sound of a blaring horn made the hair stand on

Viv's neck. A sleek gray Mercedes slid around the corner. Driving past the residential speed limit, the car headed straight toward the little boy.

Viv gasped as brakes squealed.

Rex shouted in alarm, "Look out!"

The grandfather froze, his eyes wide with horror.

The trike hit a cone which fell over as the boy tipped off the seat collapsing onto the pavement. The sound of an electric car engine whirred away as the child's piercing wail met Viv's ears.

She darted into the street toward the child. Bending closer, her eyes traveled over his body. "It's okay, sweetie. You'll be fine," she assured him. The little boy sat up, tears streaming down his face.

Smoothing back the hair on his forehead, Viv's trained fingers gently probed his small arm. *Nothing broken.* A cut on his chin oozed blood. She reached into her pocket, pulling out a wad of tissues. Dabbing at the wound, she smiled into his eyes. Her mind continuing to assess. *The wound can be cleaned, might need a stitch.* The next glance affirmed her opinion. Dirt from the road covered both of his knees. *A little skinned up.*

"Is he okay?" The grandfather bent over Viv, his hand reaching for the child.

The child thrust his arms over his head. "Grandpa," he cried. The grandfather reached down and scooped the boy into his arms. Viv watched the child cling to the chest of the older man.

The man spoke over the boy's shoulder. "My wife is going to be furious. She's always telling me not to let him play in the street." He bent his head to whisper assurances. "It's okay, buddy. I've got you. You're going to be right as rain." The child buried his face further into his grandfather's shirt. But the tears had stopped.

Viv stood. "I'd take him to the ER to have him checked out. Just in case."

Perspiration beaded down the side of the older man's face. "Good idea," he said with a nod. "I'm going to take him right now. And thank you." His voice choked with emotion.

Once the man left, Rex turned to Viv. "Are you okay?"

"What, about that?" She pointed to the trike lying in the street. The handlebars tilted backward, an orange cone trapped underneath the front wheel.

When Rex raised an eyebrow she answered his question. "I was really scared." She brushed her hands against her slacks. "I'm going to pick this up," she pointed to the trike again, "and then drag those cones out of the road."

"Why don't you let me help at least." Rex lifted the trike in one hand. Viv grabbed a cone and made her way to the sidewalk. In a matter of minutes Rex had stacked the others, leaving them on the grass.

"The car didn't even stop." Rex looked toward the community exit.

Viv's eyes narrowed. "Isn't that just what we wanted to talk to the board about? Kids playing in the streets, how dangerous that is. And now there's been an actual accident.

"I think he's going to be fine, only scrapes and bruises. Mostly, he was just frightened," Viv added, more to reassure herself and to calm down.

"Did you see who was driving?" Rex asked.

"A guy with a shaved head. Probably mid forties. He gunned that engine and didn't even stop to see if the child was okay." Viv shook her head in disappointment. "I only have first aid training. I do hope the boy is alright," she said again, feeling as if she should have insisted more strongly about having the child checked out by a doctor.

"So we'll bring that up at our first meeting," Rex assured her. "At the homeowner's meeting. We're still going, right?"

"I want to go more than ever," she stated firmly. "A fifty-five-plus neighborhood is not supposed to have children playing in the middle of the main road. Why do people think it's okay to treat the street like their backyard?"

He placed his hand on her elbow. "So we're a bit late. But let's take that indignation and put it to good use. Our first HOA meeting."

His voice sounded reassuring, but Viv still felt mad. Even though she did agree with Rex that the best course would be to take this up with the board. The list of community rules was long, but it didn't matter when there was no one to make sure they were enforced.

REX REDONDO

As they quickened their pace toward the clubhouse, Rex felt proud of Viv's indignation. She didn't just let things slide. Plus her sensitivity to the safety of babies and young children came naturally; she'd been a doula for most of her adult life.

Originally he wanted to attend the HOA meeting just to be with her. He planned on making comments about the upkeep of the Desert Tortoise Estates landscape. A safe and common topic for that kind of gathering.

But he had to admit that the artificial turf, scattered with planters of living greenery, looked very tidy and well kept. As was the outside of the community clubhouse where the HOA meetings were held.

Solar lights lined the pathway to the front entrance of the clubhouse. As for the main building, clay roofing contrasted nicely with the tan stucco outer walls. The artificial turf, trimmed to fit against a secondary sand border, added to the effect. *No weeds in sight*, Rex thought. Plus the Joshua trees, planted sparingly, made the fake turf look real.

"They remind me of Dr. Seuss illustrations." Vivienne

nodded toward the trees. "They aren't trees exactly, but they are so much more than bushes."

"It took some getting used to, when I moved here. But now I'm growing quite fond of the scraggly little fellows," Rex admitted.

Once they stood in front of the clubhouse, he nodded to a sign taped on the glass door. "HOA meeting in the conference room," he read aloud. "This is the place." Rex opened the door to let her go first.

He immediately noticed the three oversized sofas. They'd been arranged for conversation in a horseshoe shape, with an enormous coffee table in the middle. The one side, left open toward the main window, overlooked the Desert Tortoise Golf Course.

Attention to the detail of a room was a habit of Rex's. Once he took in the furniture he'd consider the next step. He called it reading the room. Using his intuition and senses, he determined, *Lots of parties have gone on here. Right underneath the facade there's a weird odor. Decay or deceit. Can't tell which.*

One glance at the bar in the corner confirmed his impression. *Deals are made in this room. Along with liberal amounts of booze.* He turned to Viv. "They're not meeting here. Let's walk down the hall and have a look." He took her hand.

Closed doors lined each side of the hallway, reminding him of a hotel. At the end of the hall a sign taped to a door read "HOA meeting in session." He hesitated, but only briefly. Without knocking, he reached for the handle.

One glance told him they were in the right place. A group of twenty or so folding chairs had been placed in the center of the room, all facing the same direction. A couple of feet in front of the chairs, men were seated around a conference table. Rex made a quick observation. *All of them caucasian. Hair mostly shades of gray. Dressed in shirts with logos.*

They stopped talking to look up.

If we sit in the back row it looks like we're afraid of the board. If we sit in the middle row, we aren't committed and we look wishy-washy. That's it. Front row for us.

Rex gestured toward the front row, where Viv sat demurely, hands folded in her lap. He sat next to her, leaning his body closer. *She's like a magnet for me.* Feeling the warmth of her skin, he concluded, *Viv runs very warm when she's anxious. One of her tells.*

Aware that his own nerves tingled, Rex narrowed his eyes. The heightened sense of excitement was a clue for him to pay attention. That something was coming next. Often the feeling was followed by images. He'd once tried to explain to Sutton how that worked, right before he hired her as his personal assistant.

"So you're not psychic," she'd said, skepticism in her voice.

"I'm just a guy with a committee in his head," Rex explained. "And I have pictures too. It may be because I've worked so many casinos, but images roll right behind my eyes like a slot machine, only no fruit. It's not like three lemons or anything. I never lose or win. I just see pictures and I have to decide what's important."

Sutton didn't ask any more questions after that.

Viv leaned over to whisper in his ear. "We seem to be the only people attending besides the group of six wearing pastel polo shirts."

She's got that right. I've never seen so many pastel polo shirts around a table at the same meeting. I wonder who's in charge? He blinked.

The image of a king-sized bed flashed briefly on his inner screen. Then a down comforter, followed by an unopened package of crisp, neatly folded white sheets. The label read: Embroidered Pinzon 400 thread count Egyptian cotton satin hotel stitch sheet set. Chic and elegant, soft and durable.

He blinked again. This time he saw fluffy pillows propped up against a quilted headboard. The images kept rolling. He blinked again, aware of a spark of excitement trickling down his spine.

Viv nudged him with her elbow. "Are you okay?" she whispered. "You have a funny look on your face."

Rex smiled, his nerves and images merging into a new sense of excitement. "I'm amazing, thank you." He took her hand in his, giving it a quick squeeze. *Now that's what I call insight.*

The images could only mean one thing. It didn't take a mentalist to figure that out. *Viv and I are heading to her house right after this meeting. All those fancy sheets and fluffy pillows. I only have one thing to say. Yowzah!*

3

VIVIENNE ROSE

The man at the head of the table looked up. "The meeting will now come to order," came his light baritone voice.

I guess he's the big cheese, Viv thought. She glanced at his name plate on the table. *Frank Salucci,* spelled in bold black letters.

Frank tipped his head toward Viv, his blue eyes looking slightly salacious. *Did he just lick his lips? Ick.* She didn't feel the smile. Not like Rex, when he directed his thousand-watt grin toward her. When he was on stage, that was another smile entirely. On stage he pretended.

A ladies' man. That's how Frank Salucci thinks of himself. I'm the only woman in the room so I get his attention. Even if I am old. Viv adjusted her seat, leaving her hands folded in her lap.

Likely in his mid sixties, Frank Salucci had that air of authority. While the other men at the table shuffled papers, he gave instructions. "We'll get the minutes approved and move on to other business as soon as Joey shows up. I'm wondering what's taking him so long?"

Viv had the feeling people did not make a habit of being

late with Frank Salucci. He had that way about him, like a jaguar stalking its prey, waiting for one slip and then *gulp*, you're dinner.

"I need to talk about the casita rentals," a man sitting next to Frank spoke out. "We're losing money."

"Not now, Pete. Like I said, we're waiting for Joey. And then Dean has to read the minutes from last month first. There's no need to rush." Salucci's voice sounded firm. He looked over at Viv again, as if waiting for her to agree. His attention made her nervous. She didn't like being the only female in the room.

Before she could issue him one of her well-honed withering glances, a loud voice came from down the hall. Viv turned to look over her shoulder right as the door swung open.

A woman stood in the threshold, tall and lean with the posture of someone used to unceremoniously interrupting people. She was dressed like a cop. Crisp white button-up shirt. Tan slacks. Brown belt. She held a badge extended in her right hand. Her voice curt.

"Stop the meeting." She made her way toward the conference table.

The officer passed Viv and Rex without a glance. Her eyes stared directly at Frank Salucci. "I am Officer Susan Farrah." The words came as a challenge, as if she dared him to disagree. "We're responding to a 911 call. A housekeeper found a dead body in one of the casitas by the golf course."

She looked at each man at the table. Dean's face registered disbelief. Samuel Daniel's jaw clamped shut. Farrah's eyes drifted past the empty seat, where Joey Baker's name plaque stood. "He's not here yet?" She pointed.

Pete Langford spoke up. "He's just running late." Even to Viv's untrained ear the excuse felt flimsy. The one guy missing at the table would most likely be the first one interviewed by Officer Farrah.

Viv gasped as Rex reached his arm around her shoulders. With a quick glance she looked at the officer again, realizing this wasn't the first time she'd seen her. The name was familiar. But the woman's demeanor was different. *She's looking good. Much better than the last time we met.*

Susan Farrah barked another order. "I'll get one of my sergeants to track him down. The rest of you sit still."

To Viv's surprise Frank Salucci had a somewhat amused expression on his face, his mouth open slightly, a smirk at the corner. From the front row she clearly saw his icy stare, taking in the officer in charge. His overall impression was one of nonchalance, like he heard about dead bodies every day.

"Who's dead?" he asked, his voice casual. As if that question came naturally, just like, "*What's for dinner?*" Then he laid both hands on the table.

Susan Farrah flinched. Her head jerked back for just a second, then she spread her legs out and squared her shoulders. Although she recovered quickly, it was obvious Salucci got under her skin.

"My team will be interviewing everyone at this table in just a few minutes. Like I said, don't go far."

Viv had to hand it to her, Susan Farrah had taken command of the room. She watched as the policewoman's eyes glanced over each of the name plates and then at the man sitting behind. After each inspection, she paused to write in her notebook. The corner of her mouth tightening.

Once she closed the notebook she turned to Viv and Rex. "Why are you two here?"

"Hello again," Viv said.

"Hello." Susan gave a small smile.

Rex stood. "Officer Farrah. Looks like you've got another situation on your hands." He kept his hands in his pockets.

The men at the table remained silent, watching the interaction.

Farrah cleared her throat. "So what brings you two to the meeting?"

"We're homeowners," Viv explained.

"We have concerns," Rex admitted. "Some landscaping issues." He glanced up at the ceiling.

"And children being allowed to play in the street." Viv sounded indignant. "On the way here we saw a child on his tricycle almost hit by a silver Mercedes. The driver was speeding on Joshua Tree Way. He didn't even stop."

"Did you now?" Farrah pulled out her notebook. "Didn't happen to jot down the license number, did you?"

"No," Viv mumbled.

"I know the plate," Rex interjected. He tapped his temple with his finger. Viv recognized one of his on-stage gestures. "It said, 'Just Win.'" He nodded with certainty.

"Shouldn't be too hard to look up." Farrah's pencil scratched across the paper in her notebook. "You two don't need to stay. I think I have everything I need here," she added.

Rex replied, "I can't argue with that. Maybe I'll head over to the casita to see what's going on." He offered his hand to Viv, helping her to her feet.

"Stay away from my crime scene," Farrah said firmly. "You're not involved with this investigation. I've got everything under control."

Viv smiled appreciatively. "I'm sure you do. We wouldn't have gotten involved last time if it hadn't been for your..." She paused and then added, "Unexpected leave of absence. But now I can see you're on duty so we'll just head home." She bumped Rex with her hip, hoping he wouldn't disagree.

Her heart pumped rapidly in her chest as they walked toward the door. Once out of earshot, she asked, "Are we really going to look at the casita and the crime scene?"

"I don't need permission to check out my own neighborhood," Rex replied. "Nice cover back there, by the way. If I didn't know you better, I'd say you outright lied to the officer. Let's get going before she can stop us."

Outside the building, Rex grinned. "This may be our next case. If there's a dead body in that casita like Farrah was saying, then Redondo and Rose are back."

"I have no intention of another case," Viv said.

"This has to be a murder," Rex continued, brushing aside her objection. "Otherwise why would the cop be so official. Like I was saying, if there's a dead body, we can pick up where we left off. I'll be Philip Marlowe." He pulled at his earlobe, tugging the brim of an invisible fedora.

Viv scowled. "You've been doing that a lot lately. Pulling your earlobe. I think I've seen that before. In a movie."

"*The Big Sleep*," he answered. "Bogart plays Marlowe in that film. He pulls on his earlobe all the time."

"And flirts with Lauren Bacall," Viv said.

"You're some kind of dame." He lowered his voice to imitate Bogart. "Let's head over to the casitas and see what's goin' on."

Rex offered his elbow with a smile.

He's irresistible, she thought. Then, despite her better judgement, she took his elbow, knowing full well she'd probably regret the decision sooner rather than later.

4

REX REDONDO

Rex massaged his temples, an index finger on each side of his head. Most people would have been shocked rather than perplexed at the sight of the dead body lying between the carefully folded sheets. Not Rex. He'd seen the bed, at least, earlier in the evening. Only it didn't mean what he thought. Not by a long shot.

Viv stood next to him. He felt her body stiffen. "He's dead all right," she said in a low voice.

It only took the one glance to confirm that the man, lying on his back, arms folded across his chest, had shed his mortal coil. The one hole in the middle of his forehead gave proof to this foregone conclusion.

"Poor guy," Rex sadly agreed.

If anyone were to ask, the sadness in his voice was mostly for the dead man, but he also felt sad for himself. Maybe more like disappointed. He'd misinterpreted the previous images of the sheets and pillows as a premonition for himself and Viv.

It turned out to be a warning that someone would end up in less fortunate circumstances. Because the man lay in the exact same sheets, fancy embroidery included. Rex sighed heavily.

"There's something kind of innocent about his arms. The freckles." Viv nodded toward the dead man.

Even Rex agreed that the freckled skin covering the dead guy's arms made him seem rather childlike. But then there were larger age spots at his wrists and on the backs of his hands. "He's not that young," Rex mumbled.

"He's at least fifty, considering those age spots." She looked down at her own hands as if to confirm.

"Let's see if we can get a better look before the cops come back." Rex glanced over his shoulder to make sure the cops were not down the hall.

"What are you two doing here?" Officer Farrah interjected. She looked fit to be tied. "I warned you. You're not allowed to step into my crime scene!"

Rex stepped away from the bed, adopting his most innocent demeanor. It wasn't hard. He'd practiced for years. As a mentalist he never let people know what he was really thinking or feeling. He even had a name for his presumed persona: the caught-with-my-hand-in-the-cookie-jar move. Eyes opening a little wider. Slight smile at the corner of his mouth. Then the lift of his right shoulder. He assumed a whiff of contriteness. Not too apologetic, just boyish, with a dash of charm and the twinkle of his eyes.

Rex knew better than to overuse this move; he saved it for the stage and when he was attracted to a woman. And he had to admit to himself, over the years he'd been able to defuse plenty of arguments with women who couldn't resist his I'm-such-a-naughty-boy attitude.

He glanced at Farrah, his eyes wide. He'd know soon enough if his persona worked.

The officer only glared at him. "Explain yourselves."

Okay, so she's not having it. He looked at Viv. Her eyebrow raised.

Finally he broke the silence. "We thought the body would have already been removed. You can't help the curiosity of two neighbors, now can you?"

Even to his ears the excuse sounded lame.

5

REX REDONDO

"Get out of here," Officer Farrah commanded. "Or I'll arrest you for obstruction."

Rex's voice, smooth as a baby's skin, rose to disagree. "Oh, surely you don't mean that. We were really quite helpful the last time." He turned to Viv. "Plus there are two of us now, a team. Working for the course of justice." He reached for Viv's hand.

When she yanked it away he casually lowered his arm. "We're only here to help." Rex added a nod to make his point sound convincing.

Farrah blinked. "So she's your partner now, is she. My recollection is that you just met a few months ago. And then you called the cops because you were snooping over her fence and saw the body when she was at work. You're that guy, right? The mentalist from the casino?"

Used to hecklers and naysayers, Rex didn't blink. Maybe Officer Farrah wasn't susceptible to his little boy charm. Okay, he knew some women who weren't. Not many, but some. He knew what to do—he'd disarm her by immediately agreeing and then changing the subject.

"That's right! I'm happy you remembered. And yes, we are friends now. That's due to the kindness of this woman standing next to me. She's something. A rare human being who keeps an open mind and doesn't jump to conclusions."

Rex knew that his power of persuasion was one of his best tools. He put subtle ideas into people's heads, which they would later assume they'd come to on their own.

But Farrah's body language, her glaring eyes, and straight-lipped mouth, made him wonder. *Am I losing my touch? Did I get into her head or not?* He waited for a clue, a softening of her expression indicating attraction or, at the very least, interest in what he was saying.

When Farrah stepped back and folded her arms over her chest, he knew he'd missed his mark again. *Okay, have it your way,* he thought. In that moment Rex felt a certain admiration for Officer Farrah. The rare woman, like Vivienne Rose, for example, who didn't respond to his moves. He remembered telling Sutton about that just a few months ago.

"I like how Viv isn't taken in by me, my little games," he'd admitted to Sutton over a beer. "She's a challenge."

"I think you may have overestimated your charm on women," Sutton commented matter-of-factly. "I don't care about your little boy act either. So that makes two of us. Viv and me. Like this." She held up two fingers close together.

Farrah's fierce glare brought Rex back to the present. The fierceness in her gaze made the color of her eyes shift slightly. From sky blue to a darker shade of indigo. Then she dropped her arms, her mouth softening at the corners. She didn't smile, but she wasn't grimacing either.

If I'm not mistaken, she's changed her mind. This is a good sign. And now I know that she's resistant yet susceptible to the power of suggestion. He glanced quickly at Viv again, hoping she'd notice how expertly he'd handled the situation. Unfortunately, Viv paid no attention to him or Officer Farrah. She kept staring at the body in the bed.

Rex followed her gaze. The dead man lay against the white embroidered pillowcases. His mouth hung open as if he'd been caught by surprise. Hands lay poised over the folded edge of the expensive sheets, which had been pulled up to touch his double chin. Rex knew the linens were pricey because they were embroidered. Black thread with D.T.E. for Desert Tortoise Estates was on every pillowcase and at the corner of the top sheet.

"He's dead, right?" Viv looked to Farrah for confirmation. "I assumed, you know, with the bullet hole and everything. But you're the professional." Her voice trembled.

"Yes, he is," Farrah answered in a lowered voice. She instantly sounded less confrontational. "And let me remind you once again, you are not invited to this crime scene. I'll give you both one more chance to go home quietly. And none of your mentalist shenanigans either!" She saved a glower for Rex.

At that moment a paramedic walked past Viv, hurrying to the bed. He bent over the dead man. Lifting the crisp linen sheet carefully, he gave it a tug, and then let it fall. The dead man's face was no longer visible.

"Very respectful," Rex said approvingly.

"We're not here to be respectful," Farrah said. "But before you leave, it dawns on me that I may have been a bit hasty to dismiss you so quickly. I may have jumped to conclusions. I forgot to ask: can you identify the victim?"

Rex kept his face immobile. *I did get to her. Because now instead of dismissing us, she's asking questions.* "Oh, I know him well. He frequents Pair-a-Dice."

"He comes to the casino for your shows?" Farrah looked surprised.

"No, not my shows. He drinks at The Roadkill and he gambles. Kind of a high roller. Plays a lot of blackjack."

"I see." Farrah pulled out the pad of paper and pencil from her pocket. She made a note. "Let's step outside. I can ask more questions and then you can go home." But before they could turn to go, she interrupted. "Did you happen to catch his name?"

"I don't know his name," Rex admitted. "Sorry about that."

"You've already helped a lot," Farrah admitted. Her voice sounded more respectful. She turned to Viv. "And you too, Miss Rose. The same question. Did you know the victim?"

"No, I did not." Viv glared at Rex. "I don't gamble. And the dead man doesn't look remotely familiar."

Sensing Viv's irritation, Rex felt uneasy. "So happy we could help." He put his arm around Viv's shoulders protectively and ushered her toward the door. This time she did not shrug away.

Standing together in the cool night air, Viv wasted no time. "So you've seen that guy? That's a real coincidence." She sounded doubtful.

Rex paused for a moment, considering his options. He decided then and there he had to tell Viv the truth, just like he would Sutton. Two of a kind. "I have no idea who that guy is. I just looked him over and made the assumption he's a gambler. His manicured fingernails made me think of a card player."

When she remained silent, he kept talking.

"Plus I wanted an excuse to give the cop, you know, to make me look more useful. She was trying to send us home," he claimed. "I didn't want to be dismissed. So I told her a few details and it worked. She stopped treating us like add-on baggage at the airport."

Viv glared. "You are incorrigible. The lies just flow from your lips. It's second nature with you!" She shook her head at him.

Rex's stomach sank. Somehow he'd gotten into trouble with the woman he'd only wanted to impress. He had hoped that she'd see his good intentions underneath the small fabrications.

He had hoped they would go back to her place and then sit by the pool. Talking about their new case would bring back the energy and intimacy he'd come to anticipate in her presence. And then they could solve the case together. Just like neighbors in crime.

But now she was mad at him. He could feel it in her body language, the way she'd stepped back. And her crisp judgment about lying. That too.

Before he could explain, Officer Farrah came striding through the open door. As she came closer, Rex closed his eyes briefly, then opened them. And in that instant another plan snapped into his head.

He'd solve the murder with Viv. He'd show her how his lies were only used for good, not evil. He'd be sitting by her pool in no time, knocking back an IPA, figuring out who killed the guy inside.

It's gonna work, he told himself. *You really are quite extraordinary, Rex Redondo.*

6

VIVIENNE ROSE

Viv moved closer to stand near a palm tree. She didn't like being triggered, especially not by Rex. He had a way of getting under her skin. She looked up into the night sky. Stars blinked overhead, indifferent and unconcerned about the dead body between the sheets. *I am not going to be an accomplice to this outrageous charade perpetuated by Rex Redondo.*

Her thoughts expressed themselves in words with one syllable. *The. Big. Jerk!*

Two other officers gathered around Farrah. They huddled in conversation as she gave them terse instructions. They immediately took off in opposite directions. Then Farrah called out to Rex. "So tell me what else you know." She lifted her pad of paper, thumbing through the pages. "You must have picked up something, with your super mentalist powers and all."

A bland expression came over his face, accompanied by a slight smile and a nod. He glanced up just enough to give Viv the impression that he was seriously considering the officer's request. She felt her anger shift to fascination. *He's a constant source of entertainment with his different personas.*

And then Rex's phone buzzed. "I have to take this," he explained quietly. Now his voice shifted to a more subdued tone, which was slightly apologetic. Rex stepped toward the casita, out of listening distance.

Officer Farrah gestured to Viv. "Let's talk while he's busy." Viv came closer. "So we meet again," the officer said quietly.

"I remember," Viv answered. She and Farrah had shared an emotionally intimate moment that time in her house. As a line of inquiry, the officer came back the next day to talk to her about her doula agency work. They'd connected right away. More than connected. Viv could tell, just by Farrah's questions, that she'd unearthed some unfinished emotional business underneath her gruff police exterior.

Viv had tried to follow up with the officer the following day by showing up at the police station. Police Chief Waldo Wilson had explained, "My best investigator had to take time off." Viv felt disappointed at the time. But she knew it wasn't her place to ask any more questions.

She'd learned over decades of working with women that a birth could be relived, especially if there was trauma. The very nature of her work brought out stories from women, some long forgotten and pushed aside. And then the stories would resurface unexpectedly. That's how it happened with Susan Farrah that morning in her kitchen.

And now they met again.

"I do remember you, Officer Farrah," Viv said quietly. "I hope you are well since your leave of absence." Viv wondered if she should have mentioned the leave. Well it wasn't exactly a secret. Everyone in the precinct knew because they ended up short-handed.

To her relief, Officer Farrah smiled. "Actually our conversation started a chain of events. I got through it with an excellent counselor, and now I know why I buried my experiences. I'm better. Thanks to you."

"Oh no, it wasn't me." Viv held up her palm as if to wave off Farrah's words. "You had to do the work. I may have been the catalyst, but it often happens that way. Women get to talking, sometimes to perfect strangers, and then a boulder is rolled aside and all kinds of memories and feelings are revealed."

Viv had to admit, looking at the officer, that she seemed different. More centered. Less fragile. She was still someone Viv could easily talk to.

"I did work with the other officer, your substitute from Lily Rock," Viv admitted. "Now she was something else!"

"Janis Jets." Farrah grinned. "She's a handful, right? Very old school and to the point."

"You can say that again," Viv chuckled.

Rex sauntered back from his phone call. He pulled on his earlobe, looking contrite. Viv glared at him, feeling a spark of her former irritation return. *Liar, liar, pants on fire.*

"Unfortunately I can't stay any longer," Rex announced. "My assistant tells me I'm needed for the early show. Last-minute cancellation. Maybe tomorrow? I can stop at the police station and tell you everything I know about..." He waited expectantly for the officer to fill in a name.

Viv knew right away what he was up to. *He's going to have Sutton do a background search and come up with the name of the deceased. Then he'll have information to share and cover up his big fat lie.*

"Carmine Nelson," Officer Farrah told them. "He owns and operates that big Fluff and Fold in town. In fact it's called Carmine's Fluff and Fold. Know the place?"

Viv glared at him, but he didn't seem to notice.

Rex smiled as if he'd known all along. *Just like my Lucas when he'd get caught doing something naughty.* As Farrah glanced at her notebook, Rex gave Viv a quick wink. And then to her annoyance, she felt her heart warm. He'd managed to take away her indignation and anger, replacing it with a tinge of admiration.

Officer Farrah flipped her notepad closed. "I'll see you at the precinct in the morning." Then she turned to Viv. "You can come too. You might know something that could be helpful." She walked toward another officer who waited for her by the door.

Rex nodded toward the path leading away from the casita. "Shall we?" he asked. Offering his elbow, she declined. She kept her arms to her side, not wanting to be touched. To give him credit, he read her signal loud and clear. He shrugged and walked ahead.

"We never got to talk to the HOA. And then the dead body," Viv said, a note of accusation in her voice. "How is it we started the evening one way and it turned in an entirely different direction?"

"The second dead body in our short time together," Rex admitted. "Surely a sign that we're meant to get involved, don't you think?"

"I am not a detective," she said, dismissing his idea. "Let's talk about something else. How about those beautiful sheets. Weren't they something?"

"Actually I had a vision about that bed before we even walked over," he said.

Viv shook her head. "No visions. Not right now. I'm pretty disgusted with you and your lies. You didn't even know the victim's name. But I bet Sutton is already on the case."

He raised both hands in surrender. "Well I did manage to send a text as we were saying goodbye. Sutton will come up with everything we need to know about the dead guy, maybe more than the cops, what with her connections."

Viv felt impatient. She didn't want to hear any more of his bright ideas. Even the talk about the sheets went back to his vision. Hoping to make her irritation go away, she looked up at the full moon, inhaling deeply.

As they strolled back in silence, Viv's previous surge of anger waned. *No use feeling upset with Rex Redondo. It's not like he'll ever change*, she concluded.

They rounded the corner and walked half a block to stand in her driveway. He spoke again.

"Why don't we talk about my big lie and the new case tomorrow over our morning coffee? I'll bring Kevin and he can play with Miss Kitty."

Viv gulped. She wasn't actually that mad, once he admitted what he'd done. In fact she felt a glimmer of excitement. She did have fun that last time they worked together. Maybe fun wasn't the right word. But it hadn't been dull, that's for sure.

Anyone can complain at a homeowner's association meeting, she reminded herself. *But how many people can get involved in a murder investigation not just once, but a second time?*

A slight smile came to the corner of her mouth. *He's so persuasive.* "I'll talk to Miss Kitty and let you know. She's not exactly a fan of Kevin's exuberant behavior." Using the cat to express her feelings had become a habit. Especially when it came to Rex. Viv wasn't ready to share her feelings directly with him. He had a certain power over her that made her feel vulnerable. *No use giving him more ammunition.*

"Understood," he said gravely. "I realize Kevin is a bit over the top. Unconventional. He's playful and full of enthusiastic affection. I get it. And I'll get him to do better. But don't forget that dog is loyal." He didn't wait for her reply. "See you tomorrow. Bright and early. Sleep tight, next-door neighbor."

She watched as he sauntered to his house, hands in pockets. Then she heard a whistle drift past in the dry desert air. She recognized the tune immediately: "The Best is Yet to Come," from Frank Sinatra's *Nothing But the Best* album. Viv knew those old '50s and '60s hits. She favored the classic tunes.

She watched as Rex disappeared through his front door.

7

REX REDONDO

The next morning Rex sat in his home office, sorting papers on his desk. When Sutton came through the door, she brought Kevin. He barked his greeting.

"Hey, you mangy mutt."

Kevin bolted toward Rex, the sound of his paws scratching against the wood flooring. He leaped into Rex's lap as papers flew across the floor. "Now that's the kind of greeting I live for." Rex reached his arms around the dog's body to give him a big hug.

"See? I told you he needs another round of obedience." Sutton Drew grinned at her employer, enjoying the swirl of papers on the floor.

With a gentle shove and a downward tilt to his thighs, Rex removed the dog from his lap. "Bork," came the happy reply. Kevin dashed back toward Sutton. Then he took a quick left. He bent over an overflowing basket of his toys tucked into the corner.

Ducking his head, he came up with his favorite. A brown bedraggled bunny, very flat because its stuffing and squeaker had been torn away. Holding it between his teeth,

Kevin raced to the door and dropped the bunny at Sutton's feet.

"Play fetch the bunny with him, would you? I'm doing some work here and then getting ready to have coffee with Viv," Rex said.

"Did you get that information I sent you last night?" Sutton tossed the bunny for Kevin. When he ran down the hallway she closed the door, blocking his way back into the office. "The dead man is..."

"I got it. Carmine Nelson. Fifty-five years old. Family with a wife and two adult children. The son is in rehab and the daughter lives up north. Two grandchildren from her first marriage."

Sutton perched on the corner of Rex's desk. She wore black tights with a bright red hoodie that stopped at her thighs. Crossing one leg over her knee, he admired her Nike running shoes. The latest edition, if he wasn't mistaken.

She looked athletic and fit. Her hair, strawberry-blonde, had been slicked back into a high and tight ponytail. After her customary three-mile run she looked cool and calm as ever.

Sutton tapped the desk with her fingernail. "So what are you going to do with that information? You never said." A text alert interrupted his reply. It was from Viv.

> Meet me at the police station. We can have coffee afterward.

Rex sighed. He sent a thumbs-up emoji and set his phone down. "Looks like I'm already late. How about you come with me to the kitchen. I can eat something quick and we can talk more about this Carmine Nelson guy." A scratch came from the door.

"And I can feed Bunny-Boy." Sutton slid off the desk.

Rex piled the papers on his blotter before following Sutton to the kitchen. He smelled coffee; his stomach growled. He didn't like it when he ran late. He loved the leisurely pace, but he had to admit a chocolate chip muffin and a fresh brew with Sutton was worth the time it took to gulp down.

He pulled out a chair at the high-top table. Sutton brought a mug of coffee and the muffin on a plate. "I only have a few minutes. You can clean up the dishes, I gotta get a move on," she told him.

He took a big bite.

Sutton glanced at her iPad screen. "So here's what I got. Have a look and I'll send you the information later." She shoved the device across the table.

Rex read, nodding over the details. "Looks like Carmine Nelson was quite the guy," he said. "Lots of Fluff and Folds in his history. Are you thinkin' what I'm thinkin'?"

"I wouldn't jump to any conclusions." Sutton reached over to grab the last bite of muffin off his plate. "But you and I both know, laundering isn't always about dirty clothes."

8

VIVIENNE ROSE

Two chairs sat across the desk from Officer Susan Farrah. She gestured with a sweep of her hand for them to take a seat. Viv took the one on the left, carefully moving it away from the other chair before she sat down.

Rex raised an eyebrow in her direction. Then he offered a friendly greeting. "So Officer Farrah, we meet again. Did you get a good night's sleep?"

Farrah stared at Rex. Doubt on her face. Viv stifled a grin. *Susan looks at Rex as if he had spinach caught between his front teeth.*

Farrah cleared her throat. "My sleeping patterns are none of your concern, Mr. Redondo." The use of his name with the Mr. made it clear that she wasn't there for chitchat.

"Let me remind you," she continued, "that I'm only interested in how you know our victim, Carmine Nelson. What can you tell me about him?"

Perspiration broke out on Viv's hands. The image of Carmine had kept her up that night. And she had to admit she felt a bit uncomfortable for Rex. Since he lied about knowing the dead man, he was more than likely going to get caught. Unless, of course, Sutton...

She glanced over at Rex. *So what's his plan?* Did he want to insert himself into the investigation because he fancied himself as some kind of detective? Viv expected Rex would come clean now that they sat in the police station. *Surely he'll tell Farrah.*

"Oh, Carmine and I are old pals," he said in an easy voice. "We go back, I don't know, maybe a decade."

Viv hid the startled look from her face by turning her head and coughing into her hand. She knew for certain that wasn't remotely true. Hadn't Rex admitted he didn't know Carmine last night? She turned her head back to stare at him. He continued to weave a tale about his supposed friendship with the deceased.

"We'd play golf occasionally." Rex held his hand up to inspect each individual fingernail on his right hand. "You had to take your time with Carmine. He spent a lot of energy with his warm-ups on the course. Never in a rush, that guy. He'd do stretches and then practice swings. He'd tell me that he needed to 'get a sense of the playing field.'" Rex used air quotes. "Of course he knew every green in Palm Desert like the back of his hand. A big player, that was Carmine."

Vivienne couldn't believe her ears. Rex had made up a story on the spot that sounded so convincing. *How does he do that?* She glanced over at Officer Farrah, who also stared at Rex. *I think she's totally taken in. Who wouldn't be with that mesmerizing voice he uses along with the attention to detail.*

Farrah slid her hand over to grasp her pad of paper. She scribbled a few notes with a pencil. "Anything else?" Farrah asked, putting her pencil down.

Viv's concern about Rex's glib lies made her wonder. *Couldn't Farrah arrest him for obstructing justice? Couldn't he be charged for an offense and go to jail?*

"Nope." Rex leaned back in his chair.

Farrah slid her notebook into a drawer. "I guess that will be all for now," she said. "Thanks for coming in."

Viv exhaled in relief. *Apparently she's not going to arrest him now or ask me any questions.*

Rex stood and Viv did the same. She followed him out the door, into the reception area. Once they stood outside, he turned to her. "How about coffee at Just Desserts?"

"Or tea..."

"You can get an herbal tea." His brows raised above his inviting gaze.

Her palms, now dry, began to itch. She felt her heart race. He wanted to explain and get back into her good graces. She could feel it in the way his eyes appraised her face, running over her mouth. He tentatively smiled again, waiting for her reply. Her heart tugged.

Why do I feel like turning him down would absolutely ruin his day...

"Oh all right. Let's walk over. We can get some steps in. I didn't get a chance to exercise this morning." Viv knew that was her fault. The visit to the police station interrupted their walk with Kevin.

"Wonderful." He smiled at her, as if she'd just delivered the best news ever. "Then I can tell you my plan. Sutton's working on getting the background on all of those HOA guys. One by one we need to track them down. It has to be one of them who killed Carmine. I just know it."

"Carmine the golf guy," she said dryly, using his own description.

"Yeah, him. I hope he does play golf. I mean, who lives

in Palm Desert who doesn't?" Rex took her by the elbow, ushering her down the sidewalk toward Just Desserts.

9

____

VIVIENNE ROSE

Rex stabbed the middle of an enormous cinnamon roll, pulling the warm gooey center out with his fork. "This is the way I see it," he said chomping down on his first bite. He swallowed. "We have work to do."

Viv took a sip of hot chamomile tea. *He actually thinks we are both investigating this murder.* She shook her head slightly, wondering, not for the first time, about his unflinching self-confidence. *Bordering on arrogance.*

She'd learned over the past months not to return his gaze. Unsure if it was his mentalist thing or that she was just attracted to him, she'd gotten into the habit of looking over his eyes to his carefully coiffed gray hair.

But this morning she took a chance. Staring into his black eyes without flinching, she inhaled deeply. His pupils widened.

And then as if to prove to herself she couldn't be mesmerized by his tricks, she didn't disconnect her gaze. She allowed herself to feel his desire, his need to get closer, to win back her full approval. And she let him feel those things without flinching or taking them on as her problem.

"Okay then," she finally said, clearing her throat. "What kind of work?" Shifting her glance back to the mug of tea, her optimism returned. *I'm pretty strong when I put my mind to it.* She felt proud of herself.

"So I sensed some extra tension when Farrah first broke into the HOA meeting," Rex began. "None of those guys seemed that alarmed when she barged into the room. Almost as if they expected her. It felt off, at least to me."

"So that's why you want to look into all of them, the HOA directors?"

Rex pulled out his phone. "Yes, it is. Like I said, they didn't act like you'd think they would. A guy was found with a bullet hole in his head in one of the casitas and they shrugged, like it was just another cleanup, nothing to worry about. So I made a list to get started with what I call my getting-to-know-you plan.

"To start with, all of these guys have jobs. Some are semiretired, like Sammy Daniels, for instance."

Viv closed her eyes to picture the names from the previous night. She opened her eyes to say, "That would be the only African American man, right?"

"That's right. He's a retired Navy admiral. A chaplain, actually. His last assignment was in Washington, DC. He's some relative of a country singer, if my information is correct. Has a bunch of kids. So they decided to retire in Palm Desert. The climate. All that sunshine."

"Does he play golf?" she asked, knowing that nearly everyone played golf in the desert.

"Probably, but golf's not our point of contact," he said.

"Really? What do you suggest?"

"What are you doing this Sunday?" A playful smile lurked at the corner of his mouth.

"The same things I do for the rest of the week," she

assured him. "That's my life now that my Desert Doulas has gone..." She hesitated to say defunct. But for all intents and purposes, she was the only doula left. As the head of the company, she could hardly call it an agency with only a couple of employees.

"So we can go to church," he immediately offered. "The Episcopalian one on Judy Garland Drive."

"The one with the big steeple? I drive past that whenever I'm heading to the freeway," Viv said.

"That's where we'll meet the retired admiral. He'll never suspect us at church. Probably think we're weekend visitors who just happened to drop by. We'll cozy up to him at the coffee hour and act friendly. Trust me, this is going to be a piece of cake."

"But we have to listen to a sermon and sing hymns. Doesn't that bother you?"

"Not at all. I was raised Catholic. I can do the rosary and maintain a happy face, still thinking about the television show I saw last night. You could say I learned to multi-task from the best.

"Plus we skip communion and watch people. Take notes. Act just like everyone else. Don't forget to bring your phone," he added.

Viv put down her mug of tea. She glanced at Rex's plate. The outside loop of cinnamon roll remained. She reached over with her finger and broke off a small piece, lifting it to her mouth.

She felt him watch her carefully, even as she chewed. When she was finished she took her napkin and dabbed at her lips. "Okay then. I'm in. I'll go home and pick out a church outfit. Can't be too careful. I don't want to stand out and alert Admiral What's-His-Puss."

Rex flagged down the waiter and then reached for his

wallet. "We'll blend right in," he told her as he dropped the plastic credit card on the table.

Since when did Rex Redondo blend in anywhere? Viv thought.

10

REX REDONDO

On Sunday morning, Rex dressed in a navy-blue sports coat and tan slacks. A crisp white shirt open at the collar, he looked desert-ready for church. Slipping his feet into a dark pair of Gucci loafers, he stepped closer to the full-length mirror for one more glance.

He paid particular attention to the wrinkles at the corner of each eye. He ran his fingertip over his chin checking for sagging. *May be time for an appointment with my doc.*

He turned away with a sense of discomfort. He suspected that Viv didn't approve of how he took such care of himself, but he also knew his profession demanded a certain look and that he had to keep up appearances. *But you're retired,* he said to himself. *You can let this vanity go and embrace the wrinkles as a sign of maturity.*

Of course he knew in the back of his mind that he said he'd retired, but the reality was something quite different. He worked the same days and hours. *But that's just for fun and some extra cash,* he reasoned with himself. *It's not like I have to work for a living.*

But it wasn't the money or the fact that he was or was not working. It was mostly that he knew Viv heard the inconsistency as soon as the excuse left his lips. He could hear her insist, to herself of course, because she was still not willing to step that far into his business. In his imagination she sounded disappointed. *You're not retired. You still work the same hours. Why lie to yourself...*

She was like that. A stickler for the truth. And to be fair, at least to himself, that's what drew him to her in the first place. Of course she was beautiful, but once he got to know her, he saw quickly that she was the yin to his yang.

But now he felt uncomfortable. For most of his life he'd played fast and loose with the facts. He could tell a story at the drop of a hat. The lies didn't matter. They never stood in the way of the truth. At least that's what he told himself. *All stories are true; some of them actually happened.*

But Viv. She was a straight arrow. He relied on her for that and he respected her for the way she cut to the heart of the matter, taking no prisoners.

Standing on her doorstep, he waited for her to answer his knock. The door opened slowly. She stood looking calm and cool in an aqua-blue sundress. The hem brushed against her knees. He inhaled sharply, appreciating the way the dress flowed down her body, showing off her legs. *She knows how to dress, my Viv.* The hem was not too short, nor too long, revealing slim calves and a pair of white low-heeled sandals. She drew a soft white sweater over her exposed shoulders while he watched with admiration.

"We need to go to church more often," he mumbled, stepping back to give her room. *How does she do that...look so amazing and put together every time.* But when he noticed she avoided his stare, he corrected himself. *Don't overreact and scare her,* he thought.

She flushed slightly but then busied herself shutting the door and testing the handle. He averted his eyes. *Most women like that kind of attention,* he rationalized.

He didn't dare take her hand. He knew in his gut that wasn't what she wanted. But he touched her elbow as they walked toward his car. Since they'd last driven together, he'd leased a new Mercedes SUV in cobalt blue.

He always felt a thrill driving the latest model off the lot. But then, in a couple of weeks, the feeling went away. The car no longer thrilled him. It became a way to get from one place to another.

"New car?" She waited for him to open her door. When he did, she slid into the passenger seat.

Once he sat beside her, he explained, "I lease a new one every year. Before you say anything, I know I'm kind of brand specific. Sutton teases me all the time about being stuck in a rut."

Once on the road he steered the car effortlessly, appreciating the quiet hum of the electric engine. "So were you ever a church-goer?" he asked, longing to reach out and take her hand. But he kept his hands firmly on the wheel instead. *Not every woman wants a hand-hold on Sunday morning. Get a grip, Rex. Viv is a classy dame.*

"My parents took me to church nearly every Sunday growing up," she told him. "I think I still remember. You know, when to stand up and when to sit down."

"The Catholics love that part. And the kneeling," he added with a nod.

"Do you feel a little, you know, guilty, about tracking a man at his place of worship? It's kind of tacky," she said.

"I have no scruples. Especially when it comes to an

investigation." The words rolled off his tongue as if he'd been a PI for years, not just in his imagination.

If the truth were known, he hadn't been to church in decades and didn't really care one way or the other about God's opinion. "Do you think God will mind that we have ulterior motives?" he asked her, hoping his question would bring a smile. But she surprised him, speaking from her heart.

"If you put it that way, I suppose God isn't that particular why you go to church, so long as you show up." She folded her hands in her lap, looking out the window.

11

VIVIENNE ROSE

Inside the sanctuary, Viv stopped to admire the surroundings. Bright primary colors exploded behind the communion table, where an expansive stained-glass window filled the entire wall. For a moment she held her breath, looking at the red, blue, green, and yellow design. Primary colors like a rainbow. *The promise of God to Noah.*

Her eyes traveled downward to a table. A white cloth covered the goblet, and another similar cloth covered the plate. An open Bible lay to one side.

Viv inhaled, detecting a touch of incense in the air, along with beeswax. The smells reminded her of church when she was a child. Appreciating the tall white candle next to the chancel, she tried to remember its significance. *A Christ Candle. At least I think that's what they called it.*

She felt her elbow being tugged. Rex whispered in her ear, "Let's sit close to the back. We can see everything from there without looking too obvious." He directed her to an empty row.

Taking the end space closest to the aisle, he pulled Viv

next to him. Their thighs touched, and she felt a tingle up her spine. She wondered if she should move away but then decided against it. Instead, she drew her dress over her knees and reached for a hymnal. Feeling self-contained, she stopped to appreciate the familiarity of church.

Rex looked toward the front of the room. He twisted his neck slightly, letting his eyes do the rest of the work. *I bet he's clocked everyone in this room already*, Viv thought. She'd seen him do the same when he was on stage. Take in everyone, his face assuming a bland expression. *Once a mentalist, always a mentalist.*

As she thumbed through the hymnal, a woman stopped at their pew, leaning over to speak. "Would you like a bulletin?" Dressed in a form-fitting red suit with large pearls at her throat, Viv assumed she was important. Maybe a head deacon or an elder. A person who had worked her way to the top of the church hierarchy.

I bet she's got matching heels, Viv thought.

Sure enough, a quick glance confirmed her suspicion. Three-inch red heels, making the woman appear taller, close to six feet.

Rex shot her a smile. "We'd love a program."

When the woman's eyes narrowed, he immediately corrected himself. "I mean a bulletin. So sorry. This isn't a Broadway show, right?"

"Welcome to St. Bart's," the woman said sharply. She handed him the bulletin and turned on her heel.

He leaned in to whisper, "I suspect that she's already sussed me out as a heathen."

She patted his thigh. "Don't worry. Heathens are churches' best customers. If they sense you're a lapsed Catholic, you're practically home free. Episcopalians love snatching up one of those." She felt him stifle a laugh.

As more people took their seats, Viv continued to look around. "Have you caught sight of the admiral yet?"

"If I could put on my sunglasses I would be more efficient and less obvious," he lamented.

"Better not, Jack Nicholson," she said. "You're not at the Oscars, you know. How about I take in the right side and you look at the left. Do you think he'll be in uniform?"

As soon as the words left her mouth, a startling sound filled the sanctuary. A throaty gasp accompanied plaintive notes. Viv did not recognize the specific piece, but she knew that the pipe organ must have cost a fortune.

"Bach's 'Fugue,'" Rex replied under his breath.

Her chin raised as she gave him a surprised glance. "What do you know about Bach?"

"I know stuff," he commented dryly. He flipped open his bulletin. "Yep, I'm right. This is a good one. Keep listening. But don't applaud at the end. Not the right thing." This time he patted her thigh.

"I know that," she hissed. As the music grew louder and the notes more frenzied, Viv felt overwhelmed. She held her breath, taking in each note. The music reminded her of a group of children each speaking over the next to get their say. One after the other, the busy notes rushed to an abrupt conclusion. Followed by the echo of the last note and then silence.

Then a man stood in the pulpit. He placed his hands on both sides as he leaned slightly forward. "Welcome to St. Bartholomew's church," he said in a deep, sonorous voice. "My name is Samuel Daniels and I'll be bringing the word today."

Viv grinned.

Rex leaned over to whisper, "I think we've found our guy."

"Looks like it," she said with a smirk.

"And now the word of the Lord," the preacher added, glaring right in their direction.

12

REX REDONDO

After the service, Viv and Rex made their way to the social hall. Rex nodded to the line of parishioners waiting to greet the pastor. Once it was their turn, the preacher extended his hand. He looked imposing, over six feet tall, shoulders back, his dark skin glowing with health. Black eyes assessed Rex first, then Viv. "Am I right to assume you're military?" he asked, turning back to Rex.

"Yes, sir," Rex answered. "Three tours in Afghanistan. Intel officer."

"I could see you casing the room from where I sat behind the pulpit." He nodded. Then he turned to Viv. "And how long have you two been married?"

"Oh, we're not married!" Viv held her hand out to shake his. "Just neighbors, as a matter of fact."

"We live close. Down the way from here. At the Desert Tortoise Estates." Rex assumed his bland pose, making Viv smirk.

The admiral's eyes narrowed. "Wait a minute. Didn't I see you two at the HOA meeting just a few days ago?"

"Yes, you did," Rex said before Viv could answer. "We

didn't get very far with the meeting, did we, what with the interference."

"And the body being found," Viv added.

"Between the sheets," Rex continued.

"I didn't go over to see for myself. I heard it was a man named Carmine Nelson. A friend of yours?" The concerned look on the pastor's face seemed genuine. But before he could inquire further, they were interrupted.

"Excuse me, pastor. Would you like a coffee?" A teenage girl, dressed in a bright yellow miniskirt and a top that showed her slim midriff, stood close by. Rex stepped back, allowing the teen some room to hand over the paper cup.

Must be nice having everyone at your beck and call.

He watched the admiral grimace after the first sip. "Reheated." His nostrils flared with distaste. "I need to have a word with the deacons."

Viv chimed in. "In answer to your question, I didn't know Carmine Nelson until I saw him that night..." she paused, searching for the right words, "...in bed." A flush came to her cheeks.

Rex smirked as the admiral looked away.

"We're thinking of joining a church," Rex said, coming to the rescue. He eased his hand to Viv's elbow to stop any denial that might come from her at his unexpected announcement.

The admiral looked surprised. "Is that so. Both of you are Episcopalians?"

"I am," Viv said.

"I'm a lapsed Catholic," Rex admitted.

The admiral's eyes shifted upward to look over Viv's shoulder. More people had lined up to greet him. "Maybe we can talk sometime this week," he said. "I can fill you in on our little congregation and add you to the email blasts. But for now..." He extended a hand to the woman standing behind Viv. "How are you today, Mrs. Lewis?"

Rex gestured with his head. "Want some coffee?" They walked away together.

Halfway to the reception table, Viv stopped. "Did you see his face after the first sip? No coffee for me either. Why don't we head back to my place and I'll fix you brunch."

"Absolutely. Your place. Sounds perfect." Rex beamed at her. He ushered her around a group of people talking, heading toward the parking lot. This time he took her hand without hesitation, his confidence returning.

Rex sat at the kitchen table, bending down to pet Miss Kitty. The cat purred, so he lifted her to his lap. His fingers idly stroked her fur as he watched Viv from behind. She stood on her tippy-toes to lean over the sink to open a window that faced the pool.

"Pancakes and bacon?" she asked him as soon as she turned around.

"Sounds good. I can help." He placed the cat back onto the floor to stand. "I'm not a great cook but I'm actually good at taking directions, if you give me a chance."

Once he'd fried bacon and she'd made a plate of fluffy blueberry pancakes, they sat down together. "Syrup?" She offered him the pitcher.

"Yes, ma'am," he said. Pouring the gooey liquid over his stack of pancakes, he asked, "Did you see the pastor's shoes?"

"What a funny question. I did not," Viv admitted. "Just his black robe with the three stripes. I never thought to glance at his feet."

"You're not gonna believe this," Rex said after a bite.

"But he was wearing Nikes. And not just any Nikes either, but the latest pair."

"Do you mean Nikes as in athletic shoes kind of Nikes?"

"Those are the ones. Air Jordan 5 Retro SE Craft style."

She looked at him, a curious expression on her face. "You know all about Bach's music and now it seems you are an expert on Nikes? You're a very intriguing man."

Rex preened, a sheepish smile on his lips. "Like I said—I know stuff."

She passed him the pitcher again. "Have the rest of the syrup and tell me why you think Admiral Daniels wears Nikes with his ecclesial robe."

"Now that, dear woman, is the question of the day. I can tell you it doesn't go with the rest of his persona. He's making a statement with those sneakers, you can just take my word for it."

"Oh, I do." Viv smiled. "But the question remains, why? The shoes may be a weird style choice, but I think it's more important that he admitted hearing of the victim, at least his name. Isn't that what we're investigating, his relationship with Carmine Nelson?"

"You remind me of my mother." Rex gestured with his empty fork.

She looked up in surprise. "You've never spoken of her."

"Oh, she passed ten years ago. You have the same way she did of cutting to the point. I go off the path and she'd bring me right back. Just like you did right now."

He lowered his fork. "Confidentially there was a brief moment when I thought of using my special skill set in..." he ducked his head in embarrassment, "...in ministry. I told Mom I wanted to be a priest because my catechism teacher kept saying that I had 'gifts of the spirit.'" He used air quotes.

Viv's eyebrows flew up. "I would never have guessed."

"And you know what Mom told me?" He cleared his throat to imitate a woman's voice. "You can't be a priest. They wear such terrible shoes."

Viv burst out laughing.

Running his fork over the last dribble of syrup, Rex lifted it to his mouth for a lick. He nodded toward the kitchen sink. "How about I help out with the dishes and then we can go outside, sit by the pool, consider how to continue our investigation."

Rex studied Viv's face carefully. When she didn't reject his offer immediately, he didn't ask again. He was learning. Like Kevin, he wanted his way right now, but Viv, she was Miss Kitty. She needed a chance to make up her own mind.

"Why not?" Viv answered.

To his satisfaction, she smiled. "Come back in half an hour. I'll be in my swimsuit by then and meet you out back. You can bring Kevin if you want. We'll make a day of it."

Be still my heart.

He stacked his plate on top of hers. "I'll do the dishes first," he announced. To his own surprise, he didn't even mind.

13

REX REDONDO

Rex extended his right hand, holding a glass of iced tea. He felt the coolness travel up his arm. His left hand dipped over the other side of the chair, grasping Kevin's collar. The dog panted. His beseeching gaze made Rex feel guilty. *I'd like to let you run loose, ol' boy, but not right now. We have Miss Kitty to consider.*

Not only Miss Kitty, but Rex wanted Viv to get used to his dog and he felt a gradual approach would be necessary. Releasing Kevin to bound through the yard, bumping into potted plants, maybe even diving into her pristine pool, may not earn the dog another invitation.

Rex felt certain that once she accepted Kevin, she'd realize that he meant no harm. And that the inconvenience Kevin brought could be set aside when one considered the dog's ability to bring joy and enthusiasm along with his bad behavior. The jumping up and licking your mouth, for example. Not everyone's taste. And then there was the incessant toy squeaking. Oh, and the sleeping on the bed. Rex admitted that Kevin was a handful.

If he were to be completely honest with himself, Rex

figured if Viv could accept Kevin, then she might be open to accepting him. *Love my dog, love me.* That kind of thing.

"Be good," he told Kevin in a stern voice. "Just lie down, would ya? Stop tugging on the collar. My fingers are getting sore."

Kevin lunged one more time. When Rex didn't release his grip, he finally sat down. He panted heavily, obviously displeased with the situation. Until Rex relaxed his hold and took a sip of his iced tea. Enjoying the cool slurp down his throat, he forgot to clamp his fingers around the dog's collar.

In a second Kevin rose and bolted toward the pool. "Kevin!" Rex hollered.

"Meow," Miss Kitty called. She peered out from behind the screen in her catio.

"Kevin!" Rex yelled again, but the dog paid no attention. He made a quick right turn and trotted toward the catio. Lifting his right paw, he scraped at the screen. Rex jumped to his feet, the glass slipping from his hand. Since it was plastic it only bounced, leaving ice cubes in its wake.

I can't have him busting through the catio screen. What would Viv say?

At that moment Viv came through the opening of the sliding glass doors. From underneath her wide-brimmed straw hat, she looked at Kevin and then Miss Kitty. "She knows that's her territory," she stated calmly.

Rex felt embarrassed. He was unwilling to look incompetent in Viv's eyes. So he stood still, calling out in a calm and reasoned voice, "Kevin?"

Kevin jumped to a crouching position, his front paws on the pavement, his rear end in the air. "Bork," he called. But that wasn't to Rex. The dog only had eyes for the imperious cat.

"He just wants to play," Rex explained.

Kevin edged closer to the screen. When he lifted his paw to scratch, Rex yelled, "Stop it, Kevin." He turned to Viv to explain. "My dog is getting frustrated."

Viv only sighed. "Miss Kitty is not amused."

"Bork!" came Kevin's next complaint. This time the sound of his paw scratching against the screen door made Rex even more anxious. It was only a matter of time and the dog would break through and race inside.

"No!" Rex commanded. "Get back here, you mutt. Don't you have any manners? Miss Kitty isn't interested in playing with you." Inching closer, he reached for Kevin's collar. The dog ducked and ran to the other side of the catio.

"You could get a leash," Viv hollered.

"I'd have to go back to my house," he replied.

Kevin now stood on all fours watching Miss Kitty, who lifted her paw for a lick.

With Kevin mesmerized by the cat's nonchalance, Rex inched himself closer. "It's okay, buddy. She'll play with you later." Reaching over, he grasped the dog's collar. "Got ya!" Rex felt back in control.

Viv spoke. "Come over here. I found this. It should help." She handed him a belt. "Hook it around the collar. It will save your hand."

"Thanks," he muttered.

Viv sat down. He sat next to her, Kevin to the side of his chair once again. This time the dog lay on the concrete with a big sigh.

As the silence grew, Rex felt a pang of worry. *She's been awfully quiet today. Was it Kevin, or maybe it's me...*

"Hey," he began hesitantly. "Is everything okay? You've seem kind of distant."

She spoke right up. "I have been kind of overly introspective lately. I think it's nice that you noticed."

His heart thumped against his chest. Was that all it took —just ask her a question to make her happy? He felt proud of himself. He got ready to ask another question but was surprised when he couldn't think of one. It wasn't often that Rex Redondo didn't have words.

"I did notice," he said hesitantly. "How can I help?"

She seemed to be considering his question because she pulled her sunglasses down the bridge of her nose to gaze at him. "I think I'm at loose ends," she began. "I thought I'd be running a doula agency at this point in my life, but now it's just me. And frankly I don't have the energy to interview more women to fill the empty places."

Is this when I tell her that I'd be happy to apply as her next full-time job? For a lifetime, if she'll have me.

Rex sat back in his chair, amazed at where his thoughts had gone. He'd never been married or even in a serious live-together relationship. A single guy to the core of his being. Oh sure, by the time he hit fifty he'd thought about settling down. But there was always another sweet young thing admiring him from the front row that had changed his mind.

Until he met Viv.

"Does it help that we've taken on another investigation?" he asked quietly.

"I have to admit I liked investigating the last time. Not the dead body part though. That was awful." Her chin drooped. "But I haven't given up on my Desert Doula plan just yet," she said in a shaky voice. "It took a lot to set up the business and interview employees.

"I still have my phone hotline, of course. And I can still do seminars on birthing for new parents. But the truth is, at this point, I'm a one-woman agency." Her voice faltered. "At my age this feels like I'm being forced into retirement."

"I think I get what you mean," Rex said. "I keep saying I'm retired, but I'm not. I mean, who am I trying to kid?"

"It's different for you. You have a distinguished career in show business. It took me years to get back into a full-time business after raising my son. And now I can't imagine not working." Viv sounded sad. Then she continued, "I do still take classes on the latest research in birth and parenting. I get energy with that part."

"You've thought this thing through," he responded, a tinge of admiration in his voice.

She turned to him, a serious expression on her face. "So you're aware that's what you do, that you say one thing but do another? 'I'm retired,' but you're not really. I was thinking that you had no idea."

"Trust me, I'm aware. For what it's worth, Sutton calls me out on a regular basis. Most people aren't brave enough. But my ego isn't that fragile."

He took a deep breath. *So that's what an honest conversation feels like. It's kind of a relief not to have to pretend.*

No longer uncomfortable with Viv's silence, he closed his eyes. Appreciating the sun on his face, he let his mind wander. Peace settled over him as he realized that for now, all he wanted to do was sit by the pool with this beautiful woman.

That's more than enough for me.

14

VIVIENNE ROSE

The following morning Viv lowered the brim of her white baseball cap over her eyes as she stepped out her front door. She was ready to start a new day. It had helped to talk with Rex by the pool.

She felt better in his company, knowing that he could be a good listener. Plus once she'd told him about facing involuntary retirement, it didn't seem that terrible. Sometimes keeping things to herself only made her feel worse.

A bump at her knee brought Viv back to the present. Kevin scrambled toward her, wagging his tail furiously in greeting. "I always know what Kevin wants," she said, reaching down to scratch behind his ears.

"Walks, food, and the occasional toss of his bedraggled brown bunny." Rex came next. "Men and dogs have a lot in common. We aren't that complicated."

"I'll remember that." She stepped out on the sidewalk.

Rex clipped the leash on Kevin's collar. Kevin moved ahead as they walked side by side, until he stopped to investigate the base of a flower bed. As he considered his options, one sniff at a time, Viv and Rex waited.

"Just when I think this is the most boring landscape I've ever lived in, something like that iris blooms and I'm surprised." She pointed to the flower that had captured Kevin's interest.

"They're kind of dainty." Rex gently tugged on the leash. "Come on, Inspector Clueless. Don't take all day." Kevin stopped to lift his leg. When he was finished they picked up their pace again.

Approaching the first intersection, Viv noticed a woman with a baby carriage coming from the opposite direction. She wore a pink baseball cap pulled over her eyes. The wheels of the oversized buggy bounced along as she pushed from behind.

Her loose-fitting gray sweatpants dragged against the pavement. A matching top fell over her front and backside. She stared ahead without a greeting.

"Isn't she a bit young to live here?" Rex commented as they passed the woman. "Fifty-five and up. Those are the rules."

"Maybe a granddaughter of a resident," Viv speculated.

"Could be," he agreed.

A cry of a young baby alerted Viv.

"Somebody's hungry," Rex commented. "Or needs a diaper change."

Viv felt herself launch into a familiar lecture. "Babies only have a few needs, at least at first. It's when they get older that they become really complicated. I usually don't tell parents that because I don't want to scare them. But in my experience infants are just the beginning of the parenting demands."

"Is that so?" He grinned down at her.

"Oh, sorry. That wasn't necessary was it. A teaching

reflex." She kept walking, only to realize that something about the young woman wasn't right. And then the wails of the child stopped as quickly as they'd begun.

15

VIVIENNE ROSE

Viv stood in front of her house. They'd finished their walk in record time. "Want to come in?"

"Thought you'd never ask." With Kevin at his heels, they walked through the open door. Kevin began sniffing the living area. "So what does your day look like?" Rex asked.

"I want to shower and then get back to work. I'm prepping for my next online class. People have already signed up," Viv said.

"And I need to move forward with the investigation," he said. "I wanted to find out more about our victim."

Viv thought for a moment. "Maybe after lunch..."

"That's perfect. I'll text later and we can head over together to check out Carmine's Fluff and Fold. Do you have any laundry we can take with us? Then we'll look like regular customers."

"So we're going incognito?" Viv smiled.

"Very clandestine. Just like a military op." Switching gears, he called out, "Kevin." The dog poked his hear from around the corner. "Meow," came a call from Miss Kitty.

"See you later. Come on, buddy." He took up the leash and opened the door.

After her phone call and shower, Viv sat outside. She liked to dry her hair naturally. Plus the warmth of the sun felt good on her skin. The clean smell of bromine wafted from the pool, accompanied by the sound of shuffling sprinklers watering the landscaping on the other side of the fence.

Her dermatologist told her early morning before ten o'clock was the best time to get some vitamin D without fear of the UV rays. Viv sighed, remembering her feelings of frustration as she'd left the doctor's office. *When I was younger my health seemed less significant. But now every little ache and pain reminds me that I have to be careful about yet another thing I used to take for granted.*

Sitting by the pool, she let her thoughts wander to Carmine Nelson. He'd looked almost content, lying in bed with the expensive sheets carefully tucked under his folded hands. Someone had made the bed with expert knowledge. The corners of the top sheet were tucked and the comforter looked freshly laundered, pristine white.

Carmine appeared happy, except for that hole in the middle of his forehead. Viv wondered for a moment, *Was there any blood? I don't remember seeing any blood.*

The dead man had a comb-over. Now that I remember. His shiny bald head showed through the thin strands. She ran her hand through her own hair.

I have half the hair I used to. She rolled a curl between her fingers, remembering how thick her hair seemed years ago.

Laundry! Viv sat up. *Better not sit here any longer. I need to get ready for the Fluff and Fold operation.*

Viv hadn't been to a Fluff and Fold for years. She'd had her own laundry room at home for as long as she could remember. Her only previous trip to a laundromat was to take care of oversized items.

By noon Viv had finished her lunch and gathered her comforter. She tossed in her bedsheets as well. Then her phone pinged.

> Be over soon. Got the laundry?

She sent him a thumbs-up emoji in reply. Before she could pick up her purse, the doorbell rang.

Opening the door, she found Rex. She handed him the overflowing basket. "Here you go."

He laughed. "Everything is fun with you, even laundry."

Once in the SUV, they drove past the security gate. After a quick right turn onto the highway, he steered the vehicle toward Palm Desert.

"So here's what Sutton found out," Rex began. "Carmine Nelson had a stable family life. He'd been married for over thirty years to his wife, Beverly. They have a couple of kids, neither of whom live in California."

"So not a close family," Viv said.

"Carmine was Italian. His parents owned a rather famous restaurant in Palm Springs and I'm not sure if he inherited the place. According to Sutton, when his name comes up, everyone thinks of him as the Fluff and Fold guy."

"I see." Viv stared out the window.

"But the interesting part," Rex continued, "is that Carmine also has a bit of a reputation. Some people say he fluffs and folds other things. Like money, for instance. He launders money for people who don't want to pay taxes."

"Like mobsters do, that kind of thing?" Viv felt her stomach tighten.

"It's not unlikely. In the desert we have a lot of high rollers who live here in the winter months. Plus there's the casino. It's also an attraction. Lots of chances to play around and pick up a poker game too."

"Where did Carmine live during the hot months?" Viv asked.

"According to rumor, Carmine spent some time back in Italy and in the Caymans. He had a house in both places."

"Well we all know what that means." Viv smirked. She'd never traveled to either place, but she wanted him to laugh.

Rex slowed down his vehicle, taking a right turn into a strip mall. A collection of retail stores lined up facing the main road: one drug store, an off-brand shoe shop, and a pizza place, along with a storefront with the sign Carmine's Fluff and Fold.

Rex muttered under his breath, "All of the parking spaces in front are taken." He stopped the car as someone honked from behind.

"Maybe we can park in the back," she suggested.

Once they found the alley behind the shops, Rex pulled his car behind a truck that had parked right at the back of the Fluff and Fold. He left a few feet between his SUV and the open tailgate. "Frustrating," he muttered.

"You do have an issue with parking," Viv giggled. Then she added, "Looks like some kind of delivery." As the SUV idled, she opened the door and stepped onto the pavement.

"Wait for me," he hollered at the slammed door.

As she walked closer to the back entrance she saw a man standing in the bed of a truck. He called out to her.

"Interested in the newest Nike? I can show you several

pairs in women's sizes." He reached down to pull out a box. "I bet these are your size. Eight and a half, right?"

He extended the box in her direction with an engaging smile. "Try these on. I can give you a good price."

Viv slipped a shoe on her foot. Before she could try the second shoe, Rex arrived, out of breath.

"Hey, aren't you Dean Marcella? I saw you at the HOA meeting just a couple of days ago." He glared at the shoe guy, who looked away.

16

REX REDONDO

"That's right." Dean Marcella nodded, then looked back at Rex. "I remember you now. How are ya?" He dropped a shoebox and extended a hand to shake.

"I thought she looked familiar." Dean nodded at Viv, who was hastily putting the shoes he'd given her back in the box. She slid the box on the tailgate as he continued to talk.

"Aren't you the couple who sat together at the meeting— right before..." He stopped abruptly. "...the cop burst in." Then he coughed into his hand. "Pretty grizzly, right? A dead man in one of our casitas?"

"Carmine Nelson." Viv stood and spoke up. "That was his name." She confronted him with a steely gaze. "Do you do a lot of laundry at the Fluff and Fold, or is this just a stop for selling sneakers?"

Her voice sounded innocent enough, but Rex knew what she was up to. That's how Viv got to know people, the combination of a sharp eye and quiet voice. The technique was a good one, especially for a detective. But she pulled it off not because she was like him, a practiced performer, but because she genuinely cared about getting to know people and didn't care to hear any nonsense.

Instead of interrupting, he kept his mouth shut. Watching the master, he kept his thoughts to himself.

Dean deliberately ignored Viv, turning around to move a shoebox. "What's your job for HOA?" Viv wasn't deterred. "I haven't seen you around. Which street do you live on? Maybe we can have you and the wife over for cocktails."

Lines etched on Dean's forehead. *So I'm not the only one, ol' Dean has had some work done too. But he hadn't disguised his age much. Probably around seventy-ish. That scar on your face is pretty well camouflaged, but it took a good surgeon. Your hair—probably plugs a few years back. Glossy and black but not natural for a guy your age.*

As Dean kept talking, Rex kept assessing. Black eyes. Kinda tall, just over six feet. The stooped shoulders of an older man. That five o'clock shadow of gray whiskers and the jutting chin gave him a seedy appearance. Rex tuned back in to the conversation with a start.

"I have a house near yours," Dean said. "It's near the golf course. But I don't stay there all the time," he added hastily. "I sing all over at different nightclubs and venues, so sometimes I stay at hotels afterward."

"So you sing for a living?" Viv said.

By now Rex grew impatient. "And here I thought you were a shoe salesman." He pointed to the boxes of sneakers lining the bed of the truck.

A sheepish grin came over Dean's face. "No, I sell these for my son. He's the shoe guy. Keeps track of all the latest brands and makes deals for a few people. When you pulled up I thought you were customers."

Sure you did, Deano. Customers for what? Knockoff Nikes from China... Let me have a closer look here. With one swift motion Rex leaped onto the tailgate. He reached forward to take a shoebox off the top of the pile. Lifting the lid, he glanced inside. "Hey, I saw a pair of these yesterday." Rex held up a shoe. "On a pastor, of all people."

"Like I said, they are the latest from Nike." Dean made his way to the end of the tailgate. Using his hand for balance, he jumped off the end. "That hurts," he groaned.

Straightening, he glared at Rex. "My hip. Had surgery a year ago but it still gives me trouble." He'd effectively changed the subject away from the shoes.

But Rex didn't respond. He kept staring inside the box.

Dean growled impatiently, "You're kinda nosey, aren't you. Get down and out of my merchandise."

Rex pretended he didn't hear, opening one more box. Dean's face contorted in anger. But before he could say anything more, Rex slid the lid back on and slowly turned around.

"Oh yeah, whatever. Just interested. I know a few things about Nikes. I can spot a counterfeit, for example. The stitching is the first thing that gives it away." His voice sounded reasonable, but the implication wasn't lost on Dean Marcella. Perspiration broke out on his forehead.

"My son is very picky about his clients. And since you're not one of them, you don't need to be assessing the merchandise."

Rex held up his hands. "Okay, I get it. Just trying to be helpful." He jumped off the tailgate, nearly colliding with Viv, who managed to step backward before getting knocked over.

"I have laundry to do," she said loudly, pointing to the SUV.

"I'll get that for you, dear," Rex said in a perfectly modulated voice. His hand reached down to his knee. He grimaced. Unlike Marcella, he didn't groan aloud. He was too proud for that.

Rex had learned from the best not to acknowledge pain or when someone got under your skin. He'd handled hecklers back in the early days by pretending he was just fine, even when he was insulted.

Refusing to limp, Rex walked toward his SUV. He opened the back to reach for the laundry basket. By the time he returned, Dean was shuffling more boxes in the back of his truck.

Meanwhile Viv moved away, ending any further conversation. She looked at her phone.

"Honey, why don't you find an oversized washing machine?" Rex suggested, loud enough for Dean Marcella to overhear.

"Of course, dear," she said. She clicked off her phone and put it back in her purse.

Rex felt a tingle up his spine. Even if she was only playing, the word *dear* from her lips had a surprising effect on him. He felt his heart beat harder in his chest, hoping it was a good sign.

17

____

VIVIENNE ROSE

Once inside the laundromat, Viv admired the machines. The back wall held five supersized dryers, with standard-sized washing machines placed across the aisle. Viv took her comforter from the basket and dropped it into the drum of an empty machine.

After dropping three pods of washing soap into the tub, she reached for the knob. *I forgot the coins.* Glancing around the room, she saw a machine on the wall by the office. The sign read: Smart Laundry Cards. Viv sighed. *Another smart card.* Feeling self-conscious, she looked around the laundromat for someone to consult. *And they say men don't like asking for directions. Me neither!*

As the other machines hummed, washers swishing and dryers tumbling, she noticed the restroom sign. Since there was no available employee, she did the next best thing. She pulled out her phone.

Where are you?

Checking out the bathroom for clues.

Need your help.

Be right there.

Viv walked toward the smart laundry card sign. *Isn't it bad enough that my phone is smarter than me? Now I have to purchase a smart card. It will get lost, knowing me. I might launder my comforter three, maybe four times a year, and every time I'll have to buy another card because I'll forget where the old one is. A smart card for a forgetful senior. That's me.*

She read the instructions on the smart card machine and started to rant again. *Twenty dollars just for the card. Definitely overpriced. Each load of laundry requires additional money. And to make matters worse, still no sign of Rex. I can figure this out myself!*

After purchasing the card with relative ease and adding twenty dollars more to it for washing and drying, Viv took the newly minted card and walked back to her washer. She tapped the card on the pad and was elated when the sound of rushing water met her ears. She let the lid slip from her hand with a slam. *It doesn't take much to bolster my confidence these days.*

"Look what I found," Rex said as he approached her. A bottle of baby oil and a pair of boots dangled from his hands. "These were in the last stall of the restroom, sitting in the corner."

She pulled a face. "Kind of disgusting, don't you think? I'm surprised you picked them up."

"What's wrong?" He dropped the boots and oil on a nearby chair. "Did I upset you?"

Viv sighed. "Not your fault. I'm too sensitive. It took a bit for me to figure out the washer and the smart card. And then when you showed up with those..." She pointed to the chair.

"They're kind of icky, right? Maybe a young girl with a baby was in the restroom. Young mothers are so vulnerable. She most likely left in a hurry, the infant crying, and she forgot her boots and the baby oil. Maybe she was running from someone?"

After a pause, he said, "Have a seat," then removed the boots and baby oil from the chair and tucked them underneath.

Viv ducked her head. She felt his concern and didn't know how to tell him that occasionally her imagination got the best of her. "Let me see those boots," she said, taking a deep breath.

Holding them in her hands, the same discomfort rose again. Looking carefully at the soles and insides of each boot, she commented, "These are very cheap. You can get them at any shoe warehouse. Size five and a half.

"The baby oil," she held it up, "looks pretty new. Almost full. Maybe not for a baby. What do you suppose it's used for?"

Rex's eyes opened wide. "Oh, now I get it. And here I thought I was the mind reader. Do you think a young woman was, you know, offering sexual favors in the bathroom for bored customers waiting for their clothes to dry?"

"I do," Viv said. "And she had to leave in a hurry without her boots. Just the thought of such desperation makes me uncomfortable."

Rex's face looked glum. "We've only been here half an hour. And we've uncovered a knockoff shoe operation in the alley and now a potential hookup place for desperate people seeking each other's company."

Glancing around at the stainless steel washers and

dryers one more time, Viv nodded. "That's creepy. But on the bright side the machines look new. State of the art with the smart readers." She showed him her newly purchased card. "Cost me twenty dollars just to get the card."

He held it in his hand. "I bet twenty bucks is way over the standard price for this card. Carmine must have been making a profit on these alone. But the question remains, did he turn a blind eye to what's going on in the alley and the bathroom?"

"The only way we can find out is to ask someone who comes here more often," she suggested.

"Or maybe there's an employee we can interrogate." Rex looked toward the other side of the room. There was a counter and a door marked No Admittance, Employees Only.

Rex spoke over the clamor of the machines. "Whenever I see a No Admittance sign, all I want to do is push my way inside. It's my nature to overcome obstacles."

Viv nodded at his self-assessment. "I don't see a person in charge." She pointed. "But that door has a keypad, in case you're considering a break-in."

"Is that a dare?" His eyes gleamed in anticipation. "Let's wager then. I'll get past that door and break into the back. Once I'm behind the counter I'll look around for clues and in exchange, you make me one of your fabulous dinners. And if I can't break in, then I'll make you a grill fest to die for. Ribs, chicken, and corn on the cob. What do you say?"

"You mean Sutton will make a grill fest," Viv scoffed.

"Either way," he chuckled.

Viv never gambled. So it took her a minute to accept Rex's wager. *It's for fun,* she told herself. *He's really a character and that's what he does. Don't be so stodgy.*

"Okay, I'm in," she said. "I'll be watching you break into

that door from here. Oops, the washer is done. I'm thinking it will take an hour for the dryer. Better get crackin'." She laughed.

After shifting the comforter from the washer to the dryer and then tapping her smart card for payment, Viv sat down. She'd deliberately chosen a place so that she could keep her eye on Rex.

He stood with his back against the counter staring at his cell. It looked as if he was waiting for service. Then he raised his eyes and winked at her from across the room. Pocketing his cell, he slid his back down the counter, inching his way closer to the locked door. He slowly turned, reaching out to try the knob.

Viv smirked. Her mouth watered at the thought of chicken on the grill and a nice green salad. Narrowing her eyes, she kept watching. Rex inspected the keypad. So far the door remained shut. *Butter and lightly salted fresh corn sounds so good right now.*

Centering himself in front of the counter, Rex placed his palms on top. Then with a slight jump he pushed himself up. One knee supported weight as he hoisted himself with the other. And then he began to topple. Losing his balance, he tilted forward and fell over onto the other side. Rex had disappeared from view.

That doesn't count for anything. He said he was going to get through the doorway. When Viv didn't see him stand up, she chastised herself. *Now that was uncharitable. He could be seriously hurt.*

She waited a moment longer before she raced across the room. *Maybe he hit his head and passed out...*

Bracing her hands, she leaned over the counter to check on him. Rex, in a sitting position, held his knee. His face scrunched in pain. "It's my trick knee," he explained. "Just give me a sec. I'll be able to stand once I pop it back in place."

As he pounded his knee, Viv caught sight of a car pulling up in front of the Fluff and Fold. Her fist tightened into a ball.

"The cops are here," she hissed.

Rex reached for the counter, struggling to pull himself to his feet.

"Hurry up." She reached to give him a hand just as the entrance door was pushed open.

"No one belongs back here except employees," came a now familiar voice.

Rex stumbled and then righted himself with a grimace. "Knee. Hurts," he told her.

Farrah spoke. "So Redondo and Rose. We meet again. Do I need to call an ambulance?"

18

REX REDONDO

The sight of Officer Farrah only made Rex feel worse. He hopped on one foot, waving his arms for balance. "Give me a minute, will ya?" He held onto the counter, gingerly touching down with the other leg. The pain in his knee made him wince.

"Just landed on it wrong," he told Viv. Tentatively balancing on both feet, he assured them, "No need for an ambulance. Viv can drive me home. Sutton will do some magic with heat and ice and I'll be right as rain."

Viv turned to Farrah. "We were looking for an employee. And when no one came Rex wondered why, so he hopped over the counter to see if he could find someone."

Officer Farrah eyed Rex up and down. Then she turned to Viv. "What are you two doing at a Fluff and Fold? Not exactly your scene. Plus I thought for sure every home at the Desert Tortoise included individual laundry rooms."

"Of course," Rex said. "But Viv has an oversized comforter that requires an oversized washer and dryer."

"Oh, she does?" Officer Farrah's lips turned up at the corners.

"Why does she think that's amusing?" He looked at Viv for an explanation.

Viv scowled and shot a dart eye toward Farrah. "If I'm not mistaken, Officer Farrah here thinks we're having sex under that comforter, and it surprises her because we're so old."

"I didn't say that," objected Farrah.

"Oh, you didn't have to. That smirk explained everything."

"I still don't get it," objected Rex. "Adults have sex. It's a perfectly good way to spend their free time. Why would you be surprised?" He addressed Farrah, a hurt sound in his voice.

Maybe it was his surprise or the tone in his voice, but this time both women burst out laughing. "Get a load of him." Farrah directed her thumb toward Rex. "That's Fluff and Fold humor," she explained, "pun intended."

"I almost feel sorry for the poor guy," teased Viv. "Except I haven't forgotten your remark." She stared down Farrah. "That was very ageist of you, Officer Farrah. It's not entirely out of the question that two people in their prime would consider conjugal bliss."

"That's a good one. Conjugal bliss. Geez. What are we, Victorians?" Rex now grinned, completely forgetting the ache in his knee.

"Okay, that's enough nonsense. You're here because of the oversized machines. You were looking for help. But that still doesn't explain why you were behind the counter, clearly reserved for employees only."

Rex bounced tentatively on his leg with the good knee. "I can explain. But not before I get some ice. Do you mind?" He pointed toward the restroom. "I saw an ice machine back there." When neither Susan nor Viv offered to get the ice for him, he shrugged. "Okay, I'll get it myself."

"You do that, Redondo," Farrah said.

As he hobbled away she called after him, "And while you're procuring that ice, I'll find out from your girlfriend why you're really here."

Despite the pain, Rex felt a jolt of delight. *My girlfriend. From her lips to God's ears.*

19

VIVIENNE ROSE

Viv and Susan Farrah sat next to each other, watching the dryer tumble around and around. Unfortunately Viv's comforter had formed a tight ball. "Give me a minute, I need to stop the dryer and do some untangling."

Stalling for time, she opened the dryer door and reached inside, the heat assaulting her face. Once finished, she slammed the door and then waited. The red sign on the payment pad flashed.

Viv shrugged. She pulled out her card and tapped it on the pad. By the time she sat down again Farrah was deep in thought.

"I was just here for the laundry," Viv explained again, realizing that once repeated it was easy to believe a half truth.

Farrah blinked. "Maybe you were here to fluff and fold, but that one," she pointed to the hallway where Rex disappeared, "he was here to snoop. He's a character, isn't he? Seems like you two are getting close."

"We're neighbors. That's all. I'm not looking for romance at my age."

Farrah shook her head. "And why not? You two look good together. Both fit and smart."

"Fit?"

"You've got a great body—for your age. Plus he's keeping up appearances. Silver fox material, from my perspective. I bet he has a lot of ladies hanging out at his back door after a casino performance."

Viv knew that Rex was still considered a catch. She didn't doubt his ability to attract, it was her ability that she lamented. *In the old days I might have gone for someone just like Rex. But that's over for me now. I'm just like Miss Kitty. I prefer my own privacy, looking down on the world from a distance.*

She pushed her feet under the chair. When they hit the boots and baby oil she felt the sadness return. Before she could mention the items to Officer Farrah, she caught sight of Rex. He held a dripping plastic bag in one hand, a big smile on his face.

"So if you don't mind I'll put my leg up." He plopped himself down, turning slightly to extend his leg on the empty chair next to him.

"Do you remember my question?" Farrah asked dryly. "What exactly were you looking for behind the counter?"

"Well that's the thing, Officer." Rex adjusted the bag over his knee. "I was looking for the person who runs this place. My dry cleaner is charging too much, raised his prices recently. I need a new place to launder my fancy work shirts. When no one came to help, I thought I'd find a price list behind the counter."

"And did you?" Farrah asked.

"Nothing close," he admitted.

20

REX REDONDO

Rex Redondo

"Thanks for dinner." Rex looked across the table at Viv. She'd been polite during their meal. But he sensed something wasn't quite right.

Viv reached for his empty plate, then hers. She stacked the utensils on top and stood from her chair. "I decided to let you win. You know because you hurt yourself. You get an A for effort."

Rex had made any number of attempts to keep the conversation going over the meal. Asking about Miss Kitty. Clever stories about Kevin. Recollecting about the times when his mentalist act went south and how he'd recovered.

She'd remained attentive but quiet. Which made him nervous. He liked it when she talked more. Viv had a way of hiding her feelings behind a very pleasant exterior.

But she did have a tell. He'd noticed when they first met. How she traced her chin with her forefinger when she was holding back her emotions. And then at dinner, she didn't initiate any conversation, just responded politely.

As the meal progressed, he began to worry. Unaccustomed to his lack of confidence in matters of the heart, his good leg began to jiggle under the table. Once he realized he wasn't getting anywhere with breaking down her reserve, he began to wonder. *Maybe she's mad at me...*

Viv brought back two pieces of cheesecake with a dollop of whipped cream and a luscious-looking strawberry on top of each slice. She placed one plate in front of Rex with a dessert fork before sitting across from him.

"In answer to your question, I rarely, if ever, gamble. I tried once at a slot machine."

He took a bite. Eyes opening wide, he swallowed and grinned. "Cheesecake is one of my favorites and this one is sublime. Make it yourself?"

"I do bake an occasional cheesecake and I freeze portions for special occasions. Happy you like it." Her matter-of-fact voice took away the pleasure of thinking that she'd made it especially for him.

"So what happened at the slot machine?" He took another bite, savoring the mixture of vanilla and strawberry on his tongue.

"I lost seventy-five cents!" Viv said indignantly. "Never again. Why would anyone use their money so carelessly."

"Honey, I watch people gamble everything they've got night after night. I don't go in for dice or cards myself, maybe the occasional gin rummy, but for some it's not just a game. It's a lifestyle."

"It's stupid. And irresponsible." She politely took a bite of her dessert.

"And that's why I appreciate you so much. You just say what you think. Put it right out there." He swallowed and then surprised himself. *I have one more trick up my sleeve to break down this impasse.*

He didn't like having to confront her, but he did it anyway. "So why don't you tell me what's really bothering you. I've felt it all night." He realized he was testing her resolve. *Let's see what she's made of.*

She put down her fork, a thoughtful look coming over her face. "I won't deny there's something on my mind. But I don't want to get into your business."

"My business?"

"You know—who you are. You have a way with people that I find off-putting. And since we're just neighbors, not that close really, it's not for me to judge."

Rex's heart plummeted. He'd been assuming, apparently falsely, that they were growing closer. Especially since they'd seen more of each other the past few days. He'd made every effort to be on his best behavior, but now something was seriously wrong.

When she resumed picking at her dessert, he knew it was up to him. He had to convince her to tell him his faults. "It's okay. If I've offended you in some way, I want to know. So that I can fix it," he hastily added.

She pushed her plate away, shaking her head in disagreement. "You don't have to fix anything. I'm not in the business of changing you or anyone else. And I'm not offended so much as perplexed."

He gulped. Despite her calm he detected a hint of sadness. She was trying to cover it up, but Rex could feel it, nestled somewhere in her past.

"Please don't be sad!" he said impulsively. "I want to hear. Go on, tell me."

She dabbed at her lips with a napkin. Acting as if she were considering his offer. Rex knew their relationship might depend on how she chose to go forward, so he lowered his eyes as his gut clenched.

"You lie," she flatly stated. "So often. So confidently. I don't always know when you're telling the truth. I feel unsettled with that. In the past I've been lied to and been hurt. I'm too old to go down that road again."

Rex liked to think that no one noticed his slight prevarications. He only used them occasionally—at work of course, and when necessary to make things come out right. That was what he told himself. No one else had complained.

Well, maybe that woman he dated last year. She said he was undependable. Please, she's wasn't exactly a straight arrow when it came down to it. She'd lied about her age. She'd lied about where she grew up. She'd even lied about her three ex-husbands.

That's the way of things. People lie. Sure, he told the occasional fib now and then. But it wasn't a deal-breaker. Not for him.

He felt a pout coming on. A lot of women tried to make him happy when he pouted. It was his go-to move. He was annoyed at Viv. She'd hurt his feelings. *No one gets to do that*, his inner voice protested.

He pushed his plate forward, thinking, *Character assassination. That's what this is.* Then he looked at her face, the way she used her forefinger to curl that strand of hair next to her ear. His heart melted. *This is hard for her too*, he realized.

Instead of standing to make a quick exit, he changed his mind. "Lost my napkin," he mumbled. He pushed his chair back. Head under the table, he admired her shapely ankles. *I'll skip the pout*, he decided.

He waved his napkin in the air. "Got it," he said.

"That's nice." She'd resumed her overly polite voice.

"Yup." He released a deep sigh, realizing his close call. He'd almost left. Now with his anger pushed aside, he reconsidered.

Viv's not trying to hurt me. What was that word she used? Perplexed.

"I don't lie to hurt people," he explained. "At least not on purpose."

He could see and feel her mind whirl as she considered his words. The familiar tingle made its way up his spine. A sign that he'd managed to shift the awareness field.

Rex was used to women wanting things from him. A good time. An expensive dinner. As they say, a superior boyfriend experience. But Rex wasn't used to someone really caring about what made him tick.

It was rare, this moment of self-reflection. *And I thought there was nothing new for a guy like me, especially at my age.*

"So help me here," he began, hesitation in his voice. "When did I lie most recently? I need an example." He tentatively smiled. And then he was rewarded with her steady gaze.

"When you told Farrah, ' I need a new place to launder my fancy work shirts.'" She used air quotes. "That seemed unnecessary to me. Why not just say you want to know who killed Carmine Nelson and that your curiosity got the better of you?"

21

VIVIENNE ROSE

Vivienne rinsed the dishes, thinking about the conversation with Rex. He'd been quite open about his reasoning, the part when he lied to Farrah.

"I figured we already told a lie about using the Fluff and Fold for your large comforter. And then one more lie, still about laundry, didn't seem that bad. Plus we are interfering with police work. Since we're not legally private investigators, at least not yet, I knew we didn't belong."

"Private investigators?" Viv said with surprise.

Rex glanced away. Viv suspected that he was searching for the right words. Now self-conscious about lying, he couldn't do what was natural to him. *I've managed to put a slight dent into his confidence.*

"Okay, about that." He cleared his throat. "I've been thinking about getting a PI license. Actually I had Sutton look into the details. It wouldn't be that hard. I would only need a couple more classes at the community college. Since I have the hours and training from the military, it would be really easy for me. Your licensing might take a little longer.

But you can work under my license while you take the necessary classes. Then we'd have every reason to show up at police scenes and not have to make...excuses."

The way he said it, the title even—private investigators—made her head spin. Even later after he left, as she added soap to the dishwasher, she couldn't quite wrap her mind around the idea. Oh sure, he'd alluded to his fascination with Philip Marlowe. But Marlowe was a fictional character.

She closed the door of the dishwasher with a thump. *That's okay for him and maybe Sutton. But he keeps saying "we" as if I'm included.*

With a mug of hot tea in hand, she made her way down the hall to check on Miss Kitty. She found her cat curled up on a fluffy blanket in the middle of the sofa. Viv sat down next to her. The low rumble of a purr began, followed by a ping from the cell in her pocket.

Thanks for dinner. The company was divine. As was the cheesecake.

He'd put an emoji with an exploding head.

See you tomorrow at the usual time.

She added a gif with two people walking a dog.

Then her eyes flew open. He'd sent the heart emoji, making his feelings known right there in plain sight.

The next morning Viv walked with Rex and Kevin, feeling a bit jittery. Despite her best intentions at keeping him in the friend category, he'd sent that emoji. She never meant to lead him on. But rather than talk about it, she preferred to let him think a heart emoji was an everyday occurrence for her. Why not? Just a cell phone thing.

She picked up her pace, realizing her discomfort. Focusing on her body, the heart and muscles, she pushed away her emotions. "So I've been reflecting about the Fluff and Fold," she told him.

"Me too," he answered immediately. "You go first."

"According to the website, it's open twenty-four seven. But no one was behind the counter. Isn't there usually an attendant; somebody to pick up laundry that's dropped off and who keeps the place clean?"

"It would make sense. I was wondering that too."

Viv's arms began to swing at her sides. She looked past him across the street. Again the woman with the baby carriage walked on the opposite side. The same blanket, draped over the front of the stroller, hid the baby from the bright glare of the early morning sun.

Viv lifted her hand to wave.

The young woman didn't look her way. She kept walking straight ahead.

"She's not that friendly," Rex commented.

"Did you notice anything about the way she's dressed?"

"The sloppy t-shirt and sweatpants? I saw that."

"No, not those. Her shoes."

"Unless women are wearing high heels, I rarely notice their shoes."

"She had on Nikes. Fairly new looking."

"Really?" He sounded interested. "So that's the third sighting this week. Were they the same style?"

"I'm not that into sneakers," Viv admitted. "I don't know if they're the same style. I did see the Nike logo though.

Which reminds me, what did you do with the boots and baby oil you found at the Fluff and Fold?"

"I put them back in the bathroom," he said.

"Probably a good idea. They're not ours. Maybe the woman who left them will come back. It could be her only pair of shoes. Have you thought of that?"

He looked at her quizzically. "That never crossed my mind," he admitted.

This time he picked up the pace. Kevin bounded ahead.

Once Viv caught up, he asked, "Will the search for Carmine Nelson continue today?"

"I think so. Why don't we have a sit-down with Sutton this evening? Maybe she's found that address."

He snapped his fingers. "Then the next day we can check out Carmine's house and go back to the Fluff and Fold and look for the behind-the-counter missing employee."

"It might be risky to go right back to the laundry so soon. If Farrah catches us again..." Viv's voice faltered.

Kevin made a quick left turn, breaking into a run. Then he skidded to a halt. They watched him sniff the corner of the grass.

"Officer Farrah showed up unexpectedly, which makes me wonder how she knew we were at the Fluff and Fold," Viv said.

"She may have surveillance or at least CCTV," Rex replied.

"Could be," Viv said.

"I did make quite the spectacle of myself. I hope it's not on some tape being passed around the precinct for laughs." He looked down at his knee. "Feeling pretty good this morning, thanks for asking."

She shrugged. "I'm not going to inquire about every ache

and pain. It's not what I do. Push through it is my motto. Just so you know."

"Understood," he said.

The sound of a wail came from across the street. "That baby certainly has a loud cry. I wish she'd pick the child up."

22

______

REX REDONDO

Sutton Drew entered the dining room. She directed her eyes forward and held her shoulders back. As she made her way to the booth in the far corner, diners at The Roadkill grew quiet.

The men looked her over. Even the women stopped speaking. Rex knew what the men were thinking, but he was unsure about the women. *Maybe they're assessing the competition or just envious of her style.*

Rex had always admired how Sutton made an entrance. Of course she was tall for a female, nearly six feet without heels. But tonight, even though it was still early, she wore a tight black sheath with her three-inch red stilettos. Her hips swayed provocatively as she navigated the space between tables.

Sutton's walk told it all. She knew who she was. Confident but not overbearing. *Okay, maybe it's not just the outfit,* Rex thought. *It's the way she wears her attitude, like a familiar piece of clothing, no lines or wrinkles.*

"Good to see you both," Sutton said, sliding into the seat across from them. "Hey, Viv," she added with a friendly nod.

She's Lauren Bacall tonight, Rex thought. He liked to figure out which movie star Sutton embodied with her choice of attire. Not averse to wigs and colorful clothing, Sutton also dressed to match her mood. *Tonight she's looking for some fun*, he concluded.

A waiter stared at Sutton, his mouth hanging slightly open. His name tag read Danny and his glance had not moved from her chest. Sutton did not return his admiration. She glanced at her menu instead.

Once they'd ordered, Rex got down to business. "Looks like you have a hot date tonight." He gestured with a finger, moving it up and down to indicate Sutton's outfit.

"Not a date yet. But the night is young." Sutton reached for her water glass.

"We're still on the Carmine Nelson case," he said in a lowered voice. "Wanted to talk to you about any information you might have gathered. We need an address to start with. Where he lived."

"I figured." Sutton put the glass down. "Been kinda busy with other stuff. Dating someone new. She's from Lily Rock. But not in town tonight."

Rex knew that Sutton appreciated both men and women. He'd noticed right away when they first met. By the time he hired her and they'd become roommates, he listened to her relationship woes without judgment. And to be frank, over the years, she, too, had extended him a lot of leeway in that department.

Sometimes it was hard to explain to women about his relationship with Sutton. They didn't like the fact that he had a live-in personal assistant who looked like a Hollywood movie star one minute and a yoga instructor slash marathon runner the next. Too much competition. Plus they didn't trust his intentions.

After the first year Rex had learned not to bring women back to his place. If Sutton happened to be home there was hell to pay. He didn't like the fights that broke out, no matter how entertaining. And no matter how hard he tried, no woman believed there was nothing between them besides an abiding friendship and the paycheck he issued once a month.

Sutton was in charge of their house, his business appointments and calendar, house maintenance, and of course, Kevin. But her main job was to help him with his shows.

The well-kept secret—that she eavesdropped and gathered intel at The Roadkill before each performance—made his act feel authentic. One quick text from Sutton and he had the name of a recently deceased or a soon to be ex.

He was very good at reading people in his audience. But Sutton's research helped fill in the places where his intuition lacked. No one paid to have the showman pause and look insecure. A fact he'd learned the hard way, when early on he'd be stumped by some people and needed to scramble.

"Psychics need tools," he'd say. "Just like every other profession."

But now that he fancied himself as a detective, he wanted Sutton to bring her skill set, internet research especially, to his new job. So he planned on paying her extra to explore the private detective avenue.

After their meal, Rex ordered coffee. "We have a show at nine." He pointed to his Rolex.

"I got ya, boss," Sutton said. "I was here a little earlier. Dressed differently. I could see and hear the entire bar and dining area. Got some good stuff."

Rex turned to Viv. "If you recall, she's honed the art of sussing people out dining before my show. She can tell by how they dress and she eavesdrops on conversations." He didn't bother to hide the pride in his voice. He pointed to his ears. "Special microphones. Very pricey. They pick up everything."

Sutton smirked. "I have my ways. I pay Jake behind the bar to start up conversations about the show, you know, talk up how talented you are." Sutton smirked at Rex. Then she looked up to nod at the bartender. He touched the side of his nose in response.

"I see," Viv said.

Rex felt a moment of discomfort. His good knee began jiggling under the table. *She's looking at us like we are red marbles in a box marked blue.*

And then he shed his discomfort to admire her instead. Viv looked amazing. Her style was less in-your-face than Sutton's, with the white linen blouse over white jeans and low-heeled sandals. With the subtle shifting of the blouse's fabric, you could see her curves beneath. He felt proud to be seen with her.

Unlike Sutton, Viv didn't welcome compliments. She'd said that the first time when he'd whistled, "I'm all about the coastal grandma look—Diane Keaton in the Nancy Meyers films. No feedback necessary." Her voice was curt.

He'd never heard of Meyers but he knew Keaton's work. Then it hit him, "*Baby Boom*, right? Keaton was in that one."

"Good guess," she said. "My favorite movie."

He put that in the back of his mind, knowing he could find the film on pay-per-view as soon as he had a free night.

Rex settled his back into the booth's cushion. It felt good to be seen with two smart and beautiful women. He hoped there wouldn't be any trouble between Viv and Sutton. That might be uncomfortable. Plus this time, he didn't want to choose.

23

VIVIENNE ROSE

Viv tuned out of the shop talk between Rex and Sutton. He expounded on the dos and don'ts of internet surveillance for the entire meal, with Sutton interjecting her opinions. Finally the conversation got back to Carmine.

"Still no address. I think he had a professional wipe his info." Sutton shrugged. "Of course, I can do a deeper dive into other resources that aren't quite legal. Call in a few favors. But that will take some time."

"You mentioned to me that Carmine may be into illegal side hustles," Rex said. "Is that a gut feeling or did you find anything we can use?"

"It is a gut feeling," Sutton admitted. "I'll have to be careful. If there is a trail, it may be in the wrong direction. I don't want to slide down any rabbit holes. Big waste of time."

As Rex and Sutton reminisced about electronic rabbit holes when they were in Afghanistan, Viv planted a small smile on her face, pretending to care. Everything she knew about internet surveillance could be summed up with her one smart phone. She didn't have a big interest in algorithms or deep dives into people's backgrounds.

Finally the check came. "I'm ready to call it a night," Viv said.

"And I've got to get ready for our show," Sutton said to Rex. "See you later."

Sutton stood up from the table. Eyes followed the tall beauty as she exited The Roadkill, until she disappeared from view.

Viv also stood. She kissed Rex chastely on the cheek. "See you tomorrow," she said.

Once in the parking lot Viv climbed behind the steering wheel, exhaling her relief. What with Carmine Nelson's death and seeing Rex every day, she knew her inattentiveness at dinner was a sign. She no longer had the energy to listen with a smile on her face to people's chitchat. She needed some alone time.

Driving on the highway helped soothe her mind. An elbow out the open window, Viv wondered if she could distract herself before settling in for the night. *I'll do a bit of shopping*, she decided. *Everything in town is open for at least another hour.*

She pulled her car into a parking space right outside of Out of the Closet Consignment. *Surely Jason has something new to show me.*

They'd gotten to know each other right away when she'd moved to Palm Desert. Viv loved shopping second-hand. She'd pick up bargains at upscale boutiques after dropping off items she no longer wore. One in, one out had been her motto for years.

Once Jason realized she'd be a regular customer and

that she took excellent care of her clothing, he'd put things aside for her next visit.

The car locked, Viv caught sight of Jason right away. He stood in the center of the shop's window, busily arranging the display. Lifting a frothy white peasant-style dress over his head, he dropped it over the form. It fell in folds, drifting with diaphanous delicacy, making Viv sigh. She loved the dress at first sight.

Maybe I'm too old to still care about clothing. This wasn't the first time she wondered if she was too old to appreciate certain things. If she was too old to pull off a piece of clothing or a certain style. The closer she came to sixty, the more frequently her doubts happened.

Not just about what she wore, but how she took care of herself. Did her aging skin deserve expensive creams, or should she just buy the drugstore variety? And that wasn't the worst part. She even wondered if she was past experiencing intimacy with a man.

Did a sixty-year-old body still want to tumble in the sheets with another human being? No matter how attractive he was. What was the point really. It wasn't as if she wanted a baby. And the pleasure, well it had shifted over the years. Even she had to admit that.

Since her divorce, avoiding sex hadn't been that hard. No one was really paying attention to her that way. Until Rex. And he was just her neighbor. Viv checked herself. *Ask Jason about the dress. That's more manageable than worrying about sex.*

Stepping into the shop, she was greeted by Jason's welcoming voice. "Hey, friend, give me a minute. I want to finish with this window dressing."

Jason adjusted a straw hat on the female form. He tilted

it to one side, then the other, and finally over her nonexistent eyes.

"Am I keeping you from closing?" she asked.

"Absolutely not! I'd stay open all night for you, sweetie. Plus I've put away a few things in the back with you in mind." Jason hopped to the floor. Coming closer, he blew one air kiss, then another, for each cheek. "Wait until you see the jacket I found. Katie Holmes wore the same thing in New York just last week. It's to die for!"

Jason disappeared into the back room, giving Viv the chance to glance through the racks of gently used clothing. He returned carrying a blazer on one hanger and a linen button-up shirt in blush pink on another. He held the shirt in front of his body. "This is so chic if you just tie the waist. Then the blazer. To die for. That's what Katie did and the look has gone viral.

"Plus the button-up in this color would be stunning on you. Not just under the blazer but with white skinnies of course, the more distressed the better. You still have those, right? The ones you bought last year." He twirled around with the blazer, his smile making Viv laugh.

"I'll try both." She looked longingly at the window. But she decided against the dress once again. Instead she pointed across the room. "And I'd like to see that skirt suit over there. I guess they're back and I may need a more formal outfit for daytime."

"Sure, honey. Let me set that aside for you." Jason snagged the hanger off the rack and then walked to the wall where the dressing rooms were located. He hung the suit on the outside of the door, and then placed the two other items inside. "Whenever you're ready," he told her.

She tried the shirt first, calling out over the closed dressing room door, "I love the color. This is a keeper."

"And I'll give you your usual discount," he immediately replied. "Plus you have a bit of credit from the items you dropped off a month ago."

Viv knew Jason offered a discount to all of his returning customers. She didn't mind not being the only one, because the shop made her feel good. Buying secondhand made her feel a bit virtuous. And now she rarely bought anything new, especially at department stores. Walking into a Nordstrom often made her anxious. It didn't take a genius to realize that all of the young salespeople seemed to think she wanted to look just like them.

Jason never made her feel that way.

By the time Viv stood at the register, she'd chosen the shirt and the blazer, plus the suit. When Jason didn't bring the dress to the dressing room for her to try, she assumed he thought it too young for her. He'd never say, of course. That was his charm. He made Viv feel good about being Viv.

"You must have a lot of regular customers," she said as he folded her shirt. Then a thought came from out of the blue. "Did you hear about the dead guy they found at the Desert Tortoise Estates? I was there when the cops arrived."

When Jason looked up with wide eyes, she continued. "I saw him. Dead. He lay between the sheets as if asleep, except for that bullet hole in his forehead."

Viv knew that Jason liked to keep up on all of the Palm Desert news. "Do they know his name?" He folded one sleeve over the body of the shirt.

"Carmine Nelson," Viv said.

To her surprise, Jason stopped folding. When he looked up she could see tears forming in his eyes. "As a matter of fact, I knew Carmine. He used to come in here with his wife, Beverly, nearly every month.

"We'd chat while she tried on clothes. She liked the mid-century short sets they used to wear, you know, the matching kind with Bermudas. I'd always keep a pair in the back for her; picked them up at estate sales when someone passed." He kept talking, rambling as he struggled with his emotions.

Then he brushed at his eyes with a rueful smile. "Beverly will be devastated. They were such a lovely couple. Got along so well, even after all those years of being together. Carmine would comment on her outfits; he loved her legs and he'd whistle when she'd come out of the dressing room."

Jason's genuine grief touched Viv deeply. After discovering the dead body, she felt mostly shock. But now Carmine wasn't just a lifeless form. He'd become real, with Jason's tears.

Plus Jason's description of the older couple, who'd been married a long while, nearly made Viv cry. Probably because she'd believed she'd be married that long. Before Laurence left her, she thought they'd make it for the long haul. *Till death do us part.*

She'd hoped her husband would grow old with her and appreciate her like Carmine did with Beverly. But after the divorce Viv needed to put away all of those hopes because it hurt too much. She finally concluded that a long marriage wasn't in the cards for her and that she just needed to move on. She pushed away the hopes and the feelings because remembering hurt too much.

"It's good to know some people have those kinds of marriages," she told Jason.

"Reminds me of my parents," he admitted, sliding her items into a decorative bag, the tissue crinkling as he drew up the string handles. "I hope to see you soon," he said softly, handing her the bag.

Viv hesitated. "Is there any chance I could get the

Nelsons' address from you? I would like to send a condolence card, but I don't want to disturb the widow."

"Oh sure. Just give me a sec." Jason turned to his computer. He slid a notepad closer and then scribbled with a pencil. Handing it to Viv, he said, "I wrote down their phone number too, in case you want to call and chat with her. She must be very lonely now without Carmine. Just tell Bev that I gave you the number."

On the drive home Viv rolled up the windows. An inky darkness clung to both sides of the roadway. Viv felt an achy loneliness, remembering Jason's tears. She reached for the screen to select some music, hoping to push away her desolation.

Then she smiled, realizing she'd gotten one up on Rex and Sutton. It didn't take any fancy computer or internet work to get Carmine's address. *Take that, you two!*

24

VIVIENNE ROSE

The next day Viv was pleased to confirm that one phone call was all it took. Plus she'd have an opportunity to wear her newly purchased skirt suit sooner than she thought. Glancing at her image in the mirror, she turned to the left then the right to see if everything worked.

The navy-blue pencil skirt fit closely over her hips. Hitting right at the knee, above her tan kitten-heel pumps. The navy-blue matching blazer, with one button in the front, fit effortlessly over a white linen sleeveless shirt. She'd ignored Jason's advice about the pink button-up. *Pink and blue remind me of babies.* Tugging at her shirt, she noted how the neckline of the blouse dipped just slightly, exposing a glimpse of her cleavage.

Viv felt a shiver of excitement remembering her early morning phone call.

"Hello, is this Mrs. Carmine Nelson?" She'd used her professional voice. Soft but firm.

"Yes, it is," came a mature woman's throaty response.

"First, may I say I'm so sorry for your loss."

Viv had experience with loss, working with so many

families and new babies over the years. Because it turned out doulas often had to deliver bad news. Not all babies were perfectly healthy or easy to bring home. And mothers had issues with postpartum depression, which required delicate conversations.

Even dads collapsed into tears on occasion. Over the years people had told her she was a compassionate woman and that she'd made a difference in their lives at very difficult times.

Viv knew it had taken a few mishaps to get her to that point. Once she'd been able to cross the threshold from her own emotions to be present for others, she'd become a better doula.

Her words of condolence began to sound more genuine because she felt them in her gut. The pull of her heart. And the resonant tears that came to her eyes when she shared someone else's grief made a difference as well.

When the grieving woman on the other end of the phone began to weep, Viv knew she should remain silent. She waited patiently, consciously inhaling in, then out. It wasn't until she heard sniffing and then a slight cough that the woman asked, "Who is this I'm speaking to?"

"We haven't met. My name is Vivienne Rose. I was there the night your husband's body was discovered. It was a coincidence, by the way, but I'd like to send a card if you don't mind. Just to say I'm still thinking about him and now you. May I assume that you are his wife..."

"Yes, I am." The woman sniffed and then hiccupped.

Viv kept her voice smooth. "My friend Jason Knew said you wouldn't mind if I called. He gave me your number."

"Oh, Jason. He's such a dear." A fresh burst of sobbing filled Viv's ear.

"I can call back later," Viv offered, as soon as she heard the woman blow her nose.

"Instead of mailing a card, why don't you come by?" An unexpected invitation lay in the air. "Come to the wake we're having for Carmine. I'm sure there will be people here interested in hearing how you found him. It's this afternoon at four o'clock."

Viv could not believe her luck. Maybe while mingling with Carmine's family and friends, she'd find out more about his life. Then she could report to Rex and Sutton and sit back as they admired how she'd gotten information on her own without any help. And without being a tech savvy genius either.

A final inspection in the full-length mirror brought a smile to her lips. *I look pretty good,* she concluded. *Maybe not bombshell good like Sutton, but good for a sixty-year-old woman who has some serious game left in her after all.*

The Nelsons lived in the expensive part of Palm Desert. Clean lines of mid-century modernism were evident throughout the neighborhood. Perhaps due to planning restrictions, none of the houses looked exactly like each other.

Named after Ronald Reagan, the custom-built Reagan Estates homes reflected expensive construction materials, including expansive glass exteriors. Each one had a different flair, but all were alike in their charming take on high desert California architecture.

Even the landscaping looked more natural than it did in her neighborhood. Money had been spent to bring in enormous boulders and stretches of river rock, which were surrounded by native cacti and succulents. If you looked carefully you could see drip irrigation, laid just under surrounding gravel, which kept the plants alive.

The hot months, nearly half the year, made watering necessary, especially if you wanted healthy-looking plants. But the water was recycled. That was how Palm Desert got past any complaints from the California State Water Board.

Viv parked along the curb and took a minute to watch people file inside the house. Most wore black, some in equally saturated dark colors. One woman had a hat with a veil over her eyes. *Now that's old Hollywood*, Viv concluded. *And kind of classy too.*

She felt confident in her skirt suit. The self-assurance showed in her erect posture and assured walk as she approached the front door.

Viv was used to entering unfamiliar homes. Offering her hand to a greeter at the door, she began the introduction, establishing her connection to leave no doubt as to why she was there. "My name is Vivienne Rose. Beverly Nelson invited me to pay my condolences."

The man nodded. His eyes took in every aspect of her dress before he offered his hand to shake. "Thank you for coming. The body is to the left and the reception to the right. There's a line, but it should move quickly."

Viv's stomach lurched. She'd not expected to view the body. She moved forward to make way for the next person. A quick glance over her shoulder at the man greeting newcomers confirmed her suspicion.

She felt certain the greeter carried a gun in a shoulder holster. She'd seen police officers' jackets bulge the same way. And even if that guy was sporting a two-thousand-dollar Armani suit, the bulge could be detected.

Viv walked into the foyer, her low heels clicking against the glossy marble floors. She instantly recognized a Carolyn

Sale sculpture placed in the center of the room. *Ceramic on steel. That must have cost a fortune.* She edged closer to glance more closely. *Yep, that's an original.*

Though Viv was not an art expert, she'd taken a class. The local High Desert of Modern Art Museum, called the MAM by locals, had offered a seminar that was attended by several well-known artists who gave talks.

She stepped away from the statue. Taking her place at the end of the line, Viv assumed a pleasant but serious expression. She tried to look detached. She planned on doing a lot of listening to the people around her. The couple standing ahead of her in line would be her first target. Fortunately they were talking loud enough for her to overhear.

"Beverly must be devastated," said the woman with the hat and veil.

"We've taken care of everything." Her companion wore a black suit and a red tie. And a hat. A fedora tilted back on his head, exposing gray hair.

Viv stepped slightly to the side to get a closer look at his profile. He seemed familiar. Then she knew. *That's HOA Frank.* She moved back in line, this time an inch closer to the couple to hear even better.

"Have you seen Joey?" the woman asked.

"He's in the dining room. Acting real nervous, you know, offering people drinks and interrupting like he does when he's hiding something."

"Do you think he's the one?" the woman asked.

"Wouldn't surprise me at all," the man said matter-of-factly. "Joey and Carmine had issues going way back. Maybe it finally came to a head and batta boom, batta bing. Carmine is dead."

The woman reached into her purse, pulling out a

hankie. "That's so terrible, Frankie. I can't bear to think about it." She dabbed at her eyes.

"You women get emotional. But I'm telling ya. The older you get, the deadlier you've got to be. You take your age and you make it a strength. A real businessman is even more dangerous the longer he lives," Frank said, then added, "I never cared about dying. That's just life."

His words sounded rehearsed to Viv. Not as if he didn't mean them, but as if he'd said them often and was trying to convince himself.

But Viv didn't entirely disagree with him. Hadn't she just been tiptoeing around the same idea, wondering how to turn her age into her strength? Maybe the dying part was a bit much, but being strong until the end? That philosophy had some merit.

25

VIVIENNE ROSE

When it was Viv's turn, she stepped closer to the casket. She held her breath before glancing at the body. Exhaling quickly, she stared at his hands clutching a Bible, which had been turned upside down. She eased her hand toward the book, causing a man behind her to gasp, but she didn't mind. She shifted the Bible to appear right side up with a pat. "That's better," she said aloud.

Closing her eyes, she hoped that people would think she was praying. When she opened her eyes she inhaled quickly, bracing herself for the next look at the body. Carmine's forehead was very smooth. To her surprise there was no evidence of the bullet hole. Someone behind her cleared their throat, breaking Viv's concentration. She moved away quickly, grateful to get away from the coffin.

On her way to the reception she stopped to sign a guest book. She added her phone number, just in case the widow wanted to get back in touch to talk about Carmine. Voices wafted in from the outdoor patio.

Viv walked through the room and then outside, stopping to order a seltzer water with a slice of lime at the portable bar. Glass in hand, she made her way to stand near an expansive potted palm. Her attention was drawn immediately to a particularly loud voice coming from a group of men standing in the grassy area beyond the patio.

One guy gestured with his hands as he spoke; the others listened attentively, laughing at appropriate intervals. Viv recognized the man talking. It was Frank Salucci.

She had a better view of his face this time. He had a strong nose and bronzed skin, accompanied by very white straight teeth, and a loud derisive laugh that she associated with a man who had just told a dirty joke.

His tan indicated that he spent time outdoors. Probably a tennis player or golfer. A taut trim body, he had not lost his sex appeal, though he probably was at least seventy.

"It's all about loyalty, men," Frank said loudly enough for everyone, even those standing around the bar, to hear. "Don't forget, no one gets out of this alive."

The men chuckled. One raised a glass to Frank.

"Am I right, Joey?" Frank looked at the bald man standing to his right. Viv shivered, sensing the words and the glare may have had a more sinister meaning.

So that must be Joey Baker, Viv concluded. The only guy who didn't show up at the HOA meeting.

After finishing her seltzer water, Viv put her glass on a tray and made her way to the front door. On her way past the sculpture, she realized that she hadn't spoken to Beverly. She'd glanced into the room but found the widow surrounded by people offering their condolences.

Viv didn't want to draw attention to herself and she didn't want to add to Beverly's difficult day. *I can talk to her another time. I signed the guest book. She'll know I came.*

On her way through the foyer, she stopped to admire the lacquer-finished grand piano. Rolled into a corner, an array of framed photos sat on top. Viv ran her finger over the shiny black finish and then stooped to look closer at the pictures.

There were shots of a younger Carmine and Beverly, their smiles directed toward the camera, taken in happier times. One photo showed a baby in a christening dress. Then another with Carmine holding the baby, along with a toddler clutching his hand.

Viv gently lifted a silver frame. People stood in a group, arms around each other, wearing swimsuits. Frank Salucci stood in the center, back row. Even in a photo he looked like he was in charge. Something about the tilt of his head and his smile. Next to him was a girl leaning into his side, eyes staring at his face.

I bet that's his daughter. She resembles him, the tilt of her chin...

Viv blinked. She stared at Frank and then the girl. She used her thumb and forefinger to try to make the image larger. Realizing her mistake, she smiled. *Talk about habits. This isn't a picture on my phone.*

Viv lifted her cell out of her bag. She looked over both shoulders. It only took a few moments for her to open the app and take a picture of the photo she held in her other hand.

26

REX REDONDO

"I can't believe you just showed up at the wake and introduced yourself." Rex knew he sounded upset. Her impulsive decision worried him.

Viv sat with her feet propped up against the stones that surrounded his fire-pit. The flames licked at the rocks, the blaze casting light on her face. *She's beautiful in the firelight. I like the way the angle of her chin lifts as she looks at the stars.*

He'd texted her earlier, hoping they could get together.

> Want to come over later and talk about our case?

> Yes!

He'd not expected her to arrive with such interesting news. She took a beer and began to tell him about showing up for Carmine's wake. He nursed his beer and paid attention. But then when she got to the part where she turned the Bible around, he leaned forward. His nerves tingled. *I forget that Viv has some nerve. Touching a dead guy like that.*

"Carmine looked so fake," she said. "Waxy and lifeless. That's to be expected. But the bullet hole? No sign on that forehead. I don't know how they managed to cover up the hole, but if I hadn't seen it with my own eyes, I'd assume he died of natural causes."

"I think the desert mortuaries hire old Hollywood makeup artists to do their work. Not surprising they're good at it. But let's get to the other part. You actually turned the Bible around right under his cold dead waxy hands?"

"Sure did." Viv nodded. "I didn't break one of his fingers off or anything, if that's what you're wondering. It needed to be done, so I did it."

There it was. That practical side of Viv. But had she gone too far this time. Maybe someone noticed what she did and took offense. He shuddered to think of what the family would do if someone messed with one of their own.

"So was the widow, you know, properly upset?" he asked.

"People lined up to offer their condolences," Viv replied. "She was devastated. In tears. I didn't stop to talk to her. But then I didn't stay very long."

"Do you think Mrs. Carmine might have killed her hubby?" Rex asked.

"I can't say for certain, not having met her face-to-face. But in case you're wondering, Beverly's tears sounded sincere on the phone. I sensed she genuinely grieved the loss of her husband. And then Jason told me they were close. So there's that."

"So what did you think of Frank?" Rex asked.

"I didn't get to talk to him face-to-face either. Most of the time he was surrounded by other men. I'm thinking he's the head of their group. The one with the power. All the men there were afraid of him," she said thoughtfully. "It was more than respect. It seemed like genuine fear."

"He is retired. I got that from Sutton. In his previous life he was a motion picture director and producer. Used his profits to promote his films. I think there was a rumor that he was a part owner at the Pair-a-Dice. At least he spent a lot of time there. Had a high-power poker game going every week in a back room. And now he's turned his eye to real estate; property dealings in the high desert."

"Mob connections?" Viv asked.

"Maybe, though I'm not sure about that. The casino is run by a Native tribe, the Cahuillas. Maybe they bought him out at one point," he mused.

"So no more poker games?"

"Could be. Either way, Frank's supposedly out of the casino business. Sutton is looking at Dean Marcella now. She thinks he may have a Fluff and Fold connection."

Viv leaned back in her chair. She continued to stare up at the night sky. "I wish I knew more about constellations," she said softly.

"Me too." He wanted to say more, but constellations were the last thing on his mind. *If only Viv was as interested in me as she is in the night sky.* He held up his empty bottle. "Want another one?"

"No thanks." She didn't look over.

When he returned to the firepit, she was still gazing at the stars. "So let's recap." He pulled his chair closer. "We know Carmine had a wife. She also has an unlimited capacity for tears, which may be who she is or may be because she's an actress and putting on a show. But you think the former is true."

"Genuine tears. From my perspective. Plus we also

know that Carmine owned or at least operated the local Fluff and Fold," Viv added.

"Carmine must be connected to Frank Salucci," Rex said.

"And the other HOA guy, Dean what's-his-name, sells shoes out of a truck in back of his place," Viv said.

"Or Dean's son does. Remember?" Rex smirked.

"Like I believe that excuse," Viv scoffed.

"It may be a father and son operation," Rex said.

"You're right. That may be true. But let's stick to what we know about the HOA guys first."

"Okay, so we have Frank, Dean, and then the preacher guy," Rex concluded.

"Samuel Daniels," Viv said. "He seemed so nice. And he's a man of God. I think he can be scratched off our list of suspects. Plus I didn't see him at the wake, so maybe he didn't even know Carmine."

Rex tapped her arm. He made a face at her in the dark. "The church is filled with lunatics and money grabbers. How do you think the Vatican got so rich?"

"That doesn't mean a retired chaplain, an admiral no less, would murder a person. I'm not seeing Pastor Daniels as a suspect. Like I said, just because he's on the HOA with others doesn't mean they are associates or even friends."

"You think he's a good guy," Rex said.

"And you think all of the HOA members are suspects," she replied at once.

Rex had to admit that she was right. It was part of his work to listen for the secrets that people did their best to hide. *Probably makes me suspicious of everyone. Kind of collateral damage in my line of work.*

He didn't respond to Viv's accusation. Instead he took her cue and looked up at the night sky to avoid defending himself. The expanse of the stars, the swath of darkness made him feel slightly out of control. He focused on her again. "I'm thinking we've found out a lot about Carmine. But the most interesting part is what you overheard when Frank was talking to his wife about Joey Baker."

"I agree," Viv replied. "Head-of-the-family Frank thinks that Joey was acting oddly. And that means he may suspect that Joey killed Carmine."

"Maybe so," Rex commented. "So I think we need to focus on Joey Baker. Let's get a good night's sleep and make our plan in the morning."

"During our walk," Viv added.

Rex's heart skipped a beat. *As long as we're investigating, I get to see her every day.*

"Get a load of that dipper," he said, pointing to the sky.

"Which one is that?"

27

REX REDONDO

Rex yanked on Kevin's lead. Slightly out of breath, he drew alongside Viv and asked, "Do you think we'll see the woman with the baby this morning?"

She glanced at him with a quizzical expression. "You read my mind. That's exactly what I was wondering."

Viv kept talking. "It's the sound of the baby crying. I worry. Maybe that isn't a healthy family. A sign of post-partum or dysfunction. Maybe it's a signal to look more closely. Maybe the young mother is in trouble. You never know."

"I'm not feeling what you are—about the baby. But then I don't have your experience. I'm not a doula and I've never actually lived with anyone that young in my home," Rex admitted.

Viv smiled. "Thank you for that."

"For what?"

"Oh, for admitting you may not be the expert in every-thing. I'm used to men who think they know more than I do, even when it's in my line of work."

"Men are pretty bossy," he laughed.

"Nice that you agree," she chuckled.

Rex felt his shoulders push back. He wanted to jump up and down, though he knew he'd look ridiculous. But Viv's words actually made him feel proud. She'd noticed that he was a bit introspective.

"Thank you," he said cautiously. "I believe that may be the first compliment you've ever paid me."

She took a longer stride, calling back over her shoulder. "You're a stage performer with women at your beck and call. You don't need me to prop up your ego."

He burst out laughing. "That's very true. I'm pretty good at keeping my ego inflated all by myself."

Until I met you.

He wanted to tell her that but didn't think it was the right time or place.

28
____

VIVIENNE ROSE

Rex leaned over to tug at the brim of Viv's baseball cap. "Do you think he can see us?" She squirmed, lowering herself in the passenger seat.

"That's why we're keeping the windows up. They are tinted, but that doesn't mean he hasn't noticed us. We've been hanging out here for two hours. If he realizes we're here he may come closer and confront us. That would blow our cover."

They sat in Rex's SUV across from the offices of Joseph "Joey" Baker. It turned out that his address was in plain sight all along. His face and smile had been painted on bus benches along the main highway. Joey even had a slogan: Everything starts with trust. The signage included a business phone number that appeared underneath his tag line in bold black numbers.

"I hope he comes out soon," Viv said. "I'm getting hungry."

"I believe I mentioned every stakeout requires snacks." Rex handed her an open bag of pretzels.

"Too many carbs. I eat veggies in between meals."

He scoffed. "It's surprising we're partners, you know, with our opposing views on what to eat when."

Viv's eyes grew wide. "Partners?"

"This is our second case. And I am moving forward on the PI license. So yeah, we're partners."

"Neighbors in crime," Viv mused. "I'm not all in. Because it sounds ridiculous. But I hear what you're saying. This is our second case. Fell into our laps. That has some merit."

"Look over there." Rex pointed to a man coming from the building. He wore a dark-colored suit, a tie, and a button-down light gray shirt. Ducking his bald head, he strode across the street. A car came to a screeching halt, barely avoiding him.

"That's him," Viv said.

Joey opened the door to his Mercedes Roadster, slipping behind the wheel.

"Follow that car!" Viv exclaimed.

"Gotta do a U-turn." Rex flicked on the ignition, then made a turn in the middle of the road as horns honked in his wake. "That was close," he said.

Ten minutes later Rex pulled into a space next to the curb, half a block down from where Joey parked in the driveway of a single-story bungalow.

"Is this his house?" Viv asked. "Doesn't seem swanky enough for a guy like him."

"I would agree." Rex flicked the engine off.

"I think these places were built just after the war." Viv looked around to take in the neighborhood.

"Some have been renovated, maybe more than once. But check out the one over there." Rex pointed.

"Single story, adobe construction. Maybe twelve hundred square feet. I actually looked two streets over before I bought my place. My son wanted me to be safe, so he persuaded me to live in a gated community."

"I'm very happy he did," Rex commented.

She changed the subject quickly. "So do you think Joey's a family man?"

"I see no evidence of family from here. No teenage-type vehicles. No basketball hoop on the garage. In fact everything looks perfunctory. As if he was..."

"Single," Viv filled in. "So our guy doesn't have a family. Or maybe he's like you. Not interested in marriage. Or he could be divorced."

When Rex didn't respond, Viv looked over. She caught a sign of discomfort in his face. He pulled on his ear and then glanced into his rearview mirror. "Well look who we have here."

Viv turned her head. A truck lumbered past their SUV. It continued several feet and then parked against the curb. "That's Dean, the sneaker guy," Viv said.

She heard the vehicle beep as Dean walked toward the front door of Joey's house. It opened immediately. Ushered inside, he disappeared from view.

"I wonder what they're talking about?" Rex sighed. "We may be done for now. Unless you want to wait to see who comes out. It could take a while." He glanced at the empty pretzel bag. "Why don't we get some lunch at Just Desserts. I have a hankering for a pastrami on rye."

"I would love a nice chicken salad," Viv agreed.

Before he started the SUV, he stopped to send a text. A

quick ping came in response. He read the message to himself as Viv watched without asking any questions.

Finally Rex started the engine and pulled away from the curb.

29

VIVIENNE ROSE

On the way back to town, Rex asked, "Do you remember what specific role Joey and Dean played on the HOA? Was it mentioned that night or did everything get lost once the cops showed up?"

"I think their job titles are on the monthly newsletter. I've looked before. There are names but no contact information, and the job titles sound kinda fake. Plus they pump out the same letter every time. All they change is the date at the top. There's the typical information. Like the hours of trash pickup and reminders about bagging your pet's waste."

"I delete the notices without reading them," Rex admitted.

"I keep the latest one in my inbox. Just in case I need to call the office about something."

"Do they pick up?"

"I have to leave a message most of the time."

"Our HOA is kinda odd. For example, why would Joey Baker have a house that's not in our community? I thought that was one of the rules to be on the board."

"He could own a house at the Desert Tortoise and be renting it out," Viv suggested.

"I suppose." Rex pulled into a parking space in front of Just Desserts. He came around the SUV to open Viv's door, and she stepped out onto the pavement. *He is kind of old-fashioned,* she admitted to herself. *I like the door being opened.*

Sitting at the table, they ordered. While they waited for their food, Viv found her thoughts returning to Carmine's wake. *I haven't told Rex about the photograph.* She cleared her throat. "There's something I found on the piano at the wake," she began. But then the waiter arrived.

Viv lost her train of thought. She picked up her fork to stab a piece of chicken, lifting it from a mound of lettuce. Rex held the overstuffed pastrami sandwich to his mouth. They ate in companionable silence. Once he'd finished, he asked, "How was your salad?"

"Pretty good." She shoved a few lettuce leaves around to make it look like she'd eaten more. The problem was she kept glancing at his face while he chewed. *Nothing wrong there.* Then she'd forgotten she was hungry.

She'd even spent some time inspecting his hands, the tapered fingers. When he caught her staring she looked away, but not before a flood of heat spread over her chest. *That could be a hot flash,* she told herself. *Or could it be something else?*

Since she'd reached middle age, she had trouble distinguishing the messages from her body. Feeling warm all the time and then moving to the desert with the dry hot climate didn't help. Sometimes the heat led to breathlessness and a sense of panic. She'd apply ice bags at night if she woke up suddenly. Place them on her chest just to calm her nervous system. All of these unfamiliar body experiences had confused her.

She had friends who took antianxiety medication prescribed by their doctors. But Viv didn't want to go that route. She liked to think that the body knew things that maybe she wasn't aware of. And that the heat and sudden flashes were a new normal, caused by fluctuating hormones and the climate. *Just changes in temperature*, she told herself. *Nothing to be alarmed about.*

Then she made an odd connection. Paying attention to the clues from her body wasn't that different than paying attention to other clues. Like in a murder investigation, for instance. Line them up and after a while a conclusion can be drawn.

"Why the smile?" Rex asked, putting his wallet back into his pocket.

"I'm thinking about my body," she said.

"Oh, I'm interested. Do tell." He grinned at her, a playful sound to his voice.

"Do you ever wonder? I mean, if your body could talk, what it would tell you?"

"I know what my body is telling me most of the time." He paused for a moment as if he wanted to say more, but then asked her, "What's your body telling you right now?"

"Maybe that I'm pushing aside a lot of my feelings." She smiled at him. "Emotions are so inconvenient, don't you think?"

"Not at all," Rex exclaimed. "In fact, I always want to know what you're feeling. I'm not one bit afraid of your emotions."

"You surprise me. In a good way." She felt genuinely pleased at his response. "Should we leave now? The tables are filling up and they most likely want to seat more paying customers."

Walking toward the exit, Viv heard Rex's phone ping. He read his screen, continuing to walk. He stopped at the curb. "So our pal Joey? Sutton's on the stakeout. He's been picked up by another guy. She'll keep us posted."

He opened the SUV's door for Viv, closing it as soon as she settled into the seat.

As they drove, Viv's thoughts returned to the HOA meeting. She thought about the men sitting around the table. There were five plaques with names but only four men in attendance: Frank Salucci, Dean Marcella, Sammy Daniels, and Peter Langford. Joey Baker was the one missing. They'd tracked down his place of work and maybe his house.

"What about Peter Langford?" she asked suddenly. "We haven't found out where he lives."

Rex made a left turn into their neighborhood.

"We haven't followed up on him yet," Viv repeated.

The entrance gate lifted as Rex drove through. "What made you think of him?"

"I'm wondering if he was at the wake and if maybe he's the guy who picked up Joey. It's a big assumption, a long hunch..."

Rex pulled into his garage, shutting off the car. Kevin's bark sounded from inside. "Let me check on Kev and I'll get back with you. Any chance I could have a swim in your pool later? That would help my..." He pointed to his knee. "It's still bothering me after that catapult over the counter."

"Swimming is very therapeutic," Viv said. She felt a tingle travel up her spine. *Stop it*, she told her body. *He's just a neighbor who wants to use the pool. No big deal. Behave yourself.*

Viv found herself humming on the way to her house. *What is that tune?* She hummed the next line. *A Frank Sinatra song: "The Best is Yet to Come."* Then she blushed. *Rex was singing that just the other night.*

Obviously meant for someone a lot younger, she told herself firmly.

30

REX REDONDO

"Nice UV-blocking shirt," Viv commented. She stood by the pool in her one-piece red swimsuit. Designed for swimming, it clung to her body but had no extra frills.

Rex nodded. "My dermatologist suggested I do more blocking with clothes at my age."

He gave no feedback about her appearance. He'd learned that she didn't believe his compliments, so he held back. *But I can think whatever I want and I'm just sayin'... That woman's got it goin' on.*

Pausing to brush her hair into a messy ponytail, Viv dove into the pool. Her arms stretched into an easy crawl stroke, as her body skimmed through the clear blue water.

Hardly any splashing when she swims, he thought. *So precise—just like the rest of her personality.* Rex pretended to look at his phone, but his eyes kept glancing toward the pool.

Twenty minutes later she emerged, a huge smile on her face. "I do love the feel of the water, so refreshing." She reached for her towel.

"I can see that." Admiration filled his voice.

"I swam all the time as a kid," she explained. "Took lessons early on. Over the years I gave it up. Funny what gets left behind when you're raising a family. Until I moved here."

"Maybe you're on to something," Rex said. "When I was a teen I used to play tennis. But I haven't picked up a racket in years."

"Pickle ball," she said. "It's all the rage."

"You play?" he asked.

"I never have. But my father played paddle tennis. I think it's the same thing. I can remember going with him to the club and hearing the smack, smack, smack of balls going back and forth."

Rex stood from his chair. "I guess it's my turn for a dip. Don't watch, okay? I'm a terrible swimmer. Just tune out my cries of distress when I get in. The water's never warm enough for my taste."

"No problem. I am very discreet. I won't look and I won't tell. How about that?" To emphasize her words, she walked to her chair and picked up her cell phone.

"Man, it's cold," he said as he stuck a toe in the water and looked over to see if she laughed.

"Buck up and get moving," she called out.

Rex rarely put his whole body in water at the same time. Unless it was a spa and there was a woman waiting for him. But now he didn't want to look like a fool, so he took the plunge and then held his breath.

31

VIVIENNE ROSE

A notification popped up on Viv's screen; someone was at her front door. She recognized him immediately. The man who'd greeted everyone at Carmine Nelson's wake. She looked up. Rex was still swimming.

"Be right back. Have to answer the door," she called to him. Since his head was underwater, he most likely couldn't hear.

"Be right there. I'm outside," she told the man waiting out front through the speaker on the doorbell's camera. Pulling on her bathing suit coverup, she yanked the scrunchy out of her hair and ran her fingers through the wet strands. Then she slid her feet into flip-flops.

The man took a step backward when she opened the door. Today, dressed in faded jeans and a white polo shirt, he looked less formal but just as efficient. Viv wondered if he was still on the job. *Maybe when he isn't working as Beverly Nelson's doorman, he runs errands.* Could he be her bodyguard? Well-muscled arms hung at his sides.

"Miss Rose," he said. "I have a message for you."

Okay, today he's the errand guy. "How did you know my address?" she asked.

"You're not hard to find." He reached into his pocket and came up with an envelope. The blush color and gold initials embossed in the corner looked like expensive stationery. Not the kind you picked up at the drugstore.

She took it from him, feeling curious and suspicious. Holding it in her hand, she appreciated the weight of the deluxe brand of paper. Her name had been handwritten in cursive on the back of the envelope.

"Why didn't Mrs. Nelson just pick up the phone?"

"She has her own way of doing things," he explained. "I'm just the messenger. But if there isn't anything more, I'll go. She didn't tell me to wait for a response."

As he turned on his heel, Viv called after him. "Are you a friend of Beverly's? I remember seeing you at the door greeting people on the day of the wake."

He turned back. "I'm her employee. Like I said, I have to go now. Have a nice day."

Behind the closed door she used her finger to open the envelope's flap.

"What do you have there?" Rex had finished swimming and stepped inside the house. A towel wrapped around his waist, his chest was bare.

She looked him over with a smile. *Okay, not the body of a twenty-year-old but definitely in shape for a man of his age. He must work out. No gut. Some muscle in the shoulders. Nice chest hair. Not too much. He doesn't wax. I like that.*

She was tempted to glance further, but when he tugged at his ear, she stopped. *I believe I've made Rex Redondo self-conscious. Well good for me.*

She waved the envelope in the air. "Carmine's widow sent me a letter. Dropped off by her employee."

Rex whistled. "You must have made quite the impression. Go ahead. Open it."

The seal already broken, Viv removed a note in the same handwriting. She read aloud. "I need help with a delicate situation. This is a matter that requires some discretion. I heard you helped the police solve a murder, so you must be something of a sleuth. Here's my private phone. Call at your earliest convenience." Viv folded the note and put it back in the envelope, a thoughtful look on her face.

Rex let out another low whistle. "So the plot thickens. What's our next move?"

She didn't answer him right away. She wanted time to think, so she headed toward the kitchen as he called after her.

"I'm going home to shower off the chlorine. Be back in twenty minutes."

She answered immediately. "I'll get in touch with Mrs. Nelson. Maybe I'll have something more to report by then." To her surprise he followed her into the kitchen, a concerned expression on his face.

"Right. But please don't make any plans to meet up with her by yourself. I want to go with you. But you can take Sutton if you think a woman would be better. Just to make sure that you're safe."

Viv swallowed hard, feeling a retort on the tip of her tongue. *I'm perfectly capable of handling the situation myself. I don't need a companion.* To her surprise, she felt angry. She wanted to shout after him and tell him, "If I were a man you'd never act this way!"

But she didn't. Instead she gulped back her opinions and the accompanying frustration and swallowed. She cleared her throat and then spoke, her voice sounding calm and rational.

"I think I can meet with Mrs. Nelson by myself. We've established a connection over the phone. I showed up at her house for her husband's wake, and she wants to talk to me alone."

And then sarcasm slipped in. "Plus I didn't see a 'plus one' on the note. Neither you nor Sutton need to accompany me."

Rex blinked. He didn't argue right away. Maybe he realized he'd overstepped Viv's boundaries. Maybe the tone of her voice, cool and calm, startled him. Maybe he just didn't know what to do when a woman turned down one of his offers.

"Okay then." His chin dipped to his chest.

Don't you dare, she told him in her head. *Do not start to pout. I am not in the mood.*

To give him credit, he walked toward the door.

She called after him, "See you tomorrow for our walk." *I hope he noticed I didn't say I'd see him in twenty minutes like he wanted.*

When he didn't respond she felt a pang of remorse. But then she recovered.

I do not need him following me everywhere I go, as if he's driving Miss Daisy.

32

REX REDONDO

Rex made his way home, more than just a little angry. *I thought she'd be happy that I wanted to come along. And did you see how huffy she got...* He stomped through his living room.

"Bork!" Kevin ran right over, wagging his tail.

"Not now, Kev," he mumbled.

Making his way to the bedroom, Rex stripped out of the wet trunks, casting them along with his towel to the floor. He headed straight to his shower. The warm water pelted his head, soothing his hurt feelings.

By the time he'd toweled off, he was able to think more clearly. *Maybe I imagined her attitude. I felt like I was dismissed. What triggered her, I wonder?*

Women!

Dressed in jeans and a button-down with shirttails out, he sat in his office.

Need to talk.

When no response came from Sutton, he smacked his

phone down on the desk. Kevin's dark eyes stared up at him. His tail slightly elevated, his eyes beseeching, he lifted his paw, placing it on Rex's thigh.

Rex patted the top of his head. "You don't have to look so glum. I'm the one in the doghouse. I hate this feeling."

Kevin's tail thumped against the floor. When Rex removed his hand from his head, the dog leaped onto Rex's lap.

"Woah, partner," Rex exclaimed, gripping the desk to keep the chair from tipping over. Kevin snuggled into his chest. Then the dog lifted his nose, his tongue swiping across Rex's mouth.

Rex buried his nose in Kevin's neck. *Dogs can really be a comfort. Especially when women are annoying.* He wrapped his arms around Kevin's warm fur. "You smell pretty good today. Kind of like a cheap vanilla candle. Must be the doggie shampoo and conditioner Sutton's using." He hugged the dog again and then gave him a gentle shove. "Now get down, you silly mutt."

"I got your text." Sutton stood in the doorway. "You shouldn't let him do that, jump in your lap," she scolded.

"He just does what he wants around me." Rex extended his leg to stretch. "I went swimming today. Very therapeutic for my injury." He pointed to the problematic knee.

"And not bad for watching your girlfriend's strokes either. I assume you swam in her pool."

"Yeah, about that." Rex sighed. Then he told Sutton how mean Viv was to him and how she'd hurt his feelings.

After talking it out and sharing several deep sighs, Rex got quiet. Sutton made her assessment. "You're a bit much. You know that, right? Viv is her own woman. She doesn't need you treating her like a weak sister who requires protection."

Surprised that Sutton wasn't more understanding, Rex shot her a hurt look.

"And that pouty thing you do with your bottom lip and the big eyes. That's not gonna work on Viv either. Don't you think she's seen enough babies as a doula?"

The truth hit him hard. He gulped back a defense. Mostly because Sutton's matter-of-fact assessment made sense. *Viv only said no, that she didn't need any help.* He sniffed, feeling even more sorry for himself now that he knew he'd most likely exaggerated the situation.

"Maybe I am pouty," he mused aloud. "Don't you find that mildly attractive in a man?"

"I find you irritating," Sutton said. "Now enough about your feelings. I have some news. My guy—he's on the inside of the Palm Springs police—told me that the Nelson family does have mob ties. Apparently Mrs. Beverly Nelson's father is Nick Luciano."

"Not the boss in Detroit—they call him Nicky L., right?" Rex felt his gut clench. "I am right. Viv can't handle a mob boss's daughter. They're a special kind of wicked. Did I not just say that Viv needed help!"

"Just stop. You said that, but your mistake was to imply that she was weak. That's why she got mad. Think about it and stop being so defensive."

Sutton left the room. She'd grown smart that way. Over the years when they'd disagreed, she'd learned to make a quick exit. She knew that he'd calm down and be more reasonable afterward.

She returned shortly with a coffee carafe and two mugs. "Give Viv some space. She'll get over it. And really, how much trouble can a doula possibly get into?"

33

VIVIENNE ROSE

Viv dropped the lion-head door knocker to announce her arrival. She tried again. *Tap, tap, tap.* She'd called ahead, so she knew Beverly expected her. Finally the door swung open, revealing a young woman wearing black jeans and a white t-shirt. Her sneakers were so white they appeared to sparkle. *Glitter on the shoelaces,* Viv thought. *Interesting touch.*

Her clothes resembled what the messenger man wore, the one who'd dropped off the letter earlier that day. Viv assumed the black and white casual was some sort of uniform. *Looks like the Nelsons have a full-time staff...*

The young woman spoke first. "You must be Vivienne Rose. Beverly is expecting you." The use of her employer's first name surprised Viv. If she were the owner of this expansive estate, she wouldn't encourage the use of her first name. Ms. Rose, she'd insist.

Following the young woman through the entryway, Viv glanced around. The furniture had been moved since Carmine's wake. The piano, no longer shoved into the alcove, took center stage. A pure statement piece, she could see her reflection in the high-gloss lacquer finish.

Viv imagined people congregating around a jazz player who crooned Sinatra hits; people mingling with cocktail glasses. Men in bow ties, women in slinky black dresses. *That's so Palm Desert. Playground to Hollywood's elite.*

The young employee gestured for Viv to follow her down the wide hallway toward two closed double doors. She opened both to reveal a grand sunroom filled with tropical plants. "I'll be going now," the young woman mumbled, leaving Viv to fend for herself.

The scent of plumeria wafted toward Viv. She inhaled deeply, appreciating the moist air in her nostrils. Twelve-foot palms rose overhead. Two wax palms had grown so tall, they pushed against the glass ceiling.

"Do you have a sunroom at your house?" came a voice from behind a fiddle leaf fig. Viv walked closer. She found Beverly Nelson seated on a wicker sofa, leaning against plush pillows.

"I don't have a sunroom," Viv answered, "but my neighbor has a smaller version than yours. He likes orchids."

"Many people in Palm Desert have sunrooms. So pleasant to come home to, especially during the hotter months."

And some lucky folks have property that backs up to a golf course. Viv looked out the window over the vast expanse of grass. "You seem to have everything you need to feel at home," she said.

"Oh, let me assure you, I wasn't raised this way. It was Carmine. He provided well for our family. This is my favorite of our houses."

Viv tried not to stare, but her eyes lingered on Beverly Nelson. She wore a loose-fitting caftan that draped to the floor. The fabric was gauzy and white, with beads sewn in a swirling pattern from the plunging neckline to the hem. *No widow's weeds for her.* Flat white sandals with straps over her toes peeked out from the dress. She looked comfortable but wildly expensive.

Beverly didn't seem to mind Viv's gaze. She glanced to the left and the right, biding her time. Then she raised her hand, gesturing for Viv to sit down. Gold bracelets on Beverly's arm made a slight clinking sound as they cascaded to her elbow. "Thank you for coming so quickly."

Beverly inhaled deeply. Before she could speak, the young woman came through the double doors. She brought a metal tray held in both hands. Three oversized glasses with short stems and large bowls sat next to a pitcher, filled with a shimmering pink liquid. The rim of the glasses glistened with salt. The pitcher's frosted glass looked cool and inviting.

The young woman settled the tray on the coffee table and then turned to leave.

"Thank you, Maria," Beverly called after her.

Then turning to Viv, she said, "Pour yourself a strawberry margarita. So refreshing this time of year." She pointed to the tray. Viv, who immediately declined, explained, "I have to drive, so I'd better not."

Beverly smiled slightly and then took a glass and filled it for herself.

I'm not here to be social, Viv reminded herself. Feeling slightly impatient, she began to speak. "You mentioned needing help..."

Beverly took a long sip. "I thought of you as soon as I realized my quandary. It started with the phone call. You were there when Carmine's body was found. When you didn't come to talk to me at the wake, I wondered. But then

I did a background check—one can't be too careful these days. I read that you run a doula agency and that you helped solve a recent murder."

Viv kept her expression blank. It didn't surprise her that Beverly knew about Desert Doulas. That was public information. But her involvement in a murder investigation had not been publicized.

She took her time answering, while Beverly reached for the pitcher. She poured herself another margarita. Filling the bowl-shaped glass to the top, she licked the salt from the rim as the bracelets slid up and down her arms. After a long gulp, she said, "That's much better." The half-filled glass remained balanced in both hands.

"I can't emphasize enough how I don't want to involve the police," Beverly stated.

A chill came up Viv's spine. The woman's voice had acquired a new intensity. No longer sounding like the grieving widow, but a woman in charge.

"Why don't you tell me how I can help?" Viv suggested.

With a quick nod, Beverly explained. "It's come to my attention that my husband Carmine was murdered. Not because he did anything wrong but because he threatened to go to the police."

Viv's eyebrows raised. "Was he a whistleblower with a company?"

"Oh no. Self-employed all his life. Most of his associates are family members. That's another reason for a discreet investigation. I don't want to upset anyone unnecessarily. I just want to punish the person who killed my husband." She took another long sip.

"Let's just say there's a group of wheeler-dealers here in Palm Desert who all know each other. They dabble in creative financing. Nothing illegal, understand."

And Viv did understand. She knew that people who had to say "nothing illegal" were in fact not exactly legal either. Otherwise why bother to explain.

Beverly continued. "The claim is that my Carmine threatened to expose one of those high-powered men. And in order to shut him up, they killed him." Tears formed in her eyes. She took another swig of her margarita, this time draining the glass.

"Please help yourself." Beverly pointed to the tray again. Her words were slightly slurred.

Viv refused demurely. "I want to keep my wits about me. You did say you needed my help."

"I want you to bring Joey Baker to me." Her lips pursed.

"Any particular reason?" Viv asked.

"I don't need a reason, do I? Just bring him. I know that you have connections with that mentalist at the Pair-a-Dice. Maybe he can help get you an introduction. Joey practically lives at the blackjack table, so it won't be hard."

Viv was shocked. "Are you asking me to go undercover?"

"More like become an acquaintance. Baker is known for having loose lips, especially when he drinks. He'll gamble for hours, hoping to beat the odds. As he plays and runs a bar tab, he chats up the people next to him. It doesn't matter who you are. But he's known to target women of a certain age. Ones who have money in the bank, who day gamble into the early evening.

"If you fluff yourself up a bit and go for that friendly granny look and then sit next to him at the blackjack table, I think he'd talk to you."

Viv wondered if she should feel insulted.

The sound of a door opening came from the other side of the room. She watched Beverly lean toward the beverage tray, her ample bosom exposed by the neckline of the caftan. Beverly filled her glass for the third time. "Hello, dear. I have your drink already." She held it aloft as an invitation. Her hand slightly swayed as Viv held her breath.

A man dressed in white shorts and a white polo shirt, along with white court shoes, walked into her line of sight. He came closer. Without acknowledging Viv's presence, he reached out to steady Beverly's hand. Then he leaned over to kiss her cheek.

Viv recognized him immediately.

He turned to her, offering a half smile. Once he sat next to Beverly, his thigh touching hers, he spoke.

"Let me introduce myself." He glanced quickly at Beverly before continuing. "My name is Peter Langford. My friends call me Pete. I run a local accounting business here in Palm Desert. That's only part-time, of course. I spend half of my time in DC, where I also have a consulting firm."

Viv held out her hand. "I'm Vivienne Rose. We haven't met officially. I was at the HOA meeting when Carmine Nelson's body was discovered."

She expected him to be shocked. But he only nodded. "That's right. A terrible night. Now I remember you. And that guy you were with. A boyfriend?"

The question about Rex felt awkward, way too personal to Viv. "We are neighbors," she explained, without adding any more detail.

Beverly's words seemed to stick on her tongue, the alcohol in the margaritas taking effect. "I've already mentioned that we're suspicious and that I need her help," she told Peter with a slur.

"Not from the police," he quickly added. "We talked about that." His voice was full of reproach.

"Not the cops. I'm not stupid, honey." Beverly patted his knee, the bracelets jingling. She removed her hand and slumped further against the cushions. Her glass began to tip. Pete leaned over her lap to take it out of her hand.

"Be careful there, baby. Slow down on the booze." He placed the empty glass on the table and then turned to Viv.

"So here's the thing. Carmine and I go way back. I've been his accountant for years. I knew his finances inside out and I'm here to tell you, he's clean as a whistle. Never been audited. He was that honest.

"I also know that Joey Baker is the opposite of Carmine. Joey's always been on the take and he cuts corners every chance he gets. He'd steal the pension from an old lady if he thought he could get away with it. In fact, he marks older women, oozes his charm. Pretty soon they hand over their savings and he up and disappears."

"That's awful." Viv felt her stomach clench.

"Not the half of it," Pete continued. "Carmine got tired of Joey. He'd had enough. They must have gotten into an argument that led to Carmine saying he'd go to the cops. Now that in itself is extreme, since Carmine was no snitch and he hated police.

"Joey killed Carmine. That's not debatable in my estimation. You bring him to us and we'll do the rest. And don't worry. He's not worth the effort of protecting."

The hair on her neck rose. Now she was convinced that Joey Baker must have killed Carmine.

Pete reached into his pocket. He removed a piece of paper that had been folded in half. "We're hoping this will be enough, a retainer for your services."

Viv took the paper and unfolded it. *Ten thousand dollars.*

"You know I'm not a licensed private investigator, right?"

"Don't want someone with a license," he said emphatically. "Our only rule is that when Joey cons you, you lure him to your house. Then call us. We'll do the rest. No cops. That has to be understood. Palm Desert is a small town. We don't want anyone to get any ideas that we have a relationship with law enforcement. Can I say that enough?"

"I've got it." Viv nodded. "So when do I start?"

"How about tomorrow? I'll send you a photo. Keep it on your cell. Just so you can identify him in the casino. The lights are terrible there. Joey starts gambling around noon..." He was interrupted by a loud snuffle followed by a throaty snore.

While Pete was talking, Beverly had eased her body onto the sofa cushions. She rested her head on a decorative pillow, her lips puffed in short bursts. Viv tucked the check in her purse and rose to leave.

34

———————

VIVIENNE ROSE

Once she left Beverly's house, a plan began to take shape in her mind. *I need a disguise. Maybe look slightly frumpy. Time to really granny up.*

Instead of heading straight home, Viv made the turn into town. Parking in front of Out of the Closet, the details flooded into her head. "I need to look my age," she told Jason. "With a street vibe. You know, like I live rough."

"Honey, you don't come to my shop to look worse. You come here to look amazing."

"I know, but this is different. A unique occasion." She stood at the counter, tapping her fingers. "Don't you have anything in the back room that would work?"

"What, like mismatched double-knit slacks with a baggy top? Maybe hearts and flowers stamped on the front?"

"Right. Like that!"

"And some oversized sandals in that ghastly shade of outdated pink?" His bottom lip turned down with disgust. "So last year." He sounded disappointed. "You know I hate those open-toed pink plastic sandals, right? The ones all the tourists wear by the hotel pool."

"I don't care if the sandals are pink," she said impatiently. "I want to know if you have anything I can use, stored away in that back room."

Jason sighed. "Okay, I do have something. But you have to promise not to tell anyone where you got the items, and most certainly do not use my name in any connection with this plan. You do have a plan?"

"I'm going undercover," she explained.

"Get out! Like a private eye?"

"My reputation for solving the other murder—the body floating in my pool—got me a new client. Just like that." Viv snapped her fingers.

The next day she stood in her bedroom feeling a tingle of excitement. With the check deposited, she dismissed any sense of guilt about not interviewing more doulas. That amount of money would hold her for some time. Plus she couldn't wait to tell Rex how she'd gone full-throttle private eye all on her own. But she'd tell him after luring Joey Baker to her house.

The clock on her nightstand read nine. *Better get dressed.*

She pulled items from the brown paper sack. It turned out that Jason did have tops and slacks in his back room, but he refused to put the boutique sticker on the outside of the bag when she left his shop.

He'd explained to her with careful detail. "I found these at a garage sale. I didn't buy them, if that's what you're thinking. They were shoved in the bottom of my bag, hiding underneath two pairs of delicious Ferragamo high heels." He stuck his foot out for her to see. "Breaking them in behind the counter." His eyes glinted.

Viv left the boutique with nearly everything she needed. And now this morning she pulled the slacks on first. The bright red pants hit just below her knees but were so baggy, she had to laugh. "Now that's a fashion statement." Then she added the oversized peasant top, a yellow stain around the neck. She felt certain that with this outfit she'd fit right in at the Pair-a-Dice blackjack table.

Viv sat on the edge of the bed. She knew that Jason didn't want to admit that he had these old clothes in the back. What he didn't know was that she knew more about women who frequented the casino than she was willing to admit.

Though she'd never told anyone, her mother often day gambled. When Mom couldn't be found hunched over her kitchen table smoking a cigarette and playing solitaire, she'd drive over the state line to a casino where people knew her by her first name.

"Judy, you got the kid with you?" the bartender would say. "How you doing, Vivienne?"

Judy was her mom. She'd been addicted to gambling until the day she passed away. Congestive heart failure from all of that smoking. At least that's what the doctor told her.

So Viv knew that no one, especially a gambling addict, seemed to care what they looked like once they walked into a casino. Even in the daylight, in this outfit, she'd blend right in. And with the photo of Joey Baker on her phone, she felt sure she'd recognize him right away, even if the room was hazy with secondhand smoke.

"Meow," Miss Kitty called from down the hall.

"Be right there. I haven't forgotten you." Viv took one more look in the mirror; she nodded at what she saw. *I don't have to be an ex-military officer or even have a license. I can be my own kind of detective. A woman whom no one looks at. Because over the age of forty, we're pretty much invisible.*

Viv inhaled sharply. If she was able to get Joey Baker to chat her up, she'd tell him about a big savings account. It would be easy. Mostly because making conversation with unfamiliar people was one of her gifts.

And she didn't need Rex Redondo or Sutton Drew. None of their specialized internet nonsense either. She'd made her own way. First she called Beverly on the phone. She'd shown up at a wake, had a meeting one-on-one and gotten a lead on Carmine's killer. And now she was dressed like an older woman who day gambled.

Viv dug in her drawer. She had tossed a pair of old progressives from ten years ago in the back. Sliding them onto her nose, she looked even more eccentric. A wool hat would cover her head and be the finishing touch.

By the time she parked in the casino lot, she walked toward the entrance with her head down. She deliberately didn't glance toward The Roadkill. She didn't want to catch Jake's attention. He might mention seeing her to Rex or Sutton, and then she wouldn't have the satisfaction of telling them about her exploits later.

Once inside the door, she stopped inside the ladies' room. It only took a minute to wash her hands. The water running through her fingers calmed her nerves.

Viv picked up the cards and took a quick glance. Then she turned them face down in front of her. She knew the rules but they didn't matter. She didn't care whether or not she won. Her job was to get talking to Joey Baker.

The dim lights made it difficult to see people's faces. Some casinos had outlawed smoking, but Pair-a-Dice wasn't one of them. Every incessant ding from a slot machine made her flinch. Trying not to panic, she felt a headache coming on.

But then forty-five minutes later, she was rewarded. Joey Baker slid through the entrance. Smiling and greeting the bartender, he made his way across the floor right toward the blackjack table.

Joey gave the dealer an easygoing grin. "Hey, Tabby." Then he sat in the only empty seat.

"You're the anchorman," Tabby told him, dealing two more cards.

Without glancing at Viv, Joey stacked his chips. He focused on his cards, not looking her way.

Several hands later Viv was still unable to catch his eye, let alone start up a conversation. Joey focused on his winnings. He'd had good card hands so far, his mood turning more and more jovial with the addition of alcohol.

"You going off shift soon?" he asked the dealer.

"Not soon enough," she said flatly. And then to Viv's relief, Joey finally shifted his body, turning toward her.

"I haven't seen you at the table before." His tone was conversational.

"In from out of town," she mumbled.

"Staying long?"

"Not sure. Depends if I'm winning."

Joey chuckled. "That's true. You must have some experience with the game."

"You could say that. But right now I could sure use a drink." She nodded toward the bar.

"Hey, I'm buying." Joey waved his hand over his head. A man with a small round tray appeared. "Get me a bourbon neat and something for the lady." This time he made it a point to catch her eye. She felt her heart flutter. Not from attraction, more about excitement. *Game on!*

Knowing she would only be sipping, Viv did not hesitate. "Same for me." As the server left, she picked up the two cards dealt to her, pretending to be interested.

After several more hands, Viv's stack of chips dwindled. Joey glanced over and shook his head. "Better luck next time." He stood from his chair, taking his winnings with him. Her heart dropped. *He's going without making his move. Now what...*

She hastily stood, moving alongside him. "I'm done," she announced to the dealer. She shuffled her way to the cashier. *I don't know why this plan sounded so good to begin with. I mean, who talks to a woman at a blackjack table unless she's young and sexy and out for a good time.*

That Pete guy must be nuts. Joey's way too smooth to con old women. Doubt pushed aside her previous confidence. *And I'm even crazier for thinking this undercover plan would work.*

Cashing in her few remaining chips, she walked dejectedly toward the exit. Once outside, she took a deep breath. To her surprise Joey Baker waited outside.

"Wanna have a drink at The Roadkill?" he asked. "It might cheer you up."

"A drink sounds good," she replied, "but not there. How about my place?"

35

VIVIENNE ROSE

Before she could explain where she lived, a loud voice hollered, "We've been looking for you." A tall woman with broad shoulders and trunks for legs loomed over Viv. She took her elbow. Before Viv could pull it away, her meaty fingers clamped down. She spoke to Joey.

"Gotta do a little background check on this one. She's been counting cards and is on our list."

Even Viv knew the accusation sounded flimsy. If she counted cards, then she'd be winning, not losing.

Joey Baker's face dropped before he pasted on a smile. "Oh, no worries. I don't even know this woman. We just met and she was trying to get me to buy her a meal."

"That's a big fat lie," Viv shouted, tugging to release her elbow. She knew her retort only made her look more guilty. But before she could explain, Joey walked away, disappearing into the casino.

As Viv kept shaking at the grip on her elbow, another woman grasped her shoulder, fingers digging into her flesh. "Stop resisting," she hissed in her ear. "Don't say a word, lady. You're coming with us."

They gripped an elbow on each side, lifting her off the ground. Viv felt herself being escorted across the parking lot by the two heavy hitters, right toward an Airstream trailer.

She squirmed, using her leg to kick backward at the woman on her right. Caught off guard, the woman loosened her grip, giving Viv the chance to twist around and kick her behind the knee.

Then a sharp pain in her other arm made her cry out. "Stop it!" she shouted.

"Don't make this more difficult than it needs to be," the other woman warned.

Viv used her free arm to make a fist. She swung and punched, connecting with the woman's chest. Drawing her arm back to land another hit, the woman caught her fist midair.

Before she could try another punch, the burly woman twisted Viv's arm behind her back, holding it firmly in her grasp. Viv tugged and tried to wiggle free. Now both women stood near, securing both of her hands behind her back.

"I told you to come easy," the woman growled. "Now we have to play rough."

"I'm not going anywhere." Viv raised her foot and kicked the woman square in the shin.

"Hey, that hurts!" the woman cried, holding her leg and letting go of Viv.

"I've got this." The accomplice kept her grip on Viv's arm, giving her partner a smirk. "Can't even land an old lady. Geez, what's the world coming to."

Viv, exhausted and out of moves, knew she didn't want to take the fight indoors. *I'll lose there and no one will hear me scream.*

Viv moaned and then closed her eyes. *I don't have to*

make this easy for you. Just try and shift my 150 pounds up into that trailer. I dare ya!

She felt herself partially lifted and half carried, half dragged up the stairway to the door of the Airstream.

36

———————

VIVIENNE ROSE

With one burly woman holding her feet and the other hefting her shoulders, they struggled to get her dead-weight body up the stairs. The woman in charge of her feet grunted. "What's wrong with you, lady?"

"We know you're not unconscious," the second woman said.

Viv willed her body to sink lower. *Make like a rock,* she told herself. *I'm not going to cooperate in my own abduction. That's for sure!*

Once they were inside the Airstream, the tall woman dropped Viv's feet and slammed the door closed. The other woman shoved her onto a sofa.

With her nose thrust into a throw pillow, Viv couldn't breathe. She struggled to stand up, but the burly woman held her down.

"You don't have to treat her like a criminal," a familiar voice scolded.

Unable to turn face up, Viv struggled. Once the woman released her hold, Viv rolled over, gasping for breath. She planted her feet on the floor, her eyes focused on the exit door. Then she looked forward, finding a man sitting on another sofa opposite her.

"What are you doing here?" she demanded.

Rex Redondo folded one calf over his knee. He wore his usual walking attire and a worried expression.

"This Airstream, despite appearances, is a safe place," he said in a calm voice. "Casino employees use it to take quick naps and hang out when they have a break. Starsky and Hutch here were only helping me out.

Viv glowered at Rex. "Starsky and Hutch?"

"That's what I call the ladies. We go way back. They've been on the Pair-a-Dice payroll since I got here. It takes a lot of muscle to keep a casino safe."

"So they aren't holding me for card counting?"

"Naw, that was an excuse. To get you away from Baker. You do know he's not a nice guy, right?"

"I don't remember inviting you into my investigation. I'm not sharing the fee. Just so you know."

"So there's a fee?" Rex paused, appearing to consider the implication.

"We had to get you out of there in one piece," the taller woman explained. "I'm Starsky, by the way. Pleased to meet you."

Viv looked at her closely. Her short-cut hair only emphasized the largeness of her body. "Hello," Viv said curtly. *She seems nice. For a bouncer.*

Viv stood up. Overcome by dizziness, she felt her knees buckle. She fell back down into the cushion. Her head pounded. She opened and closed her eyes, but it didn't stop the pain.

"Are you okay?" Rex asked in a concerned voice.

"Have a terrible headache. Been quite the morning so far."

She put her hand on the side of her face. Before she could say any more, Hutch handed her a glass of water. "Probably dehydrated," she explained. Her voice had become soft, nothing like the woman who'd conspired to abduct her in the parking lot.

"Thank you." Viv took the glass. She slurped the water down. "I think you're right. Dehydration." *Plus I haven't eaten since last night.*

When she finished drinking, she looked at Rex. "I know you're responsible for this charade. But why? I can handle myself."

"I'm sorry, but we didn't know what else to do," Rex explained. "I've had Sutton following you for the past couple of days. You went rogue and it worried us both."

"Could I have an aspirin at least? My head is pounding." She looked toward the small kitchen. "And a cracker or something so that I can take the aspirin without upsetting my stomach." The simple requests made Viv feel better. As if she were taking back some control.

Those three should be jumping at my beck and call after that treatment.

The motor home door opened, casting a light on the faded carpet. Sutton Drew called out, "You in here, boss?"

"With the lady in question," he answered.

"Can I come in?"

"You'd better. She's demanding an aspirin and some answers. Oh, do you have crackers? Viv wants those too." He grinned sheepishly.

Sutton stood between Rex and Viv. "How about some crackers and also some ice for the head? Starsky, get on that."

Starsky made her way to the kitchenette. She opened the freezer and pulled out an ice bag.

"Here you go." She wrapped a towel around the bag, holding it for Viv to take. Then she pulled saltines from a cupboard over the sink. "You can have these too."

"I can't believe you resisted so hard. A real wildcat." Rex's eyes shined with admiration. Then he leaned forward to stare more closely at Viv's face. "You okay?" he asked again.

She shifted the ice bag to her other temple. "I'm still mad at you," she said.

Viv wasn't really mad. What she felt, if she were to be truly honest, was relief. She'd known as soon as Joey Baker sat down at the blackjack table that she was in over her head. But she kept going along with her charade. And then when she'd invited him back to her house...as soon as the words left her mouth, she knew she'd made a mistake. *So Starsky and Hutch may have actually rescued me. A clumsy bit of work, but still...*

One glance of Rex in the trailer helped quell her fear immediately. Maybe it was the smell of his aftershave that made her feel very warm inside. Or maybe because as he spoke, she knew she'd be okay. No matter what, he'd make sense of things. She knew in her heart that just because Rex was unpredictable, that didn't mean he would deliberately hurt her. And that he did genuinely care about her.

"I'll be okay when I get another drink of water and that aspirin," she told him, eyes closed tight.

"Hutch, get another glass of water. Sutton, order us a light lunch to pick up at The Roadkill on our way out. And I'll be right back. I have aspirin in the SUV."

The sound of the trailer door shutting made Viv smile. *Now that's more like it.*

. . .

Rex returned with two aspirin in the palm of his hand. He sat next to her on the sofa and watched as she held the glass to her lips. "Drink it down," he told her. "The whole glass. I'll refill."

Viv's forehead wrinkled.

"Honey, you always think the worst of me." He glowered.

She handed the empty glass back to him with a question. "So you had me picked up by your female thugs because you were worried about Joey. You and Sutton. How did you know I'd be at the casino?"

"Like I started to say, Sutton followed you."

"To Beverly's house?"

"On a first name basis with the widow now?" He glanced away, trying to hide his smirk.

"Oh, I even talked to her boyfriend face-to-face. Remember that HOA guy named Peter Langford? He was there too. Gave me a whopping check to do this job. The only stipulation being that I call them to pick up Joey once I bring him back to my house."

Viv continued to explain how she'd been hired. The more she talked, the better she felt.

"So Joey Baker looks like our main suspect," Rex concluded.

"And they wanted you to play dumb and pretend to go for one of his scams," Sutton added.

"They claim that Joey is a crook and bilks unsuspecting old ladies for their savings and retirement income. He did feel pretty sleazy to me." Viv rubbed her temple. The pounding had subsided, leaving a dull ache in its aftermath.

Feeling only slightly less grumpy, she sighed.

Rex and Sutton sat across from her, both of their arms folded over their chests.

"None of this would have happened if you'd not kicked me out of your house," Rex insisted. Then his bottom lip fell into a pout. Sutton elbowed him.

"I told you to stop doing that. No one wants to look at a sixty-year-old baby."

He shrugged. "Okay. It's a habit. Sorry." His lips forming a smile, Viv had to admit he sounded truly contrite.

"I did not kick you out of my house," Viv insisted. "I merely got angry with you treating me like I couldn't handle my own business. So I asked you to leave to avoid a scene."

He rolled his eyes. "I don't mind a scene. With you," he explained.

Viv felt confused. She'd spent most of her life avoiding undue emotional outbursts. To have a man tell her he wasn't afraid of her emotions, well that would take some getting used to.

And because she was Viv, a person who always wanted to improve, she told him in no uncertain terms, "It's your job to work on your own feelings. Believe me, I have a full-time job monitoring my own."

Something about her logic must have appealed to Rex. His body language shifted. He relaxed his arms and genuinely smiled. "That's an interesting philosophy and one that we can talk more about later. But for now, how are you feeling?"

He came closer to lift her wrist in his hand. Then he leaned his head down to gently kiss the bruise, before releasing it to pick up the other.

The second kiss brought a chill up her spine. "Better," she admitted, her face flushing. "But no more about me. I want to go home and change out of these clothes, if you don't mind."

He glanced over her red pants and stained peasant top.

"Gotta admit you're looking kinda shabby chic in that getup."

Sutton spoke up. "I want to check in with The Roadkill and pick up our food. Be back in a few."

Once Sutton was gone, Viv felt less self-conscious. So she asked a question to clear the air. "After I clean up a bit, let's figure out what I'm going to tell the widow about my adventure. Since I didn't get Joey to come to my house, I suppose that I have to return the money?"

Viv stood slowly. She held her head with one hand, feeling slightly off-balance.

Rex took hold of both her shoulders. "Hold on there, let me steady you." When he didn't remove his hands, she tried to wriggle from his grasp. But then her shoe caught on the carpet. So she grasped his shirt with one hand to steady herself.

In a second he'd circled his arms around her body and pulled her close. She had to admit to herself, *I'm so tired of pulling back*. So she gave in and gladly buried her face in his chest.

She felt him duck his head to nestle his face in her neck. His warm breath hovered over her skin. She felt a tingle inside her body. A feeling she hadn't had in a long time.

She was unable to pull back, wondering at herself. Her lack of resolve. Her need for his warmth. For all of his oddness, Rex Redondo had gotten under her skin.

"Hey, boss," Sutton called through the window. Rex released her from the embrace. Viv was both disappointed and relieved.

"Sutton," he said calmly. "Viv is understandably a bit wobbly. I want you to drive her home. Leave her lunch with her. Then we can pick up her car later."

"Right," Sutton said in an agreeable voice.

Once Sutton left, Rex placed his hands back on Viv's shoulders. "Let's get you home. You can change and eat. We can talk by the pool later." He dropped his hands, a look of reluctance on his face.

"Sounds good." All her previous misgivings had been replaced with a new spirit of cooperation. "Bring Sutton with you. I want to hear her take on all of this."

To her surprise he didn't object. "Let me help you down the steps." He offered her a hand.

37

REX REDONDO

He watched Viv glide through the pool, one arm stretched over her head, then the next. He admired her red suit sliding along the surface of the water. He took a deep breath, pushing aside any thoughts of what she'd look like without her suit. If for no other reason than she wasn't ready and he was worried.

She'd gotten herself into danger at the casino. Just thinking about her being alone with Joey made him angry. He didn't trust the man. Not just because he was a daily gambler. But because Rex read desperation all over him; someone who stole money from the elderly. Though he had to admit that he wasn't surprised. No wonder Carmine's family wanted Joey out of the way.

But what bothered him even more was how carelessly Beverly and Peter were willing to use Viv. An innocent woman. A doula by profession, someone who helped women and families, to do their dirty work. That was unconscionable.

"Hey, boss, want another beer?" Sutton wore a two-piece black bikini with a cover-up that didn't cover up. The white fabric only emphasized her body underneath. This always puzzled Rex, how women managed to not cover up what they intended to cover up. Not that he minded but...

He took the IPA from her hand. "Thanks." He returned his eyes to the pool.

Viv emerged at the shallow end, reminding him of the actress Bo Derek in the old movie *10*. Though she was slightly more mature, the water streaming off her body as she pushed her hair from her face made him smile. He blinked to bring himself back from the fantasy.

Viv came closer to grab a towel from her chair. Wrapping it around her body, she sat down next to him. "Can I have a sip?" She pointed to his beer.

He handed over the bottle. She took a long draw as he admired her neck, how it dipped down toward her breasts, which still heaved slightly from the aerobic swim. She handed him back the bottle.

Rex looked toward the mountain range, now surrounded in reds and golds as the sun made its descent. "I never get tired of this view," he commented.

"Magical," Viv added.

"If you say so." Sutton handed Viv a freshly opened beer. "I, for one, am over the desert sunsets. I like the darkness, when the stars come out, the moon when it's full. More spooky."

"I like that too," Viv admitted.

Rex placed the empty bottle under his chair. "I think it's time to come up with a plan," he said. "One that includes bringing Joey Baker to justice."

"I've been paid ten grand already," Viv admitted. "Maybe I should give it back..."

Sutton nodded. "But before you do that, I've done some more investigating online. Joey's cleaned all of his information. A professional job. I got nothin' for you except what we saw on the bus bench. You two found his house, but I don't think he lives there as a permanent residence. I do know he's been married and divorced but the records are sealed."

Rex was surprised—Sutton rarely came up empty-handed. Not even when they worked intel in the military. She always had something to offer. But then he realized, she just did offer something. Not what she found but the fact that she couldn't find anything.

Joey Baker must be a crook, otherwise he'd have stuff on the internet. Regular people could be researched easily enough. For ten bucks you could get reports of where they lived and past addresses. But this was the second guy on the HOA who must have had his social media scrubbed. *So then nothin' in this case means something.*

Viv stood and dropped the towel on a chair, reaching for her cover-up. Lifting her arms over her head, Rex felt a quick inhale as he observed the dress slipping over her suit.

Viv's cover-up actually covered up. She looked beautiful in the cobalt-blue dress. And since it wasn't that chilly outside, she left her arms bare. Tempted to run his finger down the one closest to him, Rex turned away before speaking.

"I have an idea. I think we need to look into the casita where Carmine was murdered. I mean, before that night, I wasn't aware the community even had rentals, let alone a casita for that express purpose."

"Casitas," Viv prompted. "I know there are at least two. I used to walk up near the golf course and that's how I found out. Before I met you."

"I assume the HOA is in charge of the rentals?" Rex asked.

"Why don't we try this?" Viv said. "I'll call the HOA office tomorrow and find out how to rent a casita. Maybe I'll pretend my son's visiting from out of town and that he doesn't want to stay with me, preferring a little privacy. That kind of thing. Then we'll at least know the procedure for renting. That may give us a hint about why Carmine was found between the fancy sheets."

Rex agreed. "At the very least we can get keys and look the place over. Probably too late for actual clues. I'm sure the cops swept the place."

"But you never know," Sutton said. "People in a hurry, even the pros, make mistakes. Leave stuff behind. You might find something."

"That's settled," Viv said.

"Is another beer out of the question?" Rex asked Sutton.

She stood up. "Viv?"

"Not me. I'm fine with this one."

As Sutton walked away Rex felt an urge to reach out and take Viv's hand. His fingers twitched. But instead he said, "Nice evening we're having."

Viv burst out laughing. "Is that all you can say? Sounds kinda lame for a ladies' man."

This time he didn't hesitate. He took her hand in his. "I'm feeling a bit shy," he admitted. "Especially after getting Starsky and Hutch to bully you into the Airstream. I thought maybe you'd still be upset with me."

She moved his hand to rest on her thigh. "I thought I'd be more upset with you too. I don't understand it, maybe some kind of mentalist trick." She turned her head, a provocative smile on her lips. "Are you doing that mind meld thing on me, Rex Redondo?"

He laughed. "I'd do it if it worked. For some reason I can't wrap my persuasive thoughts around your sweet mind, but not from lack of trying. I tried that first night. All I got was a no trespassing message. Very clear, that was."

He thought of how he'd been attracted to her from the beginning. And how the lack of reciprocation had only made him want to be with her more.

The back door slid shut. "Here's your bottle," Sutton said.

Rex reluctantly took his hand off Viv's thigh. He lifted the bottle and smirked at Sutton.

As darkness settled over the backyard, the pool took on an otherworldly glow. The mountains in the background cast a shadow as the full moon lifted, floating its way over the highest peak. "It's a marvelous night for a moon dance," Rex sang.

"I love that song. Van Morrison, right?" Viv smiled. "I was listening to it in my car the night I drove home and found cops at my house."

"The ones I called in," Rex said, a hint of apology in his voice.

"I'm not mad at you for that." Viv's words came quickly. "In case you were wondering. The 911 led to some painful days afterward, but that's not your fault. I want you to know."

"You're remarkable," he said. "And thank you for that. I can't tell you how much it—"

"Okay then. I'm going." Sutton pushed back her chair to stand up. "And I recommend that you two get some rest too. If we're taking this investigation forward, we'll need our wits about us." She stooped to gather the empty beer bottles.

"I think Sutton has a hot date," he said. Once she disappeared into the house, he finished his thought. "But so you know, going to our separate beds is okay for now." He reached for her hand. "But not forever."

He held his breath waiting for her response.

She let go of his hand. But not as a brush-off. Just gently as if she had to move on now and didn't want to hurt his feelings. "I'm exhausted," she said slowly. "And I still have to feed Miss Kitty. How about we say good night. I'll see you for our walk in the morning."

"Sounds good." He didn't want to disagree. He didn't want to lie either. And more importantly, he didn't want to pout. He was turning over a new leaf. Rex Redondo, man of great patience. A man, not a boy.

38

VIVIENNE ROSE

The following morning Viv dressed in her walking attire. She paused to execute a few stretches while she waited for Rex. Her foot propped on a rock, she leaned over, feeling the tug on her hamstring.

Then changing positions, she bent her leg back so that the sole of her foot touched her butt. She bounced to keep her balance. "Lookin' good," Rex's voice called out.

Kevin borked a greeting as Viv stood on both feet with a smile.

"I've got some intel," she told him.

"Let's get walking," he replied.

He's looking rather pleased with himself this morning. All seems right in the Redondo universe.

Moving briskly across the sidewalk, they rounded the corner, picking up the pace. Fast enough to make Viv breathless but still slow enough so that she was able to tell him what she'd found out. "You'll be happy to know I prioritized our investigation this morning. I called the HOA first thing instead of getting back to my doula clients. And the assistant picked right up. Her name is Joan, by the way."

Kevin skipped ahead as she continued to explain, "She booked us casita number one for tonight!"

"So soon." Rex lifted his eyebrows. "You must have been very persuasive."

"Somebody canceled last minute, just before I called. To Joan's credit, she didn't want to charge the other client for the full night, so she was more than happy to sign us up."

"They only rent to people associated with homeowners, right?"

"That's my understanding." Viv picked up her pace and kept talking. "In fact, I'm wondering if our Covenants, Conditions, and Restrictions agreement lists any rules for the casitas. If they do, I don't have a copy."

"I have the CC&Rs somewhere. There's plenty of information but mostly about the trash cans," Rex muttered. "Only put your garbage receptacles out on Monday in a four-hour time window. Don't put them on the curb too early because it's unsightly. Don't forget to take them back in—"

"Because it's unsightly," Viv finished his sentence.

"And whatever you do, make sure the lid is down. No overflowing trash. Not at the Desert Tortoise Estates. That would be the most unsightly of all."

Rex stepped over the curb to give Kevin more room. The dog romped in front of Viv's legs as if asking her to play. Then he changed his mind, darting across the grass to sniff before lifting his leg. Rex yanked on the lead. "Come on, goofball. Keep up the pace."

When Kevin refused to budge, Viv stopped to catch her breath. "If you're worried about him staining the fake grass, I think he's okay. That's a special brand of artificial turf. Dog friendly."

Rex sounded skeptical. "I won't take the risk. It seems kids can ramble wherever the hell they want, in the middle of the street, in front of traffic. But my dog can be cited for peeing in the wrong place. How do I know this turf is the right stuff? I can't have Kevin ticketed for being unsightly. Now if Kev wants to poop on the fake grass, that's not a problem. I'll pick that up." Rex pulled a doggy bag from his pocket as proof.

Viv chuckled. She had to admit Rex had touched on the truth. She'd not been fined by the HOA but she'd heard other owners complain. And the fines weren't cheap either. Especially when a dog got caught off lead.

As they approached the next turn in the walking path, Viv glanced toward the casitas. "Why don't we have a quick look around the perimeter right now? I didn't get a close look that night, you know, when they found Carmine. I'd like to know if they have windows to the back, for instance." She hurried ahead.

"And if they have direct access to the golf course," Rex called after her. "The killer could have run out the back."

Viv stopped for Kevin to take another sniffing break. Rex dropped the lead to bend over and tie his shoe. In an instant Kevin took off, his tail waving goodbye. He ran straight toward the golf course.

"Kevin!" Rex called.

The dog kept running.

Viv broke into a fast trot. "Kevin," she yelled. Which only made the dog run faster. On the green he shot past a golfer, nearly knocking him over. Viv stopped, out of breath. Rex arrived to stand at her elbow.

"What's gotten into your mutt?" Viv turned to Rex.

"I have no idea. But I'd better go after him. I'll meet you at the casita." Rex left her side, sprinting across the lawn.

He'd never have a problem like that with a cat, Viv chuckled to herself.

She made a turn and then stood in front of casita number one. A three-foot retaining wall cordoned off an outdoor area, creating a courtyard big enough to include a round table and four chairs, along with two chaise lounges. Matching umbrellas created shade.

She pushed against the wrought iron gate, which opened easily. The minimal landscaping, with the path leading to the front door, felt familiar. Several houses in the gated community had similar front courtyards. Viv had not opted for that design, preferring the back bedroom as an extra. But she appreciated the appeal.

She walked toward the door, which stood partially open. Poking her head inside, she saw a mop and a plastic container filled with cleaning supplies. "Hello," she called, not wanting to startle the cleaner by appearing unexpectedly.

A man's head poked out from around the corner. "I'm not quite done," he said. "Have the kitchen to finish. Aren't you early? Check-in time isn't until two o'clock."

"Oh, I'm not checking in," Viv explained.

The man scowled. "So why are you here then?"

"I've never been inside so I wanted to scout the place out for my..." Her voice dropped off as she realized that wasn't the truth. She'd made up a story for Joan but even then, she felt uncomfortable.

Fortunately Rex and Kevin arrived, so she didn't have to explain.

"Our family," Rex finished her sentence. "We rented it tonight for our family," he repeated. "Viv's son. Staying with his girlfriend. We hope an engagement is coming soon."

How glib he sounds making up the story as he goes along.

"Sit, Kevin," Rex commanded.

The dog sat, his tongue hanging out the side of his mouth, his sides still heaving from his golf course run.

"So can we have a look around?" Viv asked.

The cleaner nodded. "Sure. Have at it. I'll be done in ten minutes. I'll have to lock up after that."

"Oh, we don't want to get in your way," Viv explained.

"You gotta leave the dog outside," the man said. "They don't rent to pets and I don't want to clean up anything he leaves behind."

"Kevin is house-trained," Rex said.

"Fur. That's the real mess. They shed and then my pay will get docked." He turned his back to them, disappearing around the corner.

Viv whispered, "I think we should start with the bedrooms down that hallway. He'll be done with the kitchen very soon and then we'll have to leave, so let's make it quick."

"I'll put Kevin in the courtyard," Rex said.

When he returned, she explained further. "According to Joan, there are two master suites, both with attached bathrooms. That door," she pointed to door closest to the main room, "is most likely the third bathroom for guests."

Rex's eyes narrowed. "As sorry as I am to say this, I'd like to begin in the bedroom where they didn't find Carmine. I'm in no hurry to go back there."

Without further explanation, he walked ahead. When he stopped in front of the closed door, she nearly collided into his back.

"Anything wrong?" she asked.

"Could you just give me a minute? I know this sounds crazy, but I can read a room. Especially if I'm the one to walk in first. If we open the door slowly and step in without talking, maybe I'll get an image or a sense of energy that may have something to do with Carmine's killer."

Questions rose in Viv's mind. She didn't believe in psychics and Rex never admitted that he was one. In fact he usually denied the label, explaining that his mentalist job required a certain skill set, which did not include superpowers. But there were times like this that Viv wondered if Rex really was psychic, only he didn't want to admit that he was. "What do you mean an image or a sense of energy?"

"I am not psychic," he insisted. "I'm a professional mentalist with observational skills. And I do have a vivid imagination." He raised his eyebrows at her.

"So you say. Except for now when you tell me you feel things and see images."

"Just give me a minute," he said impatiently. "That's all I ask." He opened the door and stepped into the room. Viv followed quietly, watching him carefully.

He closed his eyes and then took a deep breath, exhaling slowly. Holding out his arms, keeping his elbows to his sides, he turned his palms up. Then he began to rotate his body clockwise. He stopped when he'd come full circle.

Viv might have giggled had he not been so serious. The behavior seemed odd for Rex Redondo, the performer. And even odder for Rex the ladies' man.

His eyes flew open. "I'm not getting anything so far." He looked toward a closed door. "That's probably a walk-in closet. In the interest of time, we can look in there later tonight. Why don't we gather information again in the second suite? I think I'm ready."

"That's where we found Carmine," Viv warned.

Rex nodded. "It's bound to have something, an unsettled atmosphere at the very least." He walked past her toward the hallway. She followed slowly, feeling her own reluctance.

Rex opened the door and entered the room first. Viv exhaled quickly. She stood beside him as they both gazed at the carefully made bed.

Viv noted the expensive sheets, creased and folded over at the top. She inhaled the scent of lavender that pervaded the room. An array of fluffy pillows, stacked against the quilted headboard, displayed the letters DTE in black thread.

"I guess DTE stands for the Desert Tortoise Estates," she said.

"The place has been thoroughly cleaned. I don't have to do my thing. No lingering energy here."

"So you can feel energy and then see images? Does that mean you use your five senses?" Viv said out of curiosity.

"I do get a sense of things. Sometimes I can see a rolling image behind my eyes. Right here." He pointed to his forehead. "Probably a result of being around too many slot machines over the years." He tried to laugh but then turned his face away. Viv could tell it was a sensitive topic. *He's been an enigma since we first met.*

Rex began a slow amble around the room. He opened one door and closed it immediately. Then he opened another door and stepped inside. "Beautiful tub and shower in there," he called out. Then he stepped out and opened the other door again. This time he went inside.

She heard a low whistle. "You might want to have a look in here," he said.

One step inside the closet and Viv stopped. Matching velvet hangers hung to one side. Shelves had been built on the other. "You'd have to bring a lot of clothes on vacation to use all of those." She nodded to the dozens of hangers.

"Maybe they rent for longer periods of time, not just short-term." Rex looked over her head and pointed. "So there's the electric panel right there. And then if you look down, toward the floor—now what do we have here?"

It was a half-size door with two locks. "What do you suppose that's for?" she asked.

"It may be a really big safe," he said. "I suppose renters want a place for their valuables. If staff comes in to clean, that makes sense."

"But the bolt..." Viv tugged on the metal. "If it were for renters, wouldn't this be a combination lock that could be reprogrammed for each guest?"

Rex nodded his agreement. "I think we need to look into this."

"How would we do that?"

"Ask some questions. Maybe Joan would have an explanation. After this evening you can say your son wanted to know."

Before Viv could respond, barks came from the courtyard.

Viv stepped to the window to look toward the front of the house. "Look who the cat dragged in." She pointed to a woman dressed as a police officer, who bent down to pet Kevin.

39

REX REDONDO

Rex knew that he was taking a risk. Telling Viv that he wanted to feel the room, that might be more than she needed to know. And then he'd done his turning in a circle bit. He wasn't sure that she'd understand why he'd not been entirely honest when he said he wasn't psychic.

The truth was Rex had a way of knowing things. His reluctance to talk about it came from childhood. He'd had trouble as a kid trying to explain to his dad and mom how he knew what he knew. Dad patted him on the head and dismissed him. Mom only raised an eyebrow and kept washing dishes. He sensed that she was afraid for her only son, and that she suspected he wasn't quite right in the head.

When he was nine he made the mistake of trying again. Valerie McNally lived next door. He really liked her. He tried to make a dead bird come back to life. Of course it didn't. She refused to speak to him after that.

Since then Rex would always insist, "I'm not psychic." Until Viv. He told her as much as he could, mostly about the images. She looked skeptical, so he stopped. But she didn't make fun of him. *Maybe I can trust her not to think I'm crazy.* Or would she be like everyone else and distance herself just because he was different.

Rex's fingers had tingled and turned hot when he touched the lock on that door in the closet. *Something's hidden in there. Something important.* Unfortunately he had no idea what.

He wanted to explain to Viv but then Kevin barked. Once he looked out to see who was there, he knew he couldn't continue. They both made their way to the living room to greet the officer.

"Fancy meeting you two," Susan Farrah said in a bright voice. "Somebody reported a stray dog on the golf course." She pointed at Kevin, who sat with his tongue hanging out the side of his mouth. "I figured I'd keep him in the court-yard while I called animal rescue, and then I ran into you two."

"That's Kevin," Rex explained.

"He ran away," Viv added.

Susan scowled. "I'll make sure to write up the report with full detail. He's a Bernedoodle, right? I want to get the breed down correctly. Blaming Kevin's misdemeanor on a poodle or a cocker spaniel may result in a paperwork nightmare and my citation being dismissed. That wouldn't be right."

Viv giggled. "Kevin is a Berne, and you can send the fine to him." She nodded toward Rex.

"I'll take it out of his treat fund," Rex dryly responded. "I hope he didn't do too much damage—to the course, that is."

"Just annoyed the golfers." Then Susan smiled. "Okay, so truthfully, I love inconveniencing those old farts. They have so many complaints. They get even more cranky if they have nothing to complain about."

Officer Farrah looked around the room, her eyes coming back to Rex and Viv. "So what are you two doing here anyway? I thought discovering one dead body would put you off this place, never to return again."

"We're renting the casita for a family member," Viv explained. "Thought we'd have a look around." *And look at me just picking up that story.*

"Where you found a dead body?" Farrah sounded less than convinced. "You two aren't interfering with an investigation, are you? I heard all about you butting in from Janis in Lily Rock. Quite the detectives. Is that what you're thinking—that you can find the killer?"

The series of questions, coming one right after the other, made Rex squirm. His instinct was to deny Farrah's accusations. But instead he did a turnaround. Mostly so Viv wouldn't think he was lying.

"That's exactly what we're doing. I'm getting my PI license. This is something I plan to do in retirement. And this one," he put his arm around Viv's shoulders, "is going to be my partner."

"That's a terrible idea!" Farrah claimed. "You two should be thinking about retirement hobbies like playing bridge and cornhole tournaments. Settle down like the old farts on the golf course! Volunteer at the church. They always need somebody to organize the canned goods."

To Rex's surprise, Viv didn't pull away. She moved a bit closer as if appreciating the support.

"Don't dismiss his idea," she told Farrah. "We were very good at detecting the last time. And I think we'd be great partners."

Rex stood taller. He adjusted his arm around Viv's shoulders, wondering if she really meant what she'd said.

Farrah glared. "So I'm assuming you mean business part-ners, not the other kind?"

Now Viv shrugged off Rex's arm. "That's correct. Neighbors in crime. That's us."

Rex took a deep breath. *Viv may not be all in. But she did stick up for me. That's something.* He consoled himself with that thought, just as the cleaner came around the corner.

"I'm leaving," he said, propping his mop against the wall. "Have to lock up. Time for all of you to go." He stared at Officer Farrah. "I didn't know you were here."

"So you work maintenance?" She sounded surprised.

Rex felt the hair raise on the back of his neck. *There's something going on here...*

He cleared his throat and then jumped in. "I noticed a locked door in the back bedroom closet. You must know about that."

The cleaner's face froze. "What do ya mean?"

Rex pointed toward the hallway.

"Oh, now I remember. I never go in there. Maybe an owner's locker?"

"An owner's locker. I didn't know the casitas were indi-vidually owned. It was my impression that they were group owned, part of the HOA. The community pays for the maintenance and repairs."

"And improvements," Viv added.

The man scowled. "I have no idea." He picked up his tote. "You have to ask Mr. Langford about that. I'm just a cleaner. He's the one who gives me orders."

"Do you have a key to the locker?" Viv asked hastily. "Since we're technically owners, we should have access to that locker and the contents inside."

"Again, talk to Mr. Langford. He's in charge of the

casitas." His words were dismissive and impatient. Until he turned to stare at Susan Farrah. "You're lookin' good," he commented in a low suggestive voice.

Susan Farrah glared at him. "Don't be surprised if I get a warrant to search that locker."

"Like I said, you three gotta leave so I can lock up."

Walking home, Kevin pranced between them. He looked at Rex and then Viv as if expecting a treat. When neither complied, he raced ahead.

"Why don't we get a copy of those CC&Rs from Joan? Then we can look them over during lunch. I want to know more about the casitas. Who owns them, for instance, and where the money goes from the rentals," Rex suggested.

"I'll give her a call right after my shower," Viv said.

"So tonight when we stay at the casita, I want to see what's in that locker. Maybe we can get ahead of Farrah."

"Sure," Viv agreed. "I'd love getting ahead of her, especially after she insulted us."

Rex felt his nerves tingle.

The whole night with Viv on a case. My day just keeps getting better and better.

40

VIVIENNE ROSE

It wasn't until Viv stood under the shower stream that she realized what she'd done. *Did I just agree to be a private investigator with Rex Redondo and to spending the night with him as part of our investigation? What was I thinking!*

As she toweled off and then slipped into her bathrobe, she thought about how to get out of spending the night with Rex. *Maybe I can change my mind. I can just call him and explain.*

Then she remembered Farrah. Telling them they ought to find suitable hobbies for retired folks. Combing her hair back from her face, Viv had to admit—ever since Rex Redondo arrived in her world, life had gotten interesting. He'd encouraged her to use her mind, putting her experience and logic to good use. Plus he made her feel alive.

A few minutes with the blow dryer lifted her curls as they cascaded to her shoulders. Slipping on a pair of wide-leg linen slacks and a flowing peasant top, she buckled on her dressy sandals. Her customary choices: a monotone outfit accented by a pair of fancy and expensive sandals.

Picking up her cell phone, she made the call to the

HOA. "Desert Tortoise Estates," Joan answered in a crisp voice.

"Hello, this is Vivienne Rose. I'd like you to send me the HOA CC&Rs electronically as soon as you can. I'll wait and check my inbox while we're on the phone." Viv moved their conversation to speaker.

"Nobody really asks for that stuff," Joan said. "I have to do a search to find them in my electronic files. There have been a few revisions since the original agreement. Board approved, by the way. Do you want to hang up? It will take a while."

"I'll stay with you." Viv knew better than to let Joan off the hook. *She'll never get around to finding what I want.*

Pressing the app to her email, she heard a ding. A message from the Desert Tortoise HOA. Apparently the CC&Rs weren't that hard to find. She opened the attachment, still on the phone with Joan.

"These look fine for now. Send one to Rex Redondo," Viv added. "He's a homeowner and also interested."

Joan hesitated. "I have to get a personal request from him, not you. On the phone or in writing."

Viv thought quickly. "Mr. Redondo is busy today. I'm helping him out in the office. You can send the copy to him or I'll forward mine. Either way."

"I suppose," came the reluctant reply.

While Viv waited for a confirmation from Joan, she wondered why the woman dragged her feet. *One more thing for me to bring up at the next HOA meeting.*

"Sent," Joan finally said.

"Thank you." Viv hung up.

After visiting Miss Kitty, Viv made her way to the kitchen. She put together two sandwiches on sourdough, including lettuce, tomato, and avocado. By the time she made a diagonal cut across each one, her doorbell rang.

Rex's hair, slicked back, was still wet from his shower. He looked casual and comfortable wearing faded denim jeans and a plaid sport shirt. His laptop, tucked under his arm, made her smile. *This is what I'd call a working lunch.*

"I got the documents," he announced, stepping inside.

"I have sandwiches. Why don't we sit at the kitchen table and read while we eat?"

He nodded his approval.

Viv poured tall glasses of sun tea for herself and Rex. She sat down and took a bite of her sandwich before opening her laptop.

A quick glance at the CC&Rs revealed a lot of legalese. Viv yawned and took another bite of her sandwich.

Rex kept reading, his eyes clearly focused on what was in front of him. "Very interesting," he commented. "Did you get to the casita rental part yet?"

"Which page?"

"Toward the end, on page thirty-five."

Viv scrolled, her eyes widening as she read. "So we were right. The two casitas are owned by the community, not an individual. They are designated for guests of Desert Tortoise residents only. And the proceeds are to be put into the HOA general operating fund."

"Nothing about how much is charged per night." Rex chewed slowly. "The fee schedule seems a bit fluid."

"More like nonexistent," Viv commented. "Joan took my credit card over the phone. I forgot to ask how much. I guess we'll find out tomorrow after our stay." She shut her laptop. "According to this document, each casita has an owner's locker. That way people can store golf clubs and outdoor equipment. Since the casitas are owned by the community, we should all have access to that locker to share the contents with our family members who rent."

"So remind me." Rex took a sip of tea. "If Frank is the president, who is the treasurer? Maybe we need to go directly to that person for more information."

Viv opened her laptop again. She scrolled and then stopped. "Pete Langford is our HOA treasurer," she announced. "He was the one who gave me the check at Beverly Nelson's house. He told me that he's a CPA. So it makes sense he'd be the money guy for the Desert Tortoise Estates."

"And you thought there was something going on with the widow. You know. More than friends kinda thing..."

"I don't know for certain. But he sat really close to her and seemed quite friendly. That may mean something."

Rex pulled at his ear. "Are you thinkin' what I'm thinkin'?"

"It doesn't take a mind reader, now does it?" Viv sounded very matter-of-fact.

"Maybe Peter Langford and the widow Nelson decided to kill Carmine and pin the murder on Joey Baker. Maybe they are a couple."

It wasn't until later that night when Viv realized she'd better get packing for a night of investigating, like it or not.

41

REX REDONDO

Rex Redondo waited backstage at the Pair-a-Dice, ready for his second show. By ten o'clock most of the audience had eaten dinner and been liberally anointed with drinks from the bar. He had a different rhythm for the late crowd, unlike the one for the earlier show.

Dapper in his pinstripe suit, he tugged at the silk tie, then at his shirt, checking the gold cufflinks. They'd been given to him by a former girlfriend who had plenty of money. His initials, RR, had been engraved in a fancy script.

A knock came at the door. Viv stuck her head inside. "Ready for our plan to unfold?"

He turned from the mirror, letting a low whistle escape from his lips. "You look stunning," he told her. A peacock-blue cocktail dress skimmed her body. Sleeveless with a slightly scooped neckline, she had stepped out of her coastal grandma look into date-night-at-the-casino attire.

"Oh, this old thing?" Viv teased. To her credit, she seemed quite at ease with his admiring glance. *She's coming out of her shell*, Rex thought. *Maybe my attention isn't embarrassing her like it used to.*

Peeling his eyes away, he turned to the mirror to tug at the knot of his tie. "Have you packed a bag for our big night in the casita?"

He didn't turn around. Instead he watched her reflection in the mirror. She smiled tentatively. "I'm ready. Right after the show I'll meet you back here."

"Then we can head out to the casita together," he added. One look at her told him that she had something on her mind. "I hope you aren't afraid of being seen with me, you know, by the neighbors."

"Oh no," she said right away. "I just don't know what I'd say if someone asks. We both have our own homes. There's no real reason for us to rent the casita for the evening."

"Oh, I could think of a couple of great reasons," he said in a low voice. "Couples spice up their sex life with a change of scenery."

"Of course there is that," Viv admitted. "It has crossed my mind."

"In a good way?" He felt his pulse quicken.

"Let's just say, not in a bad way." At that moment her phone pinged. She read the text.

"They're here," she announced. "Second row center. Sutton saw them. They took your offer."

Rex tugged at his tie. He assured himself that no matter what happened that night, time spent with Viv was what he wanted. He'd work out the rest eventually.

"I offered them last-minute free tickets and an open tab at the bar. That's a pretty good hook," Rex admitted.

"You sent the offer to Beverly Nelson right after lunch?" she asked.

"I did. I included condolences in the email. I told her

that I'm an old pal of Carmine's, so she wouldn't be uncomfortable. I also convinced her this would be a good thing to do, to keep her mind off of her grief."

"But you had no way of knowing she'd bring Langford." Viv held up her phone, "Until now."

"I had a good hunch they'd come together. And if they didn't, I'd at least get to connect with her. Just so you know, it's common practice for mentalists to invite people to the show. Especially recent widows."

"That actually figures. It makes things easier if you already know who your mark is." Viv glared at him.

Rex looked at his shoes, absorbing the tone of her voice. "When you say 'mark,' I'm a little embarrassed. But you're right. Anything for the performance. That's my motto." But his words sounded hollow, even to himself. He buttoned the front of his tux to avoid Viv's glare of disapproval.

Almost show time, he told himself. *Focus.* Once he straightened his tie again, he felt more in charge. He'd used that movement with the tie for years. To remind himself to leave Rex Redondo the man behind and replace him with Redondo the mentalist.

He flung open his dressing room door, ushering Viv into the hallway toward the exit and stage entrance. "I'm going this way," he pointed.

Viv nodded. "Break a leg."

Rex took the stage to scattered applause. Usually the first thing he did was to take a moment. Adjusting the lights gave him time to locate where his marks sat in the audience.

But tonight he looked for Viv.

The blue dress made her stand out. She'd tucked herself into the perfect seat. Rex had explained to her earlier, "Sit in the back row where the spotlight won't find you. They rarely take in that part of the theater."

Even from the stage he could see Viv nod at him, acknowledging his glance. Then she drew a black shawl around her shoulders, hiding the color of her dress from view. She looked very put together and yet unremarkable. A middle-aged woman having a night out on her own.

Once he'd located her, he got down to business. He spotted the couple in the free seats right away. The woman with the well-coiffed platinum hair crossed her legs, her dress inching up to her thigh. A tattoo of a heart was visible on her ankle. Silver bracelets, stacked along her wrist, glinted in the stage light.

The widow Carmine, he immediately assessed, *is on a date night*. It only took one glance at her high heels to confirm.

Now he took in her companion. Langford was a bit more casual, wearing a gray suit coat and slacks, a shirt with no tie, unbuttoned at the neck. He seemed nervous, looking around to each side, taking in the crowd with side glances.

Rex knew the type. *He's used to casing the room mobster-style. I bet he's uncomfortable sitting so close to the front. That's why he looks over his shoulder so often.*

Rex, remaining silent and observant, felt the crowd growing restless. They'd come for a show and he needed to provide. So he transitioned into his warmup. With the notes Sutton had sent him via text, he already had enough information. No need to stall. He had plenty to work with.

He hadn't planned on starting with Beverly Nelson. That would be too obvious. Instead he asked, "Anyone in the audience have a chihuahua whose name begins with a W?"

The question made the audience chuckle. Except for one guy, who stood up, calling out in an excited voice, "We have Wally right here. In my wife's purse!" He lifted the dog from the oversized bag and held him in the air. The audience, realizing the show had finally begun, chuckled as the tension in the room erased.

"That's the one," Rex said with a smile. "Some people don't know, but I read pets. So bring the little guy on stage and I'll tell you what he's thinking."

With more applause the man scooted down the aisle, holding Wally to his chest. The spotlight followed him as he approached the stage. Rex didn't take hold of the dog, but he rested his hand on his head. Wally showed no alarm at the strange man's touch. "Wally loves dog treats, especially small ones that smell like beef," Rex said.

"He kinda likes those," the man looked skeptical. "But they're not his favorite."

"I see." Rex's face drew a blank. But then he smiled, pushing away any doubts. "I actually know what Wally loves. Look what I have here." Rex reached into his pocket and pulled out a square of Swiss cheese. The crowd gasped.

"Yip!" Wally lunged from his owner's grasp.

Rex held the slice away from the dog. He peeled off a bite and offered it to Wally with an open palm. The crowd approved with loud claps as the dog took the cheese.

"How did you know Swiss is Wally's favorite?" The man looked very impressed.

"Don't forget, I'm a mentalist." Rex grinned to the sound of laughter and more applause.

After that he knew he had the crowd on his side. He worked with two more people before getting to his main target. One girl had broken up with her boyfriend, and Rex assured her that the ex would be miserable and that she'd be happy very soon with a better guy.

Another man who had a lisp was told by Rex that his

speech would bring him sympathy from a very attractive woman.

And then Rex slipped his hands into his pockets. He ducked his head as if listening and then held one hand up to quiet the audience. "I feel someone's here. They're visiting us from the other side. Give me a moment of silence to see what he wants."

The crowd hushed as Rex closed his eyes. Soon he moved his head to one side then the other, back and forth as if trying to shake off a fly. When his eyes opened his voice had shifted, each word connected and trance-like. "I've got it. A man who's recently deceased. He wants to talk to his wife. A name starting with a B. Is she here?"

The spotlight drifted over the audience, searching for the right person. Finally it settled on Beverly, who had tentatively raised her hand. Her eyes glistened with tears.

"It's me. I'm a widow."

"Your name?" Rex came closer. His voice dropped, sounding intimate.

"Beverly." She sniffed. "Is it my Carmine? Is that who's talking to you?"

The audience remained quiet, waiting for Rex's next revelation.

"Does your Carmine have a gunshot wound in the middle of his forehead? Right here?" Rex pointed to his own forehead.

The widow's eyes flew open. Tears streamed down her face. Her chin jutted forward. "Yes!" she cried out. And then even louder she begged, "Don't be mad at me, Carmine!"

Beverly bent over, overcome by sobbing as everyone in the audience watched. Peter Langford eased his arm around her shoulders. Then he lifted her to her feet with one hand under her elbow, using his other arm to block out the glare of the spotlight. "Who do you think you are, preying on the grief of this poor widow?" His anger made the audience gasp.

Still clutching her elbow, he dragged Beverly down the aisle. The spotlight followed as the crowd hissed. Once the couple left through the exit, the spotlight made its way back to Rex. He'd put on his calmest expression, returning his hands to his pockets.

"So you can see, ladies and gentlemen, not everyone leaves the show feeling happy. And that goes to show us: Don't underestimate the recently deceased. Their spirits can linger as long as necessary, just to make sure justice is done."

Wild applause came over the audience as they acknowledged his words.

Rex bowed his head, taking their appreciation as his due. When he looked up, he spoke with a grin. "Tell my manager to alert the box office. Those two may want a refund."

He finished his set with a couple jokes and another reading. By the time he left the stage, he felt satisfied.

My plan worked. What with Carmine's ghost haunting them, those two will be very nervous from here on out. It's obvious to me that one or both of them are guilty. I'm just not sure who pulled the trigger.

42

VIVIENNE ROSE

Viv lifted the casita key from under the mat. With the door unlocked, she rolled her suitcase over the threshold, placing the key on the kitchen counter. Rex would follow her shortly, so she took a moment to look around.

Someone had been there since they'd left that afternoon. An upscale aroma therapy candle stood on the counter ready to light. With the snap of a match against the box, she lit the candle. The scent of eucalyptus with a hint of ylang-ylang filled her nostrils.

One light in the corner had been left on, giving the room a welcoming and romantic vibe. With the curtains closed, the stage had been set for a perfect romantic interlude. *All we need is some Sinatra music,* Viv mused.

Viv rolled her suitcase down the hall, choosing the spare bedroom for herself. She hoped Rex didn't mind sleeping in Carmine's room. "Honey, I'm home." She heard his voice calling and then the door closing. She left her suitcase in the suite to say hello.

He'd changed from his working tuxedo to casual slacks and an open-necked shirt, which he let hang over his belt.

The casual style took years off his age. "Did you bring your pajamas?" She greeted him with a smile.

"I brought everything a man needs to break into that lock." He tugged his weekender toward the kitchen, hoisting it onto the empty counter. Unzipping the sides, he reached under a sweater and then some underwear.

Viv tried not to look interested in his clothing, but she wondered what he'd packed for their first night together.

Rex held up a bulging pillowcase. "Sutton went to the local hardware store. I've got a screwdriver and a saw right in here. Plus we can always call her if we require another set of hands."

Viv's surprised face made him chuckle. "To break into the locker, silly," he explained. "She's an expert at that sort of thing."

"Phew." She pretended to wipe perspiration from her brow. "I'm not sure I know you well enough for a threesome."

His jaw dropped. "Vivienne Rose! Look at you talking all dirty." He lifted his eyebrows with a teasing grin.

Viv felt her stomach clench. "Oh, I have lots of things that I think about," she informed him. "But just so you don't get any ideas, two's company, three's a crowd. That's what my mother taught me."

"I'm only interested in you, baby." He used a seductive drawl, which made her laugh.

"Just stop. We have work to do. Bring the tools and let's see what's inside that locker. Are you thinking what I'm thinking?"

He followed her down the hall, the pillowcase with his tools thumping against his leg. To Viv's relief, he didn't hesitate opening the door to Carmine's room. He swung the bag onto the bed.

"If you find something useful in that locker, we may be able to wipe that condescending smirk off of Susan Farrah's face. Once we show her what she missed, that is."

Rex pulled out a pair of latex gloves. An hour later he had successfully removed the door to the locker. Bits of drywall clung to his arm, which he brushed off. "Okay, here we go. Time for the big reveal." Ducking down, he illuminated the area with his cell phone.

"Just a shoebox," he reported, his voice muffled from inside the locker.

"Bring it out so we can have a look," Viv said eagerly.

Once he reached inside, he emerged holding a shoe-sized box. Viv read the brand. "Nike size ten. Sounds familiar."

He handed it to Viv.

She lifted the lid for a peek inside. A slow smile came across her face. "Look what we have here." She handed the box back to him.

One glance and Rex whistled. With his gloves still on, he held up a small thumb drive, which he placed on the bed. Then he gingerly lifted a revolver out of the box and held it in the air.

"Bingo! This has to be the murder weapon!"

Viv felt herself draw back. "I don't know anything about guns. But maybe you shouldn't be waving it around in the air..."

"Don't you worry, sweetheart." Rex lowered the gun. "I'm going to tuck this little baby back in the box and leave it in the locker. We'll tell ol' Susan Farrah when we're good and ready."

"Isn't that—what do they call it...withholding evidence?"

"Probably," he admitted. "But we have no way of knowing for sure that's the gun that was used to murder

Carmine." He closed the lid and walked back into the closet.

Viv followed. She pointed to the holes in the drywall where Rex had removed the hinges. "What about those? Won't someone see and get suspicious? That cleaner guy, for instance. And they'll know it was us because we spent the night."

"He'd suspect your son, not us. Assuming he bought your story earlier." Rex's brow wrinkled. "Give me a minute." He put down the box on the floor. Taking his phone, he texted.

> I need you to do a small repair at the casita. ASAP.

> Spackle and paint?

> Yes!

> Happen to know the paint color of the repair job?

> Builder grade. Same as our house. I think it's called Egret.

> Be there in twenty.

Rex pocketed his phone. "Sutton's on the way. She even has the right color of paint. She got a gallon when we moved in just in case there were touch-ups. There's a good chance that the cleaner won't even notice that we broke in."

"You two are quite the team," she admitted with relief. She looked at her suitcase. "We can go home now that we've found what we're looking for."

When he walked back into the closet and didn't answer,

she had to admit that she wanted him to disagree. Maybe suggest that they could stay the night. *Why am I feeling this way? Up and down with my feelings. To be frank, he's acting like a perfect gentleman. And why does that annoy me again?*

Viv sat on the side of the bed. Catching sight of her unopened suitcase, she sighed. A beautiful nightgown that made her look, well, kind of sexy, lay inside right on top. And her favorite scent, which smelled like jasmine, had been tucked into her makeup bag. Obviously she'd had intentions that she might have not exactly admitted to herself.

Though she'd never make a move toward him, she'd packed just in case he made a move toward her.

But now with Sutton coming over and the need to repair the drywall, Viv felt foolish. And if she were being really honest, doubts replaced her expectation. With Sutton he had a beautiful woman who adored him, who knew him inside and out. So efficient, she bought a gallon of paint to match their interior house color before they even moved in.

Why would he want to be with someone his own age, who had barely scratched the surface of his complicated personality? It didn't make any sense.

43

REX REDONDO

The next morning Rex woke instantly, thoughts about the night before popping into his mind. *What a success, finding the revolver and the flash drive.*

Viv seemed kind of quiet as they left. The sight of the gun must have frightened her, he concluded. Pushing aside the sheets, he stood. *Gotta get up now. Time's a-wasting.* He stretched his arms over his head. Then he headed toward the shower.

By the time he pulled on his pants from the night before, Kevin pushed through the door. He bounced over to sniff the pocket of the jeans. "No treats, Kev." Rex reached in with his hand and pulled out the flash drive. "But look what I have instead." He held it in front of Kevin's nose.

The dog's head drooped in disappointment. "Come on, buddy. Let's get some breakfast."

Kevin's ears perked up. He readily followed him down the hall. The dog's head swiveled. Then he took a detour toward the living room sofa. Leaping up, he curled into a ball, resting his chin on his front paw.

Sutton stood by the kitchen table and held up a coffee mug.

"Not for me. I'm already hyped up. Did you get the job done?"

"Since you left the key under the mat, I had no trouble slipping inside. The stucco and paint should be totally dry by now. The cleaner isn't coming back until after checkout at two o'clock."

"You opened the shoebox, right?"

"Of course I did. Tidy little revolver. Very old school. Looked like a woman's gun."

"I thought the same. But I left it for the cops to figure out. What's more important is this!" He reached into his pocket and held up the flash drive.

"So that's why you're so happy." Sutton took it from his fingers.

"That drive must hold something big for sure. Since it required being hidden in a closet, behind a wall and a hefty lock," Rex said.

"I have time this afternoon to find out." Sutton grinned.

"I was hoping you'd say that. I haven't told Viv that I took this away with me. I didn't want her to worry. By the time you figure out what's on it, I can give her the full report."

Rex glanced toward his backyard. Kevin had let himself out the dog door. He sauntered past the firepit, making his way toward the fence.

"The dog door is working," Rex remarked.

Sutton nodded. "That's good. He has a thing for Miss Kitty. Waits by the fence, like he is now, hoping to catch sight of her."

"Viv does let her out to roam in the morning," Rex mused.

"Plus she uses the morning time to give Miss Kitty a run of her backyard. She doesn't leave the cat. She sits outside to watch. Then she calls and Miss Kitty comes right over. It's kind of cute. Those two have a great relationship."

Rex sighed. "Viv seemed kind of depressed when we walked home last night. I think the revolver may have upset her."

Sutton looked thoughtful. "Not everyone has a military background. Maybe that's the first gun she's seen close up. She's lived a sheltered middle-class life up until now."

"Do you think she's reconsidering—about our private investigating business?" Rex felt his voice catch in his throat.

"Ya never know, boss. But I have things to do and someone I'm meeting this morning. I'll leave you to figure that one out."

As Sutton left through the door to the garage, Rex continued to stare into his backyard. He watched as Kevin stalked the length of the fence, stopping to paw at a board. The dog reversed and walked the other way, this time lifting an ear to listen.

Rex turned away from the glass door and sat down at the table. Opening his laptop, he saw a message on his phone and stopped to read.

Time for your quarterly appointment with Dr. Ryan. Click yes to confirm. Today at nine o'clock.

He confirmed the appointment before texting Viv.

Totally forgot about a doc's appointment. Have to skip our walk.

Her return thumbs-up put a slight dent in his otherwise

happy mood. *She was way too quick with that response. I wonder if she's getting tired of walking with me...*

By the time he handed his keys to the commercial parking lot valet, he was only five minutes late for his appointment. He'd forgotten all about what he called his quarterly tune-up. Dr. Paul Ryan was the preeminent dermatologist of Palm Desert.

The larger, more popular town, Palm Springs, drew most of the big names in plastic surgery. But his doc had his share of Hollywood stars on the lineup. Most people preferred a bit of anonymity when it came to the work they had done. That's why Dr. Ryan had become so popular. If you went to the surgeons and skin care specialists in Palm Springs, you might run into people you know. And you might even be caught by paparazzi. Even though the parking garage was discreet, it was not impervious to photographers.

Rex had stumbled on Paul Ryan years ago. Recommended by one of his pals who lived in Beverly Hills. Ryan had yet to do an actual facelift on Rex. The doctor had managed to keep him youthful-looking with other techniques. Not that Rex garnered the attention of a film actor. But he did have a few thousand fans who cared.

Periodic injections and fillers worked. But for the past couple of years, Ryan prescribed more rejuvenation treatments instead. Including frequent appointments with a dermatological assistant who used LED, ultrasound, and micro-currents.

Gloria, the special assistant, slapped Rex around, nothing short of martial arts. Along with vigorous kneading, she'd assure him, "This is good for you. Waking up the skin.

Better blood flow and increased oxygen." Then Gloria would hold up her hands as proof. "My hands. They are the first technology." Then she'd slap him across the face for emphasis.

And then the quarterly retreats at Three Bunch Palms also helped. A weekend of even more intense treatments, combined with soaking in the natural hot spring water. After that, Rex felt rejuvenated. Everyone went there, especially celebrities, if they wanted the latest in skin renewal treatments.

But now Rex sat down in the waiting room. He had a few minutes before his appointment to consider the murder case. To wonder what Sutton would come up with on that drive.

"Mr. L," came a voice. A young assistant, dressed in a white nurse's uniform, held the door. She waited for the man across the room. He stood immediately, tucking his reading glasses into the front pocket of his shirt. Ducking his head, he cast a quick glance in Rex's direction before hurrying toward the door.

Rex looked amused. *If I'm not mistaken, that's Pete Langford.* As the door closed quietly, he considered the situation. *Maybe I can take advantage of this unexpected run-in.* He glanced toward the receptionist's desk. She looked completely immersed in her computer screen, oblivious to him.

Laying his magazine on the table, he stepped closer. "Seems pretty busy today." He leaned his arms on the counter, his posture relaxed as if just making conversation.

She glanced his way, her hands poised over the keyboard. Rex's eyes traveled to her name tag. "Regina, that's a beautiful name."

The woman frowned. "My grandmother's, if you must

know." She reluctantly dropped her hands to her sides and turned to face him. "How can I help?" Her voice sounded less than enthusiastic.

Rex noted her flawless skin. A slight pinkness to her cheeks gave her that enviable fresh and young look. *She certainly qualifies as the poster girl for this place.*

He cleared his throat. "I saw my buddy Pete going in for an appointment. Didn't have a chance to say hello. Would you mind giving him a message?"

The receptionist shook her head. "I don't know what you mean, unless it's the patient before you."

"Yeah, that's the guy. Pete Langford." Rex willed his mind to open, appealing to Regina's trained impulse to help a patient. He waited, and then he was rewarded. Maybe she felt a bit guilty for her previous impatience. But now she glanced toward her screen and then back to him.

"Normally we don't share names at our clinic. But yes, that was Peter Langford. So you're friends. Do you want me to tell him you said hello?"

Bingo! Ol' Pete is getting a treatment. And he's probably a regular patient like me. I bet I know where he'll be spending the weekend.

"You know what? I'll probably be seeing him this weekend," Rex said casually. "I assume he's going for the skin retreat at Three Bunch?"

"That's right. Have you already reserved your spot? We have a waiting list now. But you can certainly catch up with him then." The receptionist turned to her computer. She closed one window and clicked another, revealing a spreadsheet. "Yes. Here it is. Your prescription. A weekend of radio frequency treatments, along with collagen stimulation. May I confirm your reservation now?"

"Oh, yes you can." Rex couldn't contain his enthusiasm.

And then on a hunch, he asked, "I assume my dear friend Beverly Nelson will also be at the retreat. That would be fantastic. Maybe I'll book a dinner the first night for all three of us."

Gloria clicked again. "Yes, Ms. Nelson has also booked this weekend. She's confirmed as well."

Rex stepped away from the desk, a smile on his lips. He couldn't wait to tell Viv that he'd walked right into an unexpected opportunity to spy on their favorite couple.

44

VIVIENNE ROSE

"Miss Kitty?" Viv called. "Time to come inside." The cat disappeared behind a yucca plant, her tail swishing. Viv sighed with exasperation.

"Bork," came the call from over the fence.

"Not now, Kevin," Viv snapped and then instantly regretted her tone. "Stop barking. I've got this," she said in a more coaxing voice. Reaching into her pocket, she removed a dog cookie.

Walking to the fence, she slipped it between two boards, watching as Kevin chomped and swallowed. "Good boy. Now don't make a ruckus so that I can corral Miss Kitty."

Kevin wagged his tail as Viv called again, "Miss Kitty..."

"Meow," came the plaintive response. Out from behind the yucca, her cat sauntered toward her catio door. She stopped to wash a paw, giving Viv a chance to walk across the yard.

"Good girl." Viv shoved the screen aside, holding the door until Miss Kitty's tail cleared the space. *She never hurries*, Viv thought. Once inside, the cat scampered to the top of her carpeted castle. She turned to view Viv imperiously before lifting her other paw for a quick wash.

Viv took two treats from her other pocket and left them in front of Miss Kitty. "Thank you for coming in," she said.

Pouring herself a cup of tea in the kitchenette, she glanced outdoors. Having skipped her morning walk with Rex, she had more time to allow her cat to explore outdoors. And Viv also had more time to let go of her embarrassment from the night before.

She'd unpacked her suitcase right after her shower. Putting away all of her carefully planned outfits, including her sexiest silk nightgown and robe. This felt like cleaning up spilled milk to Viv. If she made a mistake, she always wanted to get rid of the evidence as soon as possible. And apparently she'd expected more from Rex than she was willing to admit.

He had no idea about the nightgown in my suitcase, thank goodness.

And now that she was drinking coffee, she knew what to do. Reframe the uncomfortable thoughts. That's what she'd teach her doulas, when they'd come back from a difficult birth and couldn't let go of negative emotions.

I'm perfectly fine being friends with Rex Redondo. In fact, that's a lot less complicated than the other.

Then she told herself one more time, *Rex had no idea what was on my mind. He was far too involved with his detective work to think about me. I am way past dating anyone and I need to let this all go.*

Her cell phone chimed, breaking into her self-talk. Two unheard messages. One came from a family with a new baby. The other message brought up a quick breath. *Beverly Nelson.*

Viv held her phone to her ear. "Ms. Rose. Please call me

at your earliest convenience. I want to know how your investigation is going with Joey Baker." Gone was the drunken woman with the slurred words. She had been replaced by a sober version of Beverly Nelson who wanted answers.

Viv put the phone down, agitated. *Rex warned me about going to her home alone. But she deserves answers.*

Viv's mind flashed on the scene at the casino, where she'd tried to engage Joey Baker in a conversation. She wondered if he didn't have something to do with Carmine's death. Even if Beverly and Pete looked guilty, that didn't mean Joey was blameless.

Opening up her computer at the kitchen table, she sent an email to the couple who needed advice about their new baby's sleeping schedule. *Nurse when baby is hungry. Even at night. Double your liquid intake. That's the best way. I'll check in with you this evening.*

Viv always had trouble explaining to young couples that having a healthy baby meant lots of work. If you resisted, it only felt more difficult. If you just gave in and accepted that the baby's needs came first, you had a better chance of adjusting to parenthood. Then in another eighteen years you could reclaim your life, assuming you still loved each other.

After sending that email she opened another document. From memory she typed the names of the HOA board. *I've encountered each of these men outside that meeting.*

Frank Salucci had stood in front of her with his wife at the wake. *He was the first one to mention Joey Baker.*

And then there was Rear Admiral Samuel Daniels. A man who spent a good deal of his retirement preaching at the local church. She did catch a quick glimpse of him on the golf course. *When Kevin escaped for a run.*

Viv kept typing, making notes of the things she remembered next to each name. *And there was that Dean guy. Selling sneakers out the back of Carmine's Fluff and Fold. They'd only spoken briefly, but that counted as an encounter. Plus the revolver in the locker was stored in a sneaker box. Something to consider.*

And she was hired by Beverly Nelson, who was not on the HOA board. But her friend, Peter Langford, was the treasurer of the board. And the way they bolted out of Rex's show—that surely meant something.

She tapped her fingers on the table next to the computer. All of those people, with the exception of Beverly Nelson, must have property in the Desert Tortoise Estates. Otherwise they couldn't be on the HOA board. *I want to know where they live. Beverly Nelson can wait.*

Convinced she was on to something, Viv stood from the table. *If I pay attention to the investigation, I'll stop fussing about Rex. Then he'll assume that I am interested in solving this murder, not that I'm interested in him.* She felt her chest relax.

By the time her cell phone began to rattle on the table, she was ready to answer. "Hey, neighbor," came Rex's rich voice. "I hope you kept your suitcase packed. I've booked us for a weekend at Three Bunch. And don't worry. Sutton already said she'd feed Miss Kitty."

45

REX REDONDO

On the drive to Three Bunch Palms, Rex felt anxious. He glanced over at Viv, who sat quietly looking out the passenger window. She didn't initiate any conversation, which always made him feel uncomfortable.

Why is she acting all standoffish? Plus she didn't say yes at first. She finally agreed after I explained how we were going to do some surveillance. She's still hiding something from me. More quiet than usual. Damn, I wish I knew what I'd done.

Rex pulled the SUV into the entrance of the resort. He rolled down his window to talk to the man who leaned out from the air-conditioned hut. "My name is Redondo," he explained. "I have a reservation for the weekend."

The man reached for a clipboard. "Reservation for Rex Redondo and a guest." He eyed Viv, who sat motionless in the passenger seat. When she didn't smile, he looked back at his reservation sheet.

"Got it here. For two. All the bungalows are numbered," he explained in a singsong voice. "Yours is ready." Then he slammed the window of the hut closed. The gate lifted and Rex drove through.

They found a parking spot in the gravel area shaded by palms. Signs indicated their bungalow number 122 was close by. Rex helped Viv out of the car. She stood looking toward the mountain range as he hoisted bags from the back of the vehicle.

He attempted conversation. "So have you been here before?"

"No," Viv said.

With an exasperated huff, he moved toward the path, one rolling suitcase in each hand. He gestured for Viv to walk ahead. The winding path curved away from the parking lot into the resort, through a tree-shaded oasis. He stopped to glance at a map posted on a wooden announcement board.

The low murmur of voices drew his attention. He looked over to find a group of people. They all wore white fluffy bathrobes and had their heads bound in turbans. Sunglasses hid their eyes. One couple was doing all the talking.

He turned to Viv. "So like I said on the phone, my dermatologist sends patients here for special weekend retreats. They get work done and relax too. Have you heard about the place?"

"Yes," she said.

When she didn't add any more, his frustration got the better of him. "Are you mad at me? I'm feeling the distance, ever since last night."

Viv pointed ahead. "That's our bungalow. Number 122."

"So you're not going to answer my question. Okay then,

play it that way." He lugged the suitcases down the path and toward the door.

Constructed in mid-century style, their bungalow had a courtyard and a tiled sign with the unit number prominently posted. The distinctive artwork on the tiles reminded Rex of his trips on a cruise ship. He'd done several shows for tourists traveling to Mexico. The bold cobalt-blue design matched the enormous cobalt-blue planters on each side of the door.

In the courtyard two lounge chairs had been placed in the shade of an umbrella. "Our casitas are very similar in design. Have you noticed?" Viv commented.

Relieved that she'd finally initiated some conversation, Rex agreed. "They do look similar. I think Desert Tortoise must have tried to imitate Three Bunch. This place is well known. Old Hollywood stars would come for the natural waters in the fifties."

"The grounds are welcoming," Viv added. Her voice had lost its edgy tone, much to Rex's relief.

"Like Hawaii, the atmosphere, don't you think?" He smiled at her, tapping his key card on the entry pad.

A fire had been prepared in the living room fireplace, and a bucket with a bottle of champagne sat on the hearth. Rex observed the cubes in the bucket. "Looks like the hospitality team just left." He stood in the middle of the room, giving her a moment to look things over. Viv took steps down the corridor.

"Two bedrooms?" She lifted the handle of her suitcase from his grasp and rolled down the hallway. Then she called back, "Just like the casitas. I'll take the bedroom at the back, if you don't mind."

"I'll take the other one," he called after her. *She's not gonna tell me what's really bothering her. Okay then, I'll pretend I don't notice. We're here to investigate, not to squabble.*

By the time Rex unpacked, he'd talked himself out of feeling irritated. *I'm not here to hang out with Viv. This is a surveillance opportunity.* He walked down the hallway, book for sitting by the pool in hand, and knocked on her door.

"Come in."

He found her in a bathing suit and cover-up, flip-flops on her feet, a large straw hat pulled low over her face. The brim, dipped over her eyes, giving her a casual but rather elegant appearance. His heartbeat quickened. "Reading my mind," he told her. "How about we sit by the pool for a bit before dinner? I've made reservations for seven. Does that suit you?"

"Sounds good." She sounded deliberately upbeat. But the coolness underneath was plain as day to Rex.

He'd also reserved a cabana by the pool earlier, which he explained to Viv as they strolled across the lushly land-scaped path. Palm trees shaded the way, dipping gracefully overhead.

"So you come here often," Viv said. "Is that why you reserved everything?"

"I do know my way around," he admitted. "It was by happenstance, though, that I found out the couple in question were also frequent guests. It will be challenging to find them. Most people make it a point not to interact. And most people wear the same bathrobes and head turbans. Privacy is the policy. Some people even check in with fake names."

"You didn't," she commented quietly.

"I did at first," he admitted. "Wrote us down as Frank Sinatra and Mia Farrow. Then I decided not to. I registered with my real name. I'm not hiding anything." He glanced at her. "And I thought using a fake identity might annoy you."

He saw Viv's eyebrows raise over her sunglasses. As he directed her toward the infinity pool, she said, "That was thoughtful of you and observant. You've rightly assumed that I'm uncomfortable with your easy attitude toward the facts."

"But not the truth," he said. "I am very clear on what's a story and how facts and lies can, when carefully crafted, lead to the truth. Just so you know."

Her small smile meant the world to him. He felt slightly better until she said, "But the widow and her date. What if they look at the register and realize we're following them?"

Rex frowned. He hadn't thought of that. In his eagerness to please Viv with telling the absolute truth, he'd missed the obvious. "You have a point," he muttered. "Let me think about that. I do have someone on the inside who may be able to change the check-in information."

They arrived at their assigned cabana. One oversized daybed, the main attraction, had been covered with a fitted white top sheet. Four towels, fluffy and also oversized, had been placed at the foot of the bed. Rex dropped his paperback and stretched, watching Viv from the corner of his eye.

She placed her bag on the left side, sitting down to test the mattress. Before either could stretch out, a familiar voice asked, "What can I get you two? A margarita perhaps, or a dry martini?"

The woman stood under the shade of the cabana. Dressed in blue short shorts and a red tank top, Sutton Drew held a cell phone with a cash payment device. She grinned at Viv and then nodded toward Rex.

Sutton turned around to untie the curtains on each side

of the cabana. "Hope you had an easy check-in," she said, sitting on the edge of the bed.

"Do you work here?" Viv asked.

"I do now. Got myself a weekend job with some quick talk about needing cash. I told them I'd work for free this weekend and then they could decide to hire me full-time if they thought I'd fit in." Sutton adjusted her sunglasses, which were the color of her shirt—bright red.

Rex stretched himself out on the bed, raising both arms to prop up his head. He patted the place next to him, an invitation for Viv to join him. "We need to play the part of a couple," he explained.

Viv removed her hat. She tucked the firm round pillow under her neck and leaned back. "Nice," she remarked.

Rex chuckled.

"I mean the pillow."

"They align your spine," Rex explained. "Like I said, everything this weekend is about making your body healthy."

"And about drinking and having sex." Sutton smirked.

"Oh, that won't be us!" Viv said instantly. "We're here to investigate."

Rex sighed. She'd answered so quickly. He knew for sure she was still mad at him for whatever reason. He'd been trying to give her space, but when she was so close, lying next to him, it made ignoring her impossible. If not for Sutton...

He nudged Sutton with his toe. "So did you catch sight of them yet?"

"Sure did. They checked in under the names of Fred and Ginger." Sutton grimaced. "I even know their bungalow and their weekend agenda. I think I can get surveillance on them right after dinner."

"Speaking of check-in," Rex said, "could you find our names and change them to Frank and Mia Sinatra?"

"I can so handle that," Sutton assured them. "Or how about Elvis and Priscilla just in case Frank and Mia are taken? Easily done. The receptionist owes me a favor."

"Already?" Rex exclaimed. "You've only been here a day. You do work fast!"

Sutton rolled her eyes and then winked at Viv. "He underestimates me all the time."

Viv spoke up. "So tell me how you'll do the surveillance, if you don't mind my asking. I'm interested. Are you staying in the bungalow next to them?"

"Nah. I'm not staying at Three Bunch. Commuting from home. I don't need to do anything so old-fashioned as skulking about. I have a drone for photos. It's loud, but I don't think they'll notice. Earbuds block out the sound, and everyone wears them now.

"And I slipped by early this morning to drop in my latest surveillance microphone. I've got everything they say on tape and can listen from an app on my phone. Pretty slick."

Rex sighed. "Enough details. I want a nap." He glared at Sutton, who stood up and asked, "So no drinks then?"

Viv rolled her head to the left. "Not for me." She turned to Rex. "Besides napping, what are we here for? It feels like Sutton has everything under control."

"Oh, she does," Rex admitted. "But I figured we could hang out and have a nice weekend while Sutton is on duty. She can report to us and we can do laps in the pool and soak in the hot springs. Dipping into that salty water, the palm trees swaying in the breeze. The night sky. There's nothing better.

"I don't mind the food either. All done for us. We can

sleep and chill out." He closed his eyes, hoping Viv would appreciate his plans.

"Salt water dries out my skin." She sounded a bit cross.

"Is that all you can say? Three Bunch is world-renowned. And it's all on me. So sit back and enjoy your firm pillow." Rex closed his eyes again, a smirk on his lips.

Peeking from the corner of his eye, he saw that Viv had closed her eyes. To his relief, she didn't ask any more questions.

"Well I'll leave you two then," Sutton announced. "Sure I can't get you a cocktail?"

When neither Rex nor Viv responded, Sutton lifted the curtains and slipped out, the fabric falling back into place. Rex watched Viv from the corner of his eye. She stared up to the canopy above, her arms crossed over her chest.

Women. You just can't please them.

Rex closed his eyes and drifted to sleep.

VIVIENNE ROSE

They were shown to their table, the waiter in the lead. Viv wore a shimmering off-white caftan that flowed around her body, dropping to her ankles, revealing manicured pink toenails and low-heeled sandals. Even she had to admit she'd attracted a glance or two from older men as they made their way to the floor-to-ceiling window that overlooked the steaming hot springs.

She felt proud of herself and her careful planning. Casual but elegant, knowing she'd managed to find the sweet spot for her age and body type. Not too fussy but definitely put together, as if she cared about her appearance as a mature woman. Viv hadn't felt this good since years ago, when she'd dressed to go to the theater with her former husband. A lot younger then, she'd dressed for him. But now she dressed for herself.

Seated, facing Rex, she unfolded her napkin with a slight smile. Basking in his admiring gaze, she glanced at the fairy lights surrounding the palm trees right outside their window. In no hurry, she casually picked up her menu.

Rex, already staring at selections, glanced over the top

of his menu to look at her. When she moved her head he ducked his, not wanting to be observed. Viv knew the glance. This time she did not start telling herself she was too old to be appreciated for how she looked. This time she knew that her glow made her feel confident, and that feeling was ageless.

The shift in her attitude began that afternoon. Instead of running with the feeling of inadequacy, comparing herself to the other women around the pool, she lingered on her discomfort without judgment. She made a note of everything she felt.

Maybe it was the hour spent by the pool or the dip in the hot springs when she felt a subtle shift in her attitude. The salt water and gentle current enveloping her body made her feel more alive than she had in years. Appreciating herself for once, she wanted the feeling to last. From that moment she paid close attention to her feelings, especially as she lay next to him in the cabana, her eyes closed.

Later in the afternoon she left Rex in the bungalow with a smile. "I'm going for a stroll," she told him. She laid out her evening outfit on the bed. Since her skin felt rough from the salt residue, she decided to take a shower.

Once in the bathroom she undressed, dropping her suit and cover-up on the floor. Instead of ignoring her nakedness, she paused to run her hand over her arms and body. A shiver trickled up her spine. Then a moment of gratitude filled her.

This body has accompanied me for nearly sixty years. Through thick and thin, it's been my companion. Instead of being critical, I want to be appreciative.

Rather than turn toward the mirror, she deliberately ignored her reflection. *I'm not doing that anymore, comparing my body to how I used to look or to a random woman at the pool.*

She lifted her hand to her lips and licked the back, the tangy taste of salt on the tip of her tongue. She walked to the shower, turning the knobs and testing the temperature of the water.

There were three shower heads. One on each wall, and the overhead one in the middle. Ducking under the spray, she rubbed her skin with a fresh bar of soap, lifting her hand to smell the scent. As she ran the soap over her body, washing off the salt, she thought back to Rex.

He probably knew how pampered she'd feel staying at Three Bunch. He'd spent many weekends there before. Presumably with lots of female company. Viv shuddered. She didn't want to think about that part. *Don't compare yourself*, she cautioned.

As she sat across from him at dinner, she was fully composed, having a wonderful time.

She closed her menu as he openly stared at her.

"Thinking about the food?" he asked.

"Not really." She looked outside. Steam rose up from the hot springs, glimmering in the decorative lights.

They waited for their main course; the room held the low hum of voices. A quick glance over the room assured Viv there were mostly couples, even though faces were diffi-cult to distinguish in the candlelight.

"Care for an olive?" Viv held up the small plate for Rex's inspection.

"No, thanks," he said, not removing his eyes from her face.

"So the food here is good?" She fidgeting with her napkin, avoiding his glance.

She knew her new awareness of herself would disappear once she stared into his mesmerizing eyes. She wanted to linger with herself a while longer.

"They have a famous chef on staff and serve fresh ingredients," he answered. "That's what people expect at Three Bunch. Everyone's willing to pay for the quality and service. Are you happy you came?"

"Very pleased," she said.

"And might I say you look intoxicating tonight?" His voice sounded husky with invitation.

"Yes you can," she assured him. She looked out the window, continuing to avoid his gaze.

Rex cleared his throat. "I have a surprise for this evening."

Viv's heart stopped. *Here it comes...*

"The Three Bunch Lounge booked us a table. A local crooner is performing at the bar."

She felt relieved. Her eyebrows raised. "Anyone I know?"

"That's the fun part. You do know him. Dean Marcella."

"The guy with the sneakers at Carmine's Fluff and Fold?" Viv said, intrigued.

"I thought you'd like that." He grinned. "Dean does side gigs in town. He's got a pretty good voice. Covers Sinatra tunes mostly. Doo be doo be doo," Rex sang in a low voice.

Viv grinned. "Shush. Someone will look over and recognize us." She ducked her face into her napkin.

"I was hoping we could sit in the back of the audience and not be noticed," he added.

At that moment the waiter arrived with their salad, giving Viv a chance to put her napkin back on her lap.

. . .

After dinner they walked to the lounge and were seated at the second table of the evening. Small tealight candles, along with strings of fairy lights, had been strategically placed around the room. Viv blinked, trying to see if she recognized anyone in the dim light. "This is very nice," she commented, realizing that "nice" hardly covered the intimate setting.

Seductive would be more like it.

Rex reached across the table to take her hand. "What?" he said, looking innocent. "We have to play the part of a couple, right? At least in public."

She didn't remove her hand. And to her satisfaction, she didn't feel overheated either. She leaned in closer to whisper. "Maybe we should leave. I don't think Pete and Beverly are here."

"It's hard to tell. Kinda dark and not everyone arrives ahead of time," he said.

At that moment a light shone toward the corner of the room, illuminating a platform that stood next to a grand piano. Viv was reminded of the instrument in the Nelsons' foyer—the piano with all the photos displayed on the closed lid.

Switching on a small light, the pianist sat down on the bench. He wore a tuxedo with tails. Hands poised over the keyboard, he began to play a familiar song. "Luck Be a Lady Tonight" rippled through the room. A jazz version, loose and open to interpretation. Viv tapped her toe.

A polite round of applause came at the last arpeggio. Then the spotlight focused on another man. He stood with his hand resting on the piano, and he was also wearing a tuxedo. Viv's eyes traveled to his shoes. "Is he wearing sneakers?" she whispered to Rex.

"We're not here to assess his footwear." Rex squeezed her hand.

She felt a tingle travel up her arm.

Viv slid her hand out from his, placing it in her lap. She knew she was being fickle. There was something about the suave Rex Redondo that made her want to resist. Even though only a day ago she was very hurt when she'd seen his suitcase packed with tools.

He brings out the contrary in me, she admitted to herself. Then her eyes caught sight of a familiar couple. A table with two chairs had been reserved for them close to the piano. Pete Langford stood behind a chair. Small in stature, the full head of hair—probably a toupee—was brushed back from his face.

Pete glanced over the room before helping his date be seated. Viv recognized Beverly Nelson, even in semi darkness. "Welcome to the Three Bunch Lounge," came the resonant voice of Dean Marcella. "I see we have a few regulars in the audience." His head dipped toward the table where Beverly and Peter sat.

Beverly gave a slight wave. She wore a white dress with fringe in three layers, looking like a flapper in the roaring twenties. Her hair had been combed in an updo.

"And for those of you who are new..." He grinned, his very white teeth sparkling in the spotlight. "I suggest that you order another round as soon as possible. The wait staff appreciates the tips!"

A ripple of laugher followed his remark. Then everyone grew silent. Dean drew the mic closer to his chin and began to sing in his deep baritone voice, "Fly me to the moon," as people clapped their approval.

. . .

Later that night, Viv closed the door to her bedroom. As she undressed, she thought about Rex and the evening. How he'd held her hand but not tried to kiss her, even when she'd made it clear she was sleeping alone.

"Thank you for the very pleasant evening. Who knew that private detective work would be so fun?" She'd emphasized the part about detective, hoping he'd realize it wasn't a date. Not exactly. Just an exotic locale. Where they investigated. Nothing more.

Sliding between the sheets, Viv realized that she'd only put off what she didn't want to face. At least not right now. That sometime soon she'd have to decide where her relationship with Rex would lead. And if she'd say yes to his offer and start a whole new life, become a business partner. Would the two be able to coexist?

Was she willing to have a brief fling at her age with someone who lived next door? Was she capable of having sex and keeping everything light? Or would she be the kind of woman who would get her feelings hurt and then have to awkwardly encounter him every day, living close by, when he'd moved on to other interests?

After some time Viv pushed away her concerns. *I need to sleep.* Semiconscious, she remembered the grand piano. The one at Carmine Nelson's wake.

Before Viv could recollect the significance, she fell asleep, her lips slightly parted.

REX REDONDO

Rex woke the next morning feeling a throb over his left temple. He'd had too much wine the night before. Partially to keep up the facade and partly because Viv made him lose focus.

She looked stunning in that dress. How am I keeping my hands off of her?

He didn't appreciate how silly he felt, or how he'd fallen hopelessly in love with his next-door neighbor. He'd been able to bed many younger women over the years with a quarter of the effort. But Viv, she was a challenge.

It was mostly because he cared. He just didn't want to overstep. *I don't want her to run back in her house and never speak to me again.* He realized, maybe for the first time in his adult life, that he'd gotten emotionally invested.

And those thoughts alone upset Rex. He'd not been that vulnerable for a long time. Maybe since forever, when he'd first started dating. Mary Lou What's-Her-Name in seventh grade. She'd made him feel this confused. When she dumped him for his best friend, he'd been humiliated and hurt. But not since then.

"Damn," he uttered to the empty bedroom. And then because he knew he had to stop thinking about Vivienne, he reached over for his cell phone. One message from Sutton caught his eye.

Got lots of surveillance conversations from the suspects.

[Let's talk in the cabana later?

I can come to your bungalow.

I'll shower and be ready.

Rex was making coffee when he heard a tap at their door. Sutton stood outside wearing her Three Bunch shirt. Her white sneakers looked as clean as the day before. He pointed to her Nikes.

"Are those shoes a part of the uniform they give every employee?"

"Yep, we get two sets of clothes. Even the shoes. Two pairs. Three Bunch is very particular about their footwear."

"Come on in. I have coffee."

Sutton walked through the front room toward the kitchen. She looked around. "No Viv?"

"She's sleeping in," Rex muttered.

"Did you sleep alone last night?" When he shrugged, Sutton's eyes opened wide. "Why you old scoundrel. She's keeping you at arm's length. The great Rex Redondo."

"That's true," he admitted, pouring coffee in her mug. "I am relegated to making the morning brew and licking my wounds. So what did you find out?" He gestured to a chair at the counter for her to sit.

"First of all, I'm pretty sure Pete and Beverly are a

couple. No overt flirting or anything, but they seem very familiar with each other. And then all they could talk about was Viv." She paused and then continued, "How she'd not reported in since they gave her the retainer."

"Were they mad?" He felt his stomach twist. "I mean, are they going to do anything about it, like track her down?"

"There was talk of that. Peter seems to think he can show up on her doorstep at her house and call her out."

"They did give her a whopping check," Rex admitted. "But I'm afraid they'll do more than demand the money back."

"Ten grand. They talked about that too. But mostly how Joey killed Carmine and no one, not even the cops, seemed to care."

"So what's that got to do with Viv?"

"They are depending on her to hand him over. I don't know what they want to do with Joey. That part is uncertain. But just so you know, they aren't happy with you either. In fact, Peter is furious, the way you used Beverly during the act. I believe I heard him use the words, 'phony mentalist with the fake teeth.'"

Rex tapped on his front teeth and grinned at Sutton. "Okay, so I've had some caps and gotten them straightened. And I do bleach. But I'm no more phony than everyone else around here." He nodded at her.

"I'll have you know these are my teeth. The ones my parents paid for," Sutton insisted. "I merely keep them clean and polished."

She put her empty cup on the counter. "I've gotta report in to work. I'm still serving cocktails by the infinity pool. I reserved a cabana for Elvis and Priscilla, so you two can come by any time."

She left Rex in the kitchen, closing the door with a click.

He emptied the rest of the coffee into his mug. From the other room he detected a squeak and then the drag of the front door against the tile.

"Did you forget something?" he called out.

When no one answered, Rex made his way around the corner. To his surprise, a man, facing the front door, was securing the dead bolt in place. He must have heard Rex, because he turned around quickly. "Stand over there," Joey Baker commanded, a revolver raised in the air. Nothing in his tone gave Rex the impression that he had a choice.

Before he could speak, the sight of a woman in a fluffy white bathrobe made his heart stop. He wanted to shout, to tell Viv to run the other way, but the words got caught in his throat. Fortunately Baker's back faced the hallway. Rex wasn't sure if Viv could see the small gun he held waist-high pointed right at him.

Viv stepped closer, her eyes looking past Joey to Rex. He didn't glance her way, hoping she'd realize he was in danger. She stopped in her tracks. Reaching inside her bathrobe, she pulled out a silver meat tenderizer, the kind found in a gourmet kitchen. With one swing, the mallet made a sickening thud against Baker's skull, followed by his body slowly crumpling to the floor.

Hair in disarray, her robe gaping open slightly, Viv held the mallet aloft. She waited for Baker to get up. When he didn't, she explained, "I took it with me last night. From the kitchen." A small drop of blood from the mallet dripped onto the floor.

Rex came closer. He bent down to have a better look at the unconscious man.

"I needed a weapon just in case someone broke in," Viv kept explaining. "In the middle of the night I kept thinking about Carmine. Discovering him between the sheets. I needed something for protection."

Rex put two fingers under Joey's ear. "Still has a pulse." He looked at the back of Joey's head. "Not much blood."

"It was self-defense," Viv explained.

"You protected me," he said, his voice unsteady. "With a meat tenderizer." He stood, taking in her stricken face. Then he pulled on his ear. "But now we'd better call the cops."

48

VIVIENNE ROSE

It wasn't until Viv stood outside waiting for the cops that her knees began to shake. Still in her fluffy white bathrobe, her bare toes curled up. Then she turned to Rex.

"That was quick, your call to the police." She nodded her approval.

His look of admiration made her smile. "You really walloped him. I had no idea you had that in you." A look of respect came over his face. Then the corner of his mouth quirked as if he found her amusing.

"Oh, I can defend myself quite well," Viv insisted.

"He had a gun on me, you know. Gave me second thoughts."

"Did your life flash before you, like they say it does when you're facing death?"

"As a matter of fact...yes." Rex nodded ruefully. "But I'm also wondering about the gun. It looked familiar. A revolver."

"You put it back in the box," she paused, "but then it appeared in Joey Baker's hand."

"He waved it my face, don't forget!" Rex sounded indignant. "In a threatening manner, no less." Before he could say more, sirens wailed in the distance.

"I think that may be the cops." A look of worry came over his face. "A good thing too. Joey's probably ready to wake up by now."

"Did you grab the revolver?" Viv asked anxiously.

"Got it right here." Rex patted his back pocket. "Makes me nervous. Despite my military service, I don't like guns much."

"Me neither," Viv admitted. "Though I can shoot one if I have to. My dad taught me when I was a kid."

For the second time that morning, admiration shone in his eyes. "You're quite the gal, Vivienne Rose," he said, slapping her on her back.

At that moment Susan Farrah rolled up in her police van. She exited on the driver's side, hurrying toward them. "Where's the body?" she demanded.

"Right in there." Rex gestured.

Farrah shouted over her shoulder. "Hurry up!" Her armed partner rushed past into the bungalow as Farrah pulled out her notepad.

Rex explained how the intruder had walked inside without an invitation and pulled out a gun while his back was turned. When he got to the part where Viv came down the hallway, he stopped. "She can tell you the rest."

"Go ahead, you can finish," Viv encouraged.

It didn't take another invitation. "And then Viv snuck up from behind; she came from the hallway. She had a mallet in her hand and she looked like a cavewoman in a fluffy bathrobe. Whack! She conked him right in the back of the head. He crumpled to the ground. The first thing I did was pick up the revolver. Here you go." Rex handed it to Farrah.

"Tampered with evidence," Farrah muttered, taking a plastic bag from her jacket pocket to drop the revolver inside.

Viv felt a moment of relief. *Now we won't be held responsible for finding the revolver in the locker. Farrah can do some tests and trace it back to Carmine. And then Joey will be her number one suspect. One less thing to get arrested for.*

"I wasn't going to leave it with him," Rex said indignantly. "He might have regained consciousness and come after us again."

Susan Farrah ignored his protests. She turned to Viv. "So tell me, why did you happen to have a meat mallet in your hand? As far as I know, they belong in the kitchen."

Viv looked at her feet, a blush coming up her neck. "I took it with me before going to bed," she said.

Farrah looked at Rex and then back to Viv. "Don't tell me. You two play caveman and cavewoman to, you know, spice up your love life?"

"Absolutely not!" Rex did not disguise the annoyance in his voice.

Farrah grinned, appearing to appreciate his denial.

Rex turned to Viv. "You explain to her."

Viv sighed. "Like I told him earlier, I grabbed the meat mallet from the kitchen in the middle of the night. Ever since I saw Carmine Nelson dead in bed, I've been a bit nervous, especially in unfamiliar surroundings."

As Farrah wrote on her notepad, Viv watched Rex's expression. She wondered if he doubted her explanation. *Maybe he thought I kept the mallet under my pillow in case he showed up in my room unannounced.*

"Where's the weapon?" Farrah asked.

Viv reached inside her robe and brought out the double-sided kitchen utensil. Drops of blood still clung to the metal spikes.

"I've been keeping it under my armpit," she explained. "Just in case."

Susan Farrah took out another plastic bag and slipped the mallet inside. "We can get a sample of the blood and see if he's in our database. A quick identifier."

"We already know who the guy is!" Rex exclaimed. "His name is Joey Baker. He's on the HOA. Ever heard of him?"

Farrah's face went white. Her hand flew to cover her mouth. She turned away from Rex as if to gather her composure.

"Do you know him?" Viv asked again.

When the officer didn't respond, Viv reached out to pat her shoulder. "Everything okay?"

Farrah shrugged off her hand, eventually turning to face them. "I'm fine. Didn't have breakfast yet. Feeling a bit woozy. So you're telling me that Joey Baker broke in and then held a gun on you." She wrote furiously in her notepad. "And that this is the revolver." She pointed to the plastic bag.

The door from the bungalow opened as the uniformed officer rushed outside. "I thought I had him. Read him his rights. And then I turned my back for just a second... He escaped. Pushed his way through the kitchen window and took off toward the golf course."

"Well don't just stand there, go get him," Farrah shouted. She turned to Viv and Rex. "I don't have time to talk to you right now. I'll give you a call later and you can come down to the station to sign the paperwork."

Bags of evidence in one hand, she bolted for the police van. With a screech of tires, the car pulled away from the curb.

Rex shook his head. "Okay then. Not your average morning. How are you feeling about now?"

Viv shrugged, but then admitted, "I've never been involved in anything like this before. I'm feeling terrified, if you must know the truth."

He agreed. "I hung out with some unsavory types in the military where people had weapons. But most of my time was spent in the IT tent. Sure, everyone had weapons, but no one ever pulled one on me."

They stared at each other. But then Rex broke in. "How about we unwind and sit by the pool. I'm starving. Maybe eggs Benedict?" She knew he was changing the subject to lighten the mood. And she appreciated him for it.

Viv glanced at her bathrobe. "Give me a few minutes."

He scratched his chin. "Are you sure that mallet was meant for intruders? I mean, when you explained to Farrah, I got a little self-conscious."

Viv looked him up and down. Then she smiled. "Oh please. You're a lightweight. Mallets are for dangerous criminals. Not mentalists."

Viv heard his laughter all the way into the bungalow.

49

REX REDONDO

Sutton poked her head between the curtains of the cabana. Rex lay on one side of the bed, Viv on the other, the space of a few inches in between. He held a detective novel open on his chest. It was so old the pages hung out the side.

"May I help you?" he asked. His voice implied that she interrupted.

Sutton stepped farther inside, the curtains falling behind her back. "Hey, boss, just wanted you to know I spotted another one of those HOA guys."

Viv opened her eyes. "Which one?" She'd been taking a nap. The busy morning had brought a good deal of confusion and fatigue.

"The African American guy. The one who's a pastor. The preacher guy." Sutton got a faraway look in her eye. Rex knew she was trying to imagine him standing at a lectern.

"Anyway, I looked up his background on the internet. I found lots of photos from his military days, so I knew who he was right away."

"Sammy Daniels," Rex said. "So he's here too."

Viv sat up, her round pillow dropping to the ground. "Okay, I caught most of that. Don't you think it's time for a quick review of everyone here at Three Bunch? We've got Carmine's widow and her boyfriend Pete Langford, also on the HOA. Then Joey Baker tries to hold us up at gunpoint. He's on the HOA."

Rex jumped in. "And don't forget the crooner, Dean Marcella. He's on the HOA."

"And now we have Sammy Daniels," Sutton said.

"So where exactly did you see him?" Rex asked.

"Well, boss. I'm so glad you asked. I was taking my break, flying my drone, minding my own business. Not exactly my own business, if we were to get technical about it. Anyway, I was listening in on the widow and the boyfriend, when Sammy stopped by their cabana."

"Was he dressed as a clergyman?" Viv asked. "I'd find that highly amusing, here at the spa. A man in a collar trying to convert more souls to Jesus."

"No, he had on the same white bathrobe as everyone else," Sutton said. "He was sporting some fancy flip-flops though. I want a pair of those. I checked on it. You can get them in the gift shop."

"Never mind that," Rex growled. "What did Sammy have to say?"

"That's the funny part. He was telling Beverly that he signed his wife up for a class. He wanted to know if she wanted to join. You know Three Bunch offers all kinds of instructional opportunities. The list is posted right outside the restaurant," she explained.

"I did see that," Viv admitted. "Which class? I was thinking of joining the stargazing one."

"Not the star one. He signed her up for the spirit animal class," Sutton said.

"People take classes on that?" Rex asked. "Isn't that considered not quite appropriate?"

"Not if the instruction comes from a genuine Native, it isn't," Sutton objected.

"Someone once told me, I won't mention names, that my spirit animal was a cat," Rex said thoughtfully. He remembered the woman as if it were yesterday. She was in her mid-twenties. A beautiful body and bright green eyes. Her hair, long and straight, falling around his face when they made love. She'd come to his shows and then slip backstage afterward. They'd dated for a couple of weeks back in the early 2000s. *She'd be in her forties by now.* Rex remembered everyone he'd been with from his past. But he never knew when they'd slip into his consciousness or why.

"How could that be?" Viv turned to him with a surprised look on her face. "You seem like a dog person to me. And Miss Kitty rarely pays you any attention."

"True," Rex admitted. "But that woman was an authority on spirit animals and she said mine was a cat, so there you have it." *She had a beautiful smile too. All I had to do was sit back. She'd initiate everything.*

Viv shook her head in disbelief. "Why don't you go to the class then. I'm sure the Native teacher will connect you with your real spirit animal. Which won't be a cat," she insisted.

Rex closed his eyes, still remembering. The woman never told him why she picked the cat. He didn't mind what animal she chose, just so long as it wasn't anything like a rat or a weasel.

Plus they'd ended on good terms. She hooked up with the head bouncer at the casino and that was that. The story of his life. Until he met Viv and realized not every woman threw herself at him.

By the time Sutton left, Viv closed her eyes again, leaving Rex to wonder. *Four out of five in the HOA hanging out here at Three Bunch for the weekend. Is it all about the me-time, getting facials and work done? Or is it possible that they come here for other reasons? The men sign up the wives for a class and then what...*

Rex settled his neck onto the round pillow and closed his eyes. An image arrived. Men sat around a round table. Each held a hand of cards. Women stood behind the men, scantily dressed in bikinis. Poker chips were stacked in front of each man.

There was another guy who stood at the door, his arms folded over his chest. He looked like a bar bouncer or a bodyguard. Rex inhaled, feeling his nerves tingle from the image.

It didn't take a mentalist to get the gist of that situation.

"The HOA men come to Three Bunch for a poker game. They ditch the wives and have at it. Probably high rollers and high stakes," he explained to Viv.

"What do you mean?" She swung her legs over the side of the daybed. He admired how athletic and toned they looked.

"Just like I said. I think the men are here for poker. That's why Sam hooked the wives up. It keeps them busy while they get down to business."

"I don't understand men," Viv admitted. "They come here for some relaxation and then hide in a back room, away from the beautiful setting and hot springs, to play a card game. Makes no sense to me." She stood up.

"I'm going for a swim," she announced. Pulling her cover-up over her head, she stepped into her flip-flops. Rex watched attentively. Then as she turned to face him, her face lit up. "You know something?" she asked him.

"Oh, I know lots of stuff," he said. "Like how that suit fits you so well. And the red looks great with the tan."

"Not that," she said stoutly. "I think we're doing the math wrong. We have the HOA guys all here. We added them up. But it's not good enough to keep adding. It's time to subtract. It's not who's here, but who isn't." She waited for Rex to catch on.

"Oh!" he said instantly. "Of course. I never thought of that. What about the HOA director, Frank Salucci?"

"That's right," Viv exclaimed. "Where is Frank in all of this?"

"Maybe he's just busy this weekend," Rex offered.

"Or maybe the other four don't like him that much. Maybe they cut him out of the game for some reason?" Viv suggested.

She picked up her towel. "Let's refocus. At the wake I overheard Salucci tell his wife that Joey killed Carmine. And we know that Beverly and Pete think Joey killed Carmine. I might dismiss Salucci's opinion if it weren't for the other two."

Rex looked thoughtful. "Maybe it's not Joey. Maybe Beverly and Pete wanted Carmine out of the way so they could go public with their relationship. They wanted Joey to take the fall."

Viv looked thoughtful. "So then once I brought Joey to them, they'd what? Get rid of him?"

"Think back. Did Salucci specifically say that Joey was the guy?" Rex asked.

"We were waiting in line to pay our last respects, but I think that's what he implied."

Rex cleared his throat. "Back to our first idea. Why is Frank Salucci the only HOA board member not here this weekend?"

50

―――――

REX REDONDO

"Pastor Daniels is ready to see you now," the church secretary said in a singsong voice. After Sutton was unable to get a meeting with Frank Salucci, Rex decided he'd do a work-around and get to him through Sammy Daniels. That's how he and Viv ended up back at church.

Handing Rex a stack of papers, the secretary added, "Here are the prenuptial guidelines of St. Bartholomew's. Pastor will guide you through the details and arrange three appointments prior to your ceremony."

Rex felt Viv's body stiffen. He turned to her. "Come along, darling, let's get this part done so that we can go shopping and pick out your dress." He took her by the elbow. Then he whispered in her ear, "You're the bride, remember. Act happy."

The door to the pastor's office opened, revealing Samuel Daniels. He wore an ecclesial collar with a black long-sleeve shirt. Light gray slacks emphasized his tall, slim build. "I remember you now," he said, beaming at them. "Come in and have a seat."

Rex and Viv sat in two chairs on one side of the expansive mahogany desk. A gold pen, next to a worn Bible, lay on the right-hand corner of the polished surface. Behind the desk was a credenza that held the customary photos. The largest was of a beautiful woman in her fifties and two teenage children, a boy and a girl. When Pastor Daniels seated himself, he held his hands like a steeple in front of his chest and smiled.

"I see you're ready to tie the knot," Daniels began the conversation.

Aware of Viv's eyes boring into the side of his face, Rex could barely refrain from laughing. He'd not explained earlier how he'd gotten the appointment with Daniels, just that he had one. *She must be surprised.*

It was Sutton who'd instructed him earlier on how to dress for a meeting with the pastor. "Okay, so I made the appointment for you and Viv at St. Bart's for this afternoon. I recommend that you wear clothes that look like you stepped off the golf course. Since Pastor Daniels golfs, you'll have an instant connection point with him."

Rex had yawned at the time, trying to recollect when exactly Sutton had become his clothing consultant among all the other things she was in charge of. "And Viv. What should she wear?"

"Whatever the hell she wants, Viv's a grownup. You, I'm not so sure of," muttered Sutton. Kevin chose that moment to leap on the bed and lick Rex's face.

But now that he sat in the pastor's study, he realized Sutton knew what she was doing. He hadn't anticipated feeling so disingenuous. Sitting here like this, a minister staring him down, reminded him of times in the past. *Like when I was a kid and the priest chewed me out for sampling the communion wine.* He shifted his legs, trying to get more comfortable. *The guilt makes me fidgety.* He only had to look down at his knee bouncing up and down to be convinced this wasn't the place he wanted to be.

Rex laid the paperwork on the desk. He cleared his throat. "Okay, so we're not here for prenuptial counseling." He observed Daniels's face carefully. *He's a good hider, that guy. Must be the collar.*

"Is that so," came the sonorous reply.

"We're here to talk to you about the Desert Tortoise Estates. We're all residents and you're on the HOA."

"We tried to get a meeting with the director, Frank Salucci," Viv explained.

"But he couldn't come to the phone," Rex added.

"According to the letterhead, you're the next in charge," Viv said.

"I'm the facilities coordinator," Daniels explained. "I work with Judy in the office. And then once a month we take a tour of the property, driving around the neighborhood, to see if neighbors are in compliance with the CC&Rs. That kind of thing."

Viv spoke. "So we have issues with the CC&Rs. But that's not why we want a meeting. I'd like to get a copy of the annual budget. For some reason that's not been sent out electronically or through the mail."

Sammy Daniels's jaw tightened.

Rex commented quietly, "I can see these questions bother you."

"Not at all," Daniels's voice boomed. The sheer volume of his response told Rex everything he wanted to know. *Gotcha.* Having achieved his purpose of throwing the pastor off guard, Rex knew the better part of valor was to make a quick exit.

He stood. "So if you could call Judy and tell her to send us the yearly report, we'd appreciate it."

"And then we can have a good long look." Viv stood too. "Another thing, if you could put a call in to Joey Baker, that would be great. He's the treasurer and I'm sure he can answer any questions we have after reading the report."

Pastor Daniels's face sagged. He gripped the side of the desk as he stood. "Joey is not available at the moment," he said. "He's on a cruise."

"How long will they be out of town?" Viv asked.

"I'm not sure. At least two weeks." Then he leaned closer, using a conspiratorial voice. "Joey may be in a spot of trouble. I'm only saying this because you're part of the estate community and I think you should know."

Rex took Viv's hand. "We've heard that Joey killed Carmine."

"I cannot confirm or deny, but you can put two and two together. He was the only one not at the HOA that night."

Rex inched Viv closer to the door. "Thanks for that information," he told Pastor Daniels on their way out.

Once inside the SUV, Viv spoke first. "He practically insisted Joey is hiding from the cops and that he murdered Carmine. You know, I'm not sure I believe him about the cruise. It's like a hunch."

"I like it when you have hunches," Rex said. "And I'm inclined to agree."

Viv sighed with exasperation. "So what did we learn from that charade?"

"It's a lot of paperwork to get married in a church?" he said with a grin.

"Besides that." Viv scowled.

Rex pulled the SUV into his driveway. "We learned that Sammy Daniels has confidentiality issues and that the HOA is hiding something. And that the board may just be a front for what they're hiding."

Viv shook her head. "Since Joey is the HOA accountant, he must be in way deep. Maybe he's skimming money off the top. You know, embezzling." She paused for a breath before continuing. "Maybe Carmine figured it out and tried to blackmail him. That's when Joey decided to kill Carmine."

Rex whistled. "Sounds plausible."

Viv opened the SUV door. "I'll see you later. I have some phone calls to follow up on. Plus we can't do anything until we get that report."

"See you soon." Rex waited for her to close the door before pulling into his garage.

"Bork," came a greeting from inside the house.

Rex opened the door to Kevin, who wriggled and wagged his tail.

51

VIVIENNE ROSE

With one yank, Viv pulled the comforter off of her bed. Convinced there was a connection between Carmine and Joey that went beyond the HOA, she'd decided to return to Carmine's Fluff and Fold. *There's something going on with that place besides laundry.* She dropped the comforter into a plastic basket and headed toward the garage.

At the laundromat, one glance told Viv that all three of the oversized washing machines were in use. But this time a young woman stood behind the counter folding sheets. Viv walked to the smart card machine. As predicted, her first card had gotten lost. She sighed when she saw an Out of Order paper pasted over the machine.

Viv walked to the counter. "Is there another way I can pay for a load?" she asked. The girl looked up from her folding, causing Viv to flinch. *I know her. She's the one who walks the baby in the neighborhood.*

"You live at the Desert Tortoise Estates," the girl said. "I've seen you walking with that silver-haired guy. The mentalist."

Viv did her best not to laugh. *Everybody knows Rex.*

Give a man a big smile and a stack of perfect gray hair and he becomes the immediate center of attention.

"That's us," Viv said. "And Kevin, Rex's dog," she added.

"So the silver fox owns the dog." She pushed the folded sheet aside to start on a pillowcase.

"How do I pay for a load of wash with the machine out of service?" Viv changed the subject.

"New management," the girl explained. "We only deal in cash now. You pay me. I start the washer. If you need the money, you can step across the street to the bank."

Viv looked out the plate glass storefront window to the building across the street. To her surprise there was a freshly painted sign over the door: D&M Savings and Loan. "Is that a new bank—a private one? I've never heard of it."

"Yep." The girl nodded. "Changed hands just this week." Her tone was clipped. "The guy who bought out the Fluff and Fold also owns the bank. There are branches up north." She pointed to the sign behind the counter: D&M Fluff and Fold. "Named after the owner."

"Not very original," Viv said dryly. "Naming a bank and a laundry with your own initials." She paused a moment to think. Remembering the list of members on the HOA letterhead, she made a connection. "Does that mean Dean Marcella owns both?"

"My uncle Deano," the girl said with a grin. "He got me this job." She folded another pillowcase. "Just step over and wait. I'll be there in a minute to get things going."

Viv walked away from the counter. *So now a guy on our HOA board of directors, aka the crooner at Three Bunch, has taken over Carmine's business. And if that isn't bad enough, he's opened a bank across the street. A private bank. That has to be a sign for something really bad going on.*

She stood in front of the washer, wondering what to do

with what she learned. *Maybe we're barking up the wrong tree. It's not Beverly or Pete or Joey. Maybe the real killer is the boozy Dean Marcella. His half-smashed persona aside, he owns his very own bank. And now a Fluff and Fold. Not bad for a guy who sells knockoff Nikes out of the back of his truck.*

Maybe he bumped off Carmine to get the business. Maybe the others are covering for him, trying to pin it on Joey Baker for their own reasons.

"I'll have to come back another time," Viv said, making an excuse to the girl behind the counter. "I just remembered I have an appointment."

Digging into the washing machine, she lifted her unwashed comforter. Then she turned to drop it inside the laundry basket. Instead of going across the street to the bank for more cash, she headed toward the car. Once there, she tossed the basket in the back seat of her Tesla, her mind still whirling. *I have to tell Rex.*

When she looked at her cell she found a text from him, sent five minutes earlier.

I need help

Where are you?

Pair-a-Dice. Blackjack table. Come quick.

On my way.

Viv quickly drove down Judy Garland Drive, past Barbara Streisand Way, directly into the casino parking lot. It was early, not yet four in the afternoon. She parked at the very back of the lot.

Once inside Pair-a-Dice, she hesitated, giving her eyes a chance to adjust to the semi darkness. *There he is!* She spotted his gray hair first. He stood at the blackjack table.

She walked toward him. A woman wearing a black sheath, cut very low on top and high up on her thigh, made Viv wary. Especially when she leaned into Rex, batting her eyelashes.

I thought this was an emergency! Her stomach tightened with irritation. Before she could spin around and leave the casino, a tinkling laugh wafting over the hubbub of other voices made her stop.

"Oh, Rex. You're such a devil. How about we go back to your place for a drink?" the woman said.

Viv knew her neighbor well enough by now to see that he was uncomfortable. Even she could see that he kept trying to inch away as the woman clung to his arm, tottering on her stiletto heels, bumping against his body suggestively.

Rex looked up and caught sight of Viv. The relief on his face made her smile. "Hey, honey. Thanks for picking me up. Come closer. I want you to meet Darcy." He shouted so that she could hear over the din of the casino.

Viv scowled. *I don't want to meet his casino floozy. I get it. Women like him.*

Rex nodded to the dealer. Then he put his arm around the woman's shoulder, guiding her toward Viv. Once they stood in front of her, Darcy barely glanced at Viv before returning her gaze to Rex's face. She ran her hand up his neck, her finger along the back of his collar. Then the finger snaked down his chest, where she poked at the pocket on the front of his shirt.

Rex's eyes were focused on Viv. "Honey, how about a drink before you go?" His voice pleaded and his neck had flushed red as Darcy's wandering hand traveled down his chest heading toward his belt.

Viv reconsidered. Maybe Rex really needed her help. She watched as he plucked the hand of the woman off of his belt, dropping it to her side. "Gotta go now, Darcy. The old ball and chain has come to take me away," he said.

Before Darcy could protest, he took Viv's arm, reestablishing his allegiance. Then he pulled Viv closer. "Thanks," he said in her ear as they walked away from Darcy toward the exit.

In the parking lot he continued to explain. "She was on me the minute I walked into the casino. I know most of the women who work the floor, but I didn't recognize her. I guess I looked like a ripe piece of fruit, a guy who would pay for her evening. I've been trying to say no for the past hour. That was a setup."

His earnest expression convinced Viv. *Honestly, I never thought of what it would be like for men to be sexually harassed.*

"No problem, happy to help," she told him.

Rex opened her car door. Sitting behind the wheel, she pointed to his pocket. "I think Darcy put something in there."

He reached in and pulled out a business card. A low whistle came from his lips. He turned the card over. "Now this I didn't expect. It seems Darcy was the messenger." He handed the card to Viv for her inspection.

She read aloud, "You're invited to Frank Salucci's house."

"Read the business name," he said.

"F&S Real Estate Development." *First D&M Bank and D&M Fluff and Fold, and now this? Does everyone have to have a business with their initials in the title?*

She turned the card over. A handwritten scrawl read: Tonight. Bring cash. Call me if you're in.

Viv handed the card back to Rex. "What does it mean exactly?"

"That our HOA director just invited me to his high-stakes poker game. I've heard about these invitations. Always in person. Never online because they don't want to be traced." Rex smiled.

"But you don't like gambling," Viv said.

"But I do like detecting. And that's what I'll do. I bet the rest of the HOA will be there, just like when they played at Three Bunch."

Viv was perplexed. "So is this high-roller behavior. I mean, they send an overzealous female to pick you out of a crowd and drop a number in your pocket? That seems so extreme."

"Maybe to you and me. But to Frank Salucci? Sending a potential hooker is his style. At least that's the rumor. He works deals under the table and behind the scenes."

"You sound convinced," Viv said.

"Salucci has his ways. Now I have an invite to the hottest poker game in town." He looked pleased with himself as he adjusted his shirt collar and slipped the card back in his pocket.

Viv didn't feel that pleased. All she felt was concern. She had confidence in Rex, but just watching him with that woman had shown her another side of his personality. Her neighbor was a bit shy when he wasn't in charge. The woman pushed him off balance. *He called me for help for a reason.*

And then that other incident, when Joey Baker had walked in because he forgot to lock the door. Rex didn't see it coming. All of this made her wonder. *Can Rex handle a high-stakes poker game with a bunch of men who most likely suspect he was nosing into their business?*

She leaned out her open window. "Why don't you come by after dinner. We can swim and talk this over. Plus I want to tell you what I found out today at the Fluff and Fold."

"I'll bring Kevin," he said and then turned away.

52

―――――――――

VIVIENNE ROSE

That evening as Viv swam laps in her pool, she had time to think. *Even I have trouble holding my own with a man who has so much charisma. I feel like a yo-yo, up one minute, down the next.*

After she'd gotten home and realized her feelings, she'd called Rex. "Just so you know, I am not your rescue squad," she told him firmly. "You don't have to let women cling to you like that. It's inappropriate and frankly beneath you."

Even her go-to, swimming laps, did not diminish her concern. And the realization that her annoyance with Rex wasn't nearly as intense as her annoyance with herself. It started with the girl at the laundry and her asking about him. And then when she'd seen that woman clinging to him at the casino, well she'd just had it. *I don't want to be his babysitter. He has to stick up for himself.*

Viv patted the pool water off of her face. Her eyes took in the cooler, which was filled with IPAs. Sutton and Rex were coming over later to talk about their investigation. She wanted to be prepared.

Sitting in her chair, she leaned back, stretching her legs in front of her body.

When Rex arrived, Viv offered him a beer with a smile. He sat down, took a swig, and then tucked the bottle under his chair. "So Sutton reminded me that Joey Baker gambles nearly every day of the week. The same time, late afternoon."

"That's what Beverly told me," Viv said.

His face looked grim. "I don't know if I believe Joey's on a cruise. So I did my own surveillance to see if he was hanging out at the blackjack table, and that's when Darcy found me."

"That explains it. You were looking for Joey?" Even Viv had to admit that sounded reasonable.

Rex nodded. "And then this evening before I came over, I called the number on the card from my pocket. The game is at ten o'clock tonight. I've got a couple more hours and then I'm heading over to Frank's house."

Viv felt her heart rise to her throat. "And where does Frank Salucci live exactly?"

"Two doors down on the left." He reached under his chair to retrieve his beer. Then he tipped his bottle toward her with a grin.

Viv couldn't believe her ears. "Do you mean to tell me that the big-time real estate investor and HOA president lives on our street?"

"Yep. Apparently he's got model number three. Like yours. Only I figure there's no catio on the back. I bet ol' Frank built himself a state-of-the-art poker room, no cameras or microphones. Clean swept and ready for action.

"And you know what else I figure?" He leaned toward her with a satisfied smirk on his face. "I figure Joey Baker may show up for the game. And then I can call the cops and get him arrested."

Viv sighed. "If the cops get Joey, I'll feel obligated to give the money back. That was the only stipulation, that the police would not be involved."

"That's true," Rex admitted. "I'd like you to keep the dough. But this poker game may be the only way to lure Baker out of hiding."

"Assuming he's not on a cruise," Viv added.

53

REX REDONDO

A burly six-foot giant patted Rex down, his hands moving under his armpits, then along his legs. Rex felt confident. *This poker game is gonna matter—it'll help solve the investigation.*

He knew he'd come to the right place because the guy, a bouncer or a bodyguard, looked exactly like the guy he'd seen in his inner vision at Three Bunch. "Having fun?" Rex asked. "Try my shoes. Just in case I have a knife."

"Don't tell me my job," the man muttered. Then he stood to his full height.

"You're a big guy. Work out?" Rex kept his voice deliberately playful to offset how nervous he felt. He also knew that once he got to know everyone in the room, he'd be able to do some mind shaping. Then he could ask questions and find out why everyone had it out for Joey Baker. In his way of thinking, Beverly and Pete were the most likely suspects.

"This way," the man muttered. He stepped back, waiting for Rex to walk in front of him. Down the hallway, Rex pursed his lips to whistle a few notes. *My bright and sunny demeanor will keep them off balance.*

"Sit there." The burly guy pointed to a chair in the hallway.

Rex complied, taking a moment to think about an earlier conversation. He'd spent an hour briefing with Sutton before arriving at the poker game. Though he knew that Viv was worried, Sutton had no concerns. "It's just another op," she'd told him, straightening his bow tie. "You sure you don't want a camera? I could tuck it right under this knot."

"Come on, you know they'll find it right away. The thug who does the pat downs. It would make his day and give me away, and most of all make my job a lot harder. I'm going in clean and sober and camera-free. No wires either," Rex added. "Have to use my wit and intelligence for this one."

Sutton rolled her eyes. "Will you be reading every player or just Frank?" She stepped away, so he turned to admire himself in the full-length mirror.

Rex ignored her question, mesmerized with his appearance. "What does that guy on TV say? The one who's the writer who's in love with a cop..." He grinned at his reflection. "*Castle*. That's it. Let me quote him: 'I really am ruggedly handsome.'"

"And you're not Nathan Fillion," Sutton muttered. "I saw him once at Just Desserts. He's even better in person. A lot younger too."

Rex knew it was best not to let Sutton know how nervous he felt. *I'm invited to a card game with a bunch of thugs. Not my usual gig.* Ever since the invitation he'd felt unsettled. But he'd made light of it so as not to alarm Viv. And now Sutton was getting all overly protective. *A camera? Please.*

Half an hour later he was out his front door. On the way down the sidewalk, he glanced toward Viv's front window. *I'd much rather be hanging out with her than playing poker with the desert mafia.* He'd started calling the HOA that in his own mind.

Half a block later he nearly collided with the woman with her baby stroller. She wore earbuds and a grim expression. He smiled and stopped. "Mind if I see your baby?" he said in a friendly voice. To his surprise, she shoved the stroller off the curb into the street.

"He's asleep," she told him.

"Maybe another time," he'd called after her, walking briskly away.

"Hey, Redondo." A voice now interrupted his thoughts. A woman greeted him. "Right on time. Come this way."

Rex stood with an ingratiating smile. "Hey there. I'm here for the game."

"I know," she said sharply. "Stop talking. Then hand over your phone. Then take a step to the right and hold out your arms."

He handed her his cell, submitting to the second pat down. She ran her hands over his chest and then under his armpits. Then she spread out her hands to run down his back, lingering at his belt. Kneeling to run her hands down both sides of his legs without a smile or a nod.

Finally the woman pulled a clear metal detector from her back pocket. She spent a very long time using it to circle his crotch. "Clear," she announced. Then she pointed to a chair. "Sit there for now." Once he was seated, she left him, finding her place behind the bar.

Across the expansive room, four familiar men sat around a large round table. Even without the HOA name signs, Rex knew he'd come to the right place. *HOA guys. Just like I thought. Frank, Sammy, Peter, and Dean.* But it was the three empty seats that drew his attention. *One for me and one for Joey; who gets the other one?* His heart quickened.

The men acted as if he wasn't in the room. They continued to talk among themselves.

"Good evening," he called toward the table. At first no one acknowledged him. But then Frank Salucci looked up.

"Come grab a seat at the table," Frank finally told him. "Glad you could come." His hand reached over his head as he snapped his fingers. "Bring him an IPA," he said. The woman who'd recently run the wand over his crotch pulled up a bottle and opened it. Rex stood to take the bottle from her hand.

"You know my brand." He stared at the familiar label with a black Labrador.

"It's my job to know everyone in this neighborhood," she said.

Salucci called from across the room, "Do you think I don't do my homework before I invite a guy to my table? Do you think I'm stupid?" Rex heard the defensiveness in his voice. He also knew he was being tested.

Rex took a small sip. He'd nurse that bottle all night. He didn't know how Salucci knew what he drank, but he wasn't exactly surprised. Not that hard to ask around, especially at the casino.

Rex loosened his shoulders to take on a nonchalant pose. He sauntered closer to the table.

Salucci glared. "I expect people to answer my questions when I ask them. Do you assume I'm stupid? That I wouldn't know you lived in this neighborhood? I recognized you right away when you and the dame came to the HOA meeting."

Rex realized that he was tap dancing around Salucci's trigger, at least one of them. Everyone was expected to respond to Frank with answers he wanted to hear, even if they had to lie.

Yet Rex also knew that Salucci would respect him more if he refused to be intimidated. So he shrugged and took another sip of beer.

Salucci jumped to his feet. Face red, eyes narrow, he growled under his breath. "What are you lookin' at?"

Rex glanced over his shoulder, expecting to feel a gun in the back of his head. He spoke calmly. "Actually I'm expecting that tall woman to show me her gun. And then point it right here." Rex grinned as he tapped the back of his head. "Not a bad way to go, if you know what I mean. She's very attractive."

Salucci's face turned redder.

"Come on, Frank," Rex coaxed, "that was pretty funny. You gotta admit. Lighten up or I'll think you're a real gangster."

With the woman behind him and the burly guy next to him, Rex smiled. He looked as if he didn't have a care in the world. Salucci tightened his lips into a thin angry line. Then he muttered, "Funny guy." The oversized bouncer took that as a cue. He came closer to hold out Salucci's chair.

Once Frank was settled, he addressed Rex. "Okay, smart guy. I'm done with the small talk. Take another sip and then let's you and me have a private conversation outside."

"I could use some fresh air." Rex stood.

Outside, Rex admired the backyard. The sound of water splashing into the spa caught his attention. The spa was big enough for a dozen people.

"You like it?" Salucci's voice sounded harsh, ominous and intense. "Maybe someday you could come over and have a dip with me and a few friends." He leaned closer to

Rex. "When you aren't playing footsie with your next-door neighbor."

"Not impossible." Rex used his most charming voice. He hoped the alarm would not show on his face. *So he knows we're friends.* Instead of stepping back, he leaned in. With a quick exhale of his breath, he shifted his fear into energy. *That's the stuff,* he said to himself.

A slow smile crept over Salucci's lips. "Like I said earlier, you're a funny guy. And that's why I'm gonna break one of my rules. Just for you. Give you a second chance, since you're mental and all."

"I'm a mentalist," Rex corrected him. "Very different than just being mental, though I'm probably that too, to be honest." He drew his face into a bland expression, watching Salucci's reaction.

"Ha-ha, I like that. A guy who doesn't take himself too seriously. Well let's just say, pretty boy, your act the other night—with Beverly—that impressed me. I heard about it; Pete told me everything. I don't know many who'd stand up to that woman. So now I want you to do something for me."

"Why would I do that?" Rex asked.

"Because you owe me," he said flatly.

54

REX REDONDO

"How do I owe you exactly? I hardly know you." Rex used his most certain voice.

"You owe me because you are still alive, fella. You realize that, right? You and your dame have been in my way ever since Carmine took the big sleep. I could have eliminated you both. Just for being at the wrong place at the wrong time."

So that's the criteria for killing someone...inconvenience. It wasn't our fault we showed up at the HOA meeting that night and that Carmine Nelson was found dead. Before he could point out Salucci's lack of logic, he stopped himself.

He didn't bother to explain, knowing that a big stakes poker player who was known to be a real estate mogul might not take kindly to any inconvenience. Plus there was Viv's safety to consider.

He cleared his throat. "Okay then, how can I make it even? That's what you want, right?"

Salucci looked him up and down. "My solution is simple. It's kind of a test. If you pass, you'll earn my respect.

If you don't, you're done. I'll drive you out of town and maybe keep your dame for fun. Get my drift?

"Incidentally, you'll never need a therapist so long as you pass my tests. I think everyone needs to be challenged to shape their character. Much better than paying a shrink."

He got close to Rex's face to add, "So this is your challenge, pretty boy. Find Joey Baker. Turn him in to the cops. When you drop him off, make sure they know you and you alone tracked him down. He'll be arrested and that's all you need to do. Got it?"

"I have a better idea." Rex smirked. "Let the cops find Joey on their own. That's why we pay them our hard-earned tax dollars."

Salucci growled. "If the cops could, they would have by now. Susan Farrah ain't as clever as she thinks she is." He leaned away from Rex with a faraway look in his eye. "She's like her mother. Beautiful but dumb. I knew her back in the day."

Rex felt relieved. "Don't worry. I'm on it. I will find Joey Baker and drop him off at the local police station." *But I do have one more question...* "Why is it that you want Joey Baker stitched up for this murder? Why not just let bygones be bygones?"

Salucci's face flushed red. "I didn't say you could ask questions. But so you know, loyalty is everything to me. My grandfather and my father did not tolerate snitches like Carmine or weak men like Joey Baker. Carmine's handled already and Joey's not worth my time. He has no follow-through and he's broken a commitment, a personal one he made to me. Let's just leave it at that."

The burly man popped his head out the door. "She's here," he announced.

"Good. Time to play cards. That's what you came for, right?" Salucci waved for Rex to go first.

Rex took his seat at the round table. A quick glance told him that one chair had been removed from the table. That left one empty, which had been pulled away, waiting for someone to be seated.

The bouncer stood behind the chair back, glancing at the ceiling. The door behind Rex opened.

"Ah, the lady's arrived," Frank Salucci announced.

55

VIVIENNE ROSE

Viv was restless. Lingering by the pool, she fluffed her hair with a towel, her mind drifting. Even the stars glimmering overhead didn't shift her mood.

With Rex at the poker game, she knew she had an unfinished job of her own. To report to Beverly Nelson and give the money back before the cops arrested Joey. She was no longer concerned about the cash. Ever since Baker had threatened Rex with the revolver, she'd lost interest in helping the widow. *Just too dangerous.*

Viv showered and put on a comfy pair of wide-legged pants. Selecting an equally soft sweater, she pulled it over her head, disregarding her bra with a sigh of relief. She was ready for a quiet evening with Miss Kitty. Hopefully Rex would text her after the poker game.

Settled in on the sofa, she tried Beverly on her cell. No one picked up. Unwilling to leave a message, she felt even more agitated. "Miss Kitty?" Viv called. No sign of her feline friend.

Unable to cuddle with her cat and feeling anxious waiting for Rex to call, she decided to take a walk. Viv put on her athletic shoes and a light jacket. *Keep moving,* she reminded herself. Once outside, she took a deep breath.

Heading past Rex's house, Viv glanced over. *I hope he's okay.*

She kept walking. The sound of wheels rolling across pavement caught her attention. *It's the young woman from the Fluff and Fold.* Viv picked up her pace. *Kind of late to be out walking a baby. Maybe she's in some sort of trouble. I'll strike up a conversation, tell her I'm a doula, ask if she needs any help.*

The young woman wore earbuds. As Viv drew closer she heard the woman talking. "I'm coming. Stop nagging me. It'll only be twenty more minutes. Yeah, I got everything. With me, you idiot. Stop being so nervous. No one knows. You are such a jerk!"

The vehement one-sided conversation sent a chill up Viv's spine. *Maybe she's a victim of domestic abuse? That might explain why she walks so often with her baby.* Viv dropped back farther, her heart beating wildly.

The young woman began to jog, the stroller bumping along the pavement. By the time she turned the corner of Joshua Tree and Fairway, Viv lost sight of her.

Once she turned the corner, she pulled up short. The young woman had stopped in front of a house that Viv assumed was hers. "What do you want?"

Viv edged closer.

"I know you're following me," the young woman accused. "Is that why you came to the Fluff and Fold? This is harassment."

Viv froze in her spot, not daring to come closer. "I just

wanted to ask you about the baby," she said. "I'm a doula," she added, hoping that would explain her interest.

The woman's eyes narrowed. "Oh, I see. So that explains it. Come on over and check out my baby, satisfy your curiosity."

Despite feeling apprehension, Viv knew she'd trapped herself. *I can't run away now that she's offered.* So she stepped up the walkway toward the house, coming closer to the stroller. The young woman lifted the baby blanket that covered the bundle.

Viv looked in and gasped.

The front door swung open right as the young woman gave her a quick shove, pushing her through the doorway. Before she could call out, a man took her by the arm. "A nosy neighbor. Just what I need," he growled.

The woman rolled the carriage inside and slammed the door shut. But not before Viv's back met the wall with a thud.

She struggled to free her arm. "Let me go or I'll call the cops!"

She didn't use his name but recognized him instantly.

Joey Baker dropped her arm. But the young woman took over, twisting one hand then the other behind Viv's back. She turned Viv around to push her nose to the wall. "You had to butt in, didn't ya? You could have left everything alone but oh no, you just had to see the baby."

"What have you done with the child?" Viv demanded.

"Don't be stupid," the woman retorted. "There never was a baby. Couldn't you tell the crying was fake?" She turned to Joey Baker. "Hold her for a minute."

Once he'd taken Viv's wrists, the young woman shoved her cell phone in Viv's face. Pushing a button, the familiar wail of a child met her ears. "It's an app, dummy."

Viv struggled against Joey's grip. "Just let me go," she said. "I won't tell anyone. I promise."

"Tell anyone what?" Joey's lips came close to her ear.

As soon as the words left her lips, she regretted them. But instead of trying to lie her way out of the mistake, she stated in a clear voice, "That you're Joey Baker and that the cops are looking for you."

The young woman took Viv's hands. Tying them behind her back, she dragged her away from the wall and shoved her into a chair. "Sit there. Stop talking!"

Then the woman grasped the handle of the stroller. Reaching inside, she removed the blanket and a mattress, dropping them on the carpet.

Joey lifted a box from the carriage interior, grasping it in both hands. Then he disappeared with the box down the hall.

Obviously they'd been hiding something underneath the baby blankets and mattress. *Something's been stored inside. Something they don't want me to know about.*

Baker returned to the room empty-handed. Viv raised her chin, directly engaging him with a stare. He turned to his accomplice. "Did she see what's in the stroller?"

"She only got a glimpse," the woman assured him.

"I only got a glimpse," Viv repeated. "So let me go."

When they made no move to release her, Viv gulped. She wasn't sure how to get free. But then she remembered Rex. *What would he do in this situation?*

He'd put them off balance. He'd start asking them questions.

"So the other day, how did you get the gun, the one that killed Carmine?"

Joey Baker scowled. Clearly, he didn't like being confronted. That was obvious.

"It's my revolver. I was just keeping it in the casita locker," he sneered.

Viv almost believed his answer, if it weren't for how he shifted his eyes back and forth.

The young woman's jaw hardened. "Stop talking, you idiot."

"I'll talk when I want to," he retorted.

Viv hurtled another question. "Why did you kill Carmine anyway?"

Joey blurted, "The boss said Carmine was trying to get out of the business. He thought it was disloyal to just up and retire, leaving us hanging. So he told me that it was one of his tests, to make Carmine go away.

"I owed him," Joey exclaimed. "He'd lost his trust in me since..." He glared at Viv. "None of your business," he snapped.

"Like I said, you are an idiot," the woman jumped in. "You killed Carmine right in our own backyard."

"Hey, the boss told me to. But I did Carmine a solid. I made his death all nice. You gotta admit, I left him in a really fine bed, on one of those pricey mattresses, very expensive linens, all tidy and looking peaceful. Right between the sheets. Not a bad way to go."

For a moment Viv wondered if she was supposed to compliment Joey, tell him what a good job he'd done. He had that look of a child waiting to be affirmed. His eyes pleaded with her for, what, acceptance?

She shook her head. "If you admit you killed him, why not turn yourself in? Things would go easier that way. You could cut a deal with the cops."

"I can't do that!" Joey cried. "They'll have to find me first. There's not a cop on the force who would listen to me anyway. They have it in for me."

"And for good reason," the young woman blurted. "You burned that bridge, baby, a long time ago."

The two faced off, giving Viv a chance to consider her options. She could ask another question to keep the focus away from her. So far that had worked. They were fighting with each other. This might give her a chance to wiggle out of the tie on her wrists.

As voices rose, she yanked at the restraint. Despite the pain of the tie cutting into her skin, she kept tugging. When it didn't yield, she stretched her fingers to make her hand narrow. Pulling her thumb closer to her palm, she tugged again.

By now the couple were nose to nose. Joey continued to scream. "I can't believe this, Gina. You were supposed to protect me and look what you did. Led this woman right to our doorstep." He glanced over toward Viv. "What are we gonna do with her now?"

Viv froze. She held her wrists behind her back, hiding the hand she'd wrenched free.

"You are so stupid," Gina hissed. "Uncle D hired me to keep you busy. I thought you knew that. I wouldn't spend one extra minute with you otherwise. You are really boring, you know. Like snoozable dull. I can't wait to get out of here."

"I bought you those boots," he cried. "I'm a nice guy."

"Cheap pleather," she muttered. "And too small. Even the baby oil didn't help. I couldn't get my foot inside so I left them in the bathroom of the Fluff and Fold.

"You really think those boots worked as a peace offering? Come on. I like real stuff. Real diamonds, real leather, and real men!"

Gina shot a glance at Viv, who looked up at the ceiling.

Silence filled the room. When they didn't keep fighting, she grew anxious. *I need to distract them again.*

She scrambled in her mind for another question. Since Joey Baker outright admitted killing Carmine, she didn't need to go there. But Joey did say that someone else—the boss—told him what to do. Who was the boss exactly?

It could be anyone. Maybe Gina's Uncle D. After all, he hired his niece to keep track of Joey. That had to mean something.

When Joey reached into his pocket, Viv flinched. *He's just remembered that I'm a big liability. I'm probably next,* Viv realized. *I'll be the next body found between the sheets.*

She closed her eyes tightly, waiting for the pop of his gun.

When nothing happened, she opened one eye. Joey Baker's head had drooped to his chest. He'd let the hand with the revolver dangle by his side.

Gina snatched the gun from him. Then she swung her glance toward Viv, her eyes narrowed.

Viv sat up straight. "Does the boss tell you what to do as well?" Her question sounded desperate even to her. *Just keep her talking, that's your best hope.*

Gina gave her a disparaging look. Then she shrugged. "Not me. I don't answer to him. I'm just helping out my uncle. He told me that Joey needed a little supervision. So we've been hanging out, pretending to live in this old folks neighborhood. They'll move him very soon and I'll be done."

Joey muttered, "I know Mom has a plan. She always does."

"Stop it," Gina commanded. "Your mother doesn't hold a candle to the boss. Everyone knows that."

With both feet firmly planted in the carpet, Viv stood.

"You better sit back down if you know what's good for ya!" Gina pointed the revolver at her face.

Someone started pounding on the door. Viv gulped. But she remained standing.

"Open up. Police!" came a voice from outside.

"Looks like you'd better answer the door," Viv advised. She'd used her calmest doula voice to point out the obvious. But then she couldn't resist adding, "I think the jig is up."

56

REX REDONDO

Back at the poker game, all heads at the table turned toward the door. To Rex's surprise Beverly Nelson slid in, swaying her hips. To say she was a vision in pink was an understatement.

She wore a pink dress, very tight, with pink heels. A pink boa covered her shoulders, dropping to her thighs like a cloud of cotton candy. Big dangling earrings, made from feathers, brushed her shoulders. Her platinum-blonde hair, with a pink streak over her right eye, had been expertly curled to wave around her face. She smiled right at Rex.

"Hello, fellas," she said in a throaty voice.

Rex assumed that she'd made an effort to impersonate the old-time movie star Mae West. As the bodyguard held her chair, she sat down daintily. "Margarita, pink salt, double tequila," she purred.

"Right away, ma'am," the bodyguard said.

Looking over each man at the table individually, her eyes stopped on Rex. "We meet again." No longer purring, her voice held an edge. Looking away from him, she asked matter-of-factly, "Where are the cards?"

The bodyguard pulled a deck from his pocket and laid them on the table.

Beverly removed the cellophane with the flick of a manicured fingernail. Sliding the cards out from the box, she cast off the two jokers with a smirk. "Jokers are always men," she commented. And then she began to shuffle while Rex stared at her hands.

Mesmerized by the smooth action of her pink-tipped fingers, he blinked. *Oh no, I'm not falling for that trick.* He looked away, pausing to gather his thoughts. Being a conjurer himself, he knew that a repeated action, like pocket watches swinging and cards being shuffled, would attract anyone susceptible to being hypnotized.

Once disconnected, he returned his focus to Beverly. She made a bridge with the cards and then gently released, as each one fell into place. He exhaled, admiring her expertise. *Stop it*, he ordered himself. *Focus on something else.* He turned away again listening to the hum of the refrigerator to clear his mind.

A series of ideas pricked Rex's consciousness. *She's a professional. Probably worked the blackjack table. That's where Carmine must have met her.* He knew that assumption was intuition and that it may not be true. But he'd been right before.

"Caribbean stud, my deal. Here, Sammy, cut the cards," came her crisp instructions. "Cash ready, gentlemen," she directed. "Ten grand to start." Then she looked over at the woman standing behind the bar. "Chips, please."

Rex reached into his pocket for his money. Despite being searched twice, no one bothered to remove the bills.

"Here you go." Rex slapped the hundred-dollar bills on the table.

Beverly's eyebrows rose. "Ten grand even? How did you know how much to bring?"

Somehow he knew answering her would be the most important thing he'd do that evening. Everything rested on his reply. He'd been able to convince Salucci that he wasn't a threat. He'd even gotten Salucci to include him in the search for Joey Baker.

But Beverly Nelson...she was the one he had to look out for. Somehow he'd missed that during his performance. He'd taken her for a grieving widow; okay, maybe not so much a real grieving widow, but one who was trying to play the part.

But in the midst of conjuring up his stage trick, bringing the dead man's words to life, Rex now knew that he had missed something important. *The woman's confidence came from her control.* She knew what she was about and she was probably smarter than any of the men at the table. *Except for me, of course.*

In that moment he decided to ignore her question about the exact amount of money he brought to the table. Instead he smiled knowingly, playing the fly to her spider. *Come on, Beverly. I dare you to spin your web and gobble me up!*

Once she realized he wasn't going to answer, she gave a curt nod. She turned to Salucci. "Before we start, I want a word with Redondo," she told him.

To Rex's surprise, Frank didn't object. In fact, all the other men, as if attached at the hip, stood together. The bodyguard opened the door to the backyard as they headed outdoors one by one. The door closed, leaving Beverly Nelson staring across the poker table right at Rex.

"I don't know what Frank's been telling you about Joey Baker, but it's all a lie. He'd never kill Carmine. He doesn't have the guts. No stamina. I want you to find my son and bring him home to me. I'll double Frank's fee and raise you another ten grand if he's unharmed."

Rex used every ounce of his willpower not to show his surprise. Joey was Beverly's boy? *Why didn't I see that coming...*

His mind spun. Now he understood. *She hired Viv to find sonny boy and keep him away from Salucci's grasp. Beverly would then get Joey out of the country.*

Rex looked at the woman in pink with new respect. Of course, he couldn't imagine her as a mother. At least not the kind of mom that a boy could turn to when in trouble. But Beverly had done the next best thing and found Viv, her opposite in every way, to do the job of rescuing her offspring.

For Rex, all the cards were on the table. This connection explained everything. Why Beverly had hired Viv, for instance. Once he brought her Joey, Viv would be safe.

"I'd be happy to find your son," he told Beverly Nelson with a bright smile.

The look of relief that came over her face surprised him. *Maybe she does have a motherly heart beating somewhere underneath that pink plunging neckline and heaving cleavage.*

"Good. That's settled." For a moment her face softened. Then she ducked her chin behind the fan of cards she held in her hand.

To hide her emotions, Rex thought.

Once Beverly raised her head, her face had returned to normal. No more softness. Her eyes sparkled with anticipation. Then she hollered over her shoulder, "Come on, fellas. Get back in here and let's play cards."

57

VIVIENNE ROSE

Officer Susan Farrah leaned over her desk. "So now that you've made your phone call, tell me: how long have you known that Joey Baker was holed up around the corner?"

Viv couldn't help but notice that Officer Farrah looked terrible. As if she hadn't had any sleep for days. Of course Farrah's appearance was secondary to her other concerns. She'd been able to call Rex earlier. And then when she couldn't get hold of him, she called Sutton.

"I'm not under arrest," she'd explained. "Farrah wants my testimony." She'd disconnected still worried about Rex and his poker game.

Viv cleared her throat, refocusing on Farrah's question. "Oh, I just found out this evening." She rubbed her wrists in her lap. Tender to the touch, sore from being bound, she'd have to put ointment on them when she got home.

"And what exactly did Baker tell you?" Farrah took out her notepad.

"That he'd killed Carmine Nelson and left him between the sheets."

"And what about Gina—did she admit to anything?"

Her grim expression only emphasized the dark circles under her eyes. Farrah nervously twisted her pencil between her thumb and forefinger.

"Only that there was no baby and that her uncle told her to watch out for Joey, keep him hidden." Viv thought for a moment. "And they don't seem to be getting along, I overheard them arguing on the phone and then they kept it up once they abducted me off the doorstep."

I was abducted. Me. A mere doula. A woman of a certain age. Who should be home contemplating her retirement hobbies.

Farrah's jaw tightened. She lowered her glance to write in her notepad.

Compassion welled in Viv's chest for the police officer.

"Is everything okay?" Viv finally asked, knowing full well it wasn't her place to interfere.

"Business as usual." Farrah brushed her off. "So let's make sure I have everything. Nothing was in the baby stroller. Is that your official testimony?"

"Well," Viv hesitated, "I'm just saying there was no baby. But there was something hidden underneath the blankets and the mattress. A box."

"Like what? A box of drugs, maybe?" Farrah's voice took on new interest.

"I never said that," Viv exclaimed. "But it would be possible."

The officer scribbled with her pencil in her notebook. "Okay then, anything else?"

"Gina mentioned something about her uncle."

"Did she now..."

"I didn't catch his name," Viv said.

"That would be Dean. Good old Uncle Dean Marcella." Farrah looked away for a moment.

Viv felt her pulse quicken. "Like the secretary of the Desert Tortoise Estate's HOA? That Uncle Dean?"

"Yep, that's him. He owns the house they were staying in. That's how we finally found them." Farrah looked away again. "I think Marcella was hiding Joey Baker for some reason we haven't figured out yet."

"Everyone on the HOA has to own property in the community," Viv said thoughtfully. "That may explain why no one objected to Gina and her pretend baby. She looked like a young relative of a resident. She's too young to live here, but she passed as a family member." Viv looked thoughtful.

"Not just passed. As Marcella's niece, she qualified," Farrah insisted. "That's the way with these close-knit crime families."

"Like the mob kind of family?" Viv asked.

"That's right. They're everywhere. Loyalty is their motto first and foremost. They don't mind asking the kids to do the dirty work either, so long as no one blabs." Her voice sounded weary.

"But now we've got real evidence. A firsthand testimony." Officer Farrah shared a brief smile with Viv. Then she closed her notebook with a sigh. "After this you might have to hire private security for your own protection. We don't have enough staff to pull someone from our force for very long. I can send some muscle to your house for a few days. A guy I know. At least until we've finished with the official booking of Joey Baker and his accomplice."

Viv's heart dropped. *I don't want a bodyguard.* Rubbing the red marks on her wrists, the thought upset her.

Farrah tilted her chin for a moment to stare at the ceiling. Viv's eyes widened. *The familiar curve of her jaw when she looks up... Oh no!*

58

REX REDONDO

Rex left the poker game two thousand in the hole but feeling quite good about himself. He'd managed to disarm both Frank and Beverly, while bringing light to the inner turmoil circling the Joey Baker case. He'd done that by keeping his cards close to his chest; not losing, not winning. And during the game he'd managed to keep his focus on the people around the table.

Rex's intuition told him that Frank and Beverly were former lovers. Most likely in the distant past. They held that kind of animosity that people did when they'd run hot and cold and then called the whole thing off. Yet they still played poker together.

And they both had a real concern for Joey Baker. Except that Frank and Beverly had opposite opinions about how to handle the situation. Frank wanted Joey arrested and sent to jail, while Beverly wanted her son to get out of the country. Somewhere the US couldn't get him. Maybe an exotic locale off of Cuba or even Venezuela. *I hope Joey speaks Spanish.*

No matter how challenging, living away was not as

confining as a jail cell. Rex felt a deep sense of pride, having figured out all of this. He couldn't wait to tell Viv.

On the walk home he looked up at the moon and began to whistle. Then he sang "Fly Me to the Moon," feeling happy with himself and what he'd learned. It wouldn't be hard to find Joey and deliver him to Beverly. *Case number two nearly in the bag.* Then he tugged on his ear for good luck.

The truth was that Beverly scared him more than Frank. She had a certain cat-like quality, an indifference, that made Rex nervous. He knew he couldn't charm her the way he did most women. *Maybe that's why I decided not to turn her boy in to the police, but aid and abet her plan. Scary woman. Just sayin'.*

Unlike Viv, who was impervious to him for different reasons, Beverly was cold. Nothing seemed to bother her, except if something happened to Joey. And then look out. She'd be dangerous, like a tiger protecting her young. One swat with the paw and it would be all over.

Rex slowed his pace. He thought back to his previous conjectures with Viv. Was it her idea that Beverly and Pete were a couple? Okay, Viv may have jumped to conclusions. Of course it looked that way and she was pretty intuitive. It was her kindness that disarmed people.

Probably comes from bringing all those babies into the world.

By the time he reached home, he was surprised to find Sutton standing in the open doorway. She was dressed in her undercover surveillance outfit—black T, black jeans, black shoes, and a black baseball cap pulled over her head.

"Where have you been?" she demanded.

"You know, at the poker game." His good mood slipped away.

"I've been trying to text you. Viv called my cell when she couldn't get a hold of you. She's been taken to the police station. She was abducted by Joey Baker and that woman with the stroller. Turns out that gal in the neighborhood was hiding Joey right under our noses."

Rex gasped. "Is Viv all right?"

"Come on." Sutton pulled on his arm. "I'm driving."

Sutton sped through a stop sign while Rex sat in the passenger seat, a stunned expression on his face.

"I can't believe Viv found Joey while I was playing poker."

"You had no way of knowing, boss," Sutton commented. "You didn't take your personal cell, remember?"

"I should have been there to protect her. She falls into situations without even trying. The funny part is Viv is so careful, but it happens anyway. She starts asking innocent questions, and that caring way she has, and then boom, she's in trouble."

"We're almost there. Can I change the subject for a second?"

"Go ahead, tell me."

"I've got another between the sheets story," Sutton explained.

"With a dead guy?" Rex asked incredulously.

"I'm talking about Google Sheets. You know, the kind they use for accounting. I've dug up some information that may shed light on the HOA."

"Keep talking," Rex said.

"Pete Langford does all of their taxes. He has numerous accounting sheets for each business. But they don't say much that matters. I did a deep dive, spent hours poring over the flash drive. That's where the real accounting is saved. Nothin' but holes, boss. More money coming in than going out."

"So Joey Baker—is he the number one scammer?"

"He's not the only one. It's bigger than him, boss. It seems that whole gang—Frank, Joey, Dean, Sammy, and Peter—are in this together."

"What do you mean 'in this?'"

"They've been laundering money through the Desert Tortoise homeowners' account, using lots and lots of cash."

Rex let out a long low whistle. "So that's why they stalled us when we asked for the books."

"I think they've been planning this for years. Once Desert Tortoise was built, they made sure to vote themselves on the board before anyone else could volunteer. Salucci's at the top of this heap." Sutton nodded.

"Not Beverly Nelson?" he asked.

She pulled into an empty parking space. "She may be involved behind the scenes. We're here. Let's go see what kind of trouble Viv's gotten herself into. I'm beginning to realize we can't take our eyes off of that woman for a second."

59

VIVIENNE ROSE

Alone in the interview room, Viv contemplated her situation. *A bodyguard...for me? That's a first. All because I got involved with a desert crime family. Damn you, Rex Redondo.*

Holding her hands in her lap, Viv's anger rose. *I don't deserve to be treated this way by a couple of youngsters who wave guns and kill people.* And then as suddenly as the anger erupted, Viv calmed again. *Don't forget, Viv,* she said to herself. *Susan Farrah thinks I helped capture a murderer.*

The door behind her opened. She looked over her shoulder. A tall, handsome man entered. He wore black jeans and a black polo shirt under a faded jean jacket. *Probably in his early fifties,* she assumed. *Nice brown eyes.*

"Are you the bodyguard?" she asked.

"Yes, ma'am," he replied smartly. "Officer Farrah said I'm to escort you back home. And then hang out for a couple of days to make sure you're safe."

To give him credit, he didn't seem to mind his assignment. He smiled at Viv and offered to shake her hand. "My name is Fernando Gutierrez."

Viv grasped his hand. "I'm not happy about this," she said. "But it's not you. I want that to be clear. It's the situation."

He let go of her hand politely and came closer. He pulled an extra chair from the corner to sit down, then leaned in. "What's making you so unhappy? Don't forget you helped the police catch a killer. That's a good thing."

"I was just telling myself that. But Officer Farrah assures me there will be repercussions and that I've messed with the mob, so to speak."

Before Fernando could respond, a commotion came from the other side of the closed door. Face impassive, he rose to his feet.

"We're here for Vivienne Rose," came Rex's strident voice.

"Try that door, boss," Sutton suggested.

Fernando pulled out his weapon. Holding it in one hand chest-high, he used his other hand to turn the knob.

Rex crashed into the room. "Who are you!"

Face-to-face, Fernando lowered his weapon. He shoved it in his belt. "You got the wrong door, buddy. Do I need to cuff you?"

"For what?" Rex's face turned red. "I'm here to pick up Vivienne Rose. Are you holding her hostage?"

Fernando reached up to grab Rex's arm, pulling him farther into the room. But before he could close the door, he caught sight of Sutton. "Hello," he said calmly. "How can I help you?"

"Let go of him right now." Sutton pointed to Rex.

"Why don't you come with him? I have chairs for both of you," suggested Viv's bodyguard.

He shoved Rex into the empty chair. "Sit there while I deal with the lady."

Rex looked relieved to see Viv. "What happened?" he asked.

She rolled her eyes.

As Sutton pulled out another chair, Officer Farrah showed up holding some papers. She glanced briefly at those assembled. "Joey Baker is now under arrest. Oh, and we also got his accomplice.

"Plus we searched the house where they were holed up and found valuable evidence stashed in the back room. Cash. I think we have a very good chance of bringing down the rest of this thieving family.

"Actually, I'm not even going to call it a family." Farrah shrugged. "They may be related, but they're not the kind of people anyone would want to pull a wishbone with at Thanksgiving dinner. Anyway, this woman here," she pointed to Viv, "is a crime-solving warrior."

Viv was shocked. It was one thing to tell her she had helped out, but Farrah was convinced that she'd actually been an asset in solving a crime.

Farrah kept talking. "This is the biggest bust in Palm Desert history."

Viv felt herself flush. *Okay, maybe I did do a good thing. A really good thing.*

Rex cleared his throat. "Does that mean I can take the crime-fighting warrior home? If she wants to leave, of course..." He smirked at Viv.

"I am tired," Viv admitted, standing. "Maybe I can come back tomorrow to finish up with any loose ends. Like the paperwork." She pointed to the stack Farrah had deposited on the table.

"Not quite yet you don't. I'll get you coffee. I can't afford to let you out of my sight. The family may find you, and let's just say you could disappear. So you need to stay put. I need you to sign the paperwork so that we can file with the court."

Viv turned to look at Fernando. He stood in the corner, his face expressionless as he surveyed the room.

Viv settled back in her chair. Then she turned to Rex. "Even though you've already met, I'd like to introduce you to my bodyguard. This is Fernando Gutierrez."

Fernando nodded, his eyes looking Rex up and down.

Rex's jaw dropped. "Is that really necessary? Sutton and I can take care of you."

Farrah pointed toward the door. "Gutierrez. You can wait in the break room for now."

Once the door was shut, Sutton spoke to Farrah. "I've got information on everyone on the HOA board that you might be interested in."

Then she turned to Viv with a look of admiration. "May I just say for the record that I totally underestimated you, Vivienne Rose. A doula. I mean, how can a woman who works with mothers and babies know anything about crime? But now I see who you are. And just so you know, you've got game!"

REX REDONDO

"Tell me everything." Farrah reached for her pad of paper.

"I found all the information between the sheets," Sutton began. "The accounting sheets, that is. It took some time, but I got there in the end."

"You unearthed illegal activity from the paperwork?" Farrah sounded doubtful.

"Not exactly. At first I found what wasn't in the paperwork. Like I was telling Rex earlier, I looked hard at the HOA accounts, where a load of money had been deposited, and then it disappeared without explanation. And then I realized what I was seeking was most likely a second set of accounting books. There were two. One for the residents, should they ask to see them. And the other real set of books for the guys behind the money."

"A false set of books. I see." Farrah scribbled. "I assume you're talking about money laundering. The HOA was involved?"

"You might already know. It's called layering. A not so uncommon way for criminals to launder their illegal funds.

When a big bundle of cash needs to disappear to avoid tax liability. Pretty clever, really. The money is sent through numerous transactions and various forms, so it's nearly impossible to trace.

"Rex and Viv led me down this path by requesting the HOA financials. Just to be clear, the HOA isn't where the proceeds ended up. Not by a long shot." Sutton paused to catch her breath. Then she started again.

"First someone invests in a cash-only real estate deal. It's not uncommon for deals to involve large amounts and even legitimate financial systems such as banks and mortgage companies."

"I'm very familiar with that process." Farrah turned to a fresh page in her notebook.

"I thought you might be. I don't have to explain all the details to you." Sutton paused to give Farrah a chance to agree.

Farrah's face paled. She fidgeted with her pencil. "No, you don't have to tell me." She sighed. "Frank Salucci. He's the guy. He's the head of the whole operation."

"That's what I figured," Sutton said. "So then Frank Salucci would collect the proceeds of a sale, paid for in cash. He'd take the cash and deposit it into a legit bank account. Or put it in a safe deposit box. That also works.

"Then Frank would start layering. He'd donate the cash to St. Barthomew's church. No one blinks when you donate to a church. Especially when it's put into an obscure but legitimate-sounding building fund. Like the consolidated repair initiative.

"Anything with 'initiative' is dubious in my opinion. At least that's what I've found. Anyway the St. Bart's account, on the second set of books, held millions of dollars. Then the money would disappear. It never showed up in the annual report for the congregation. So no one wondered. Like I was saying—separate books.

"But I followed the money, at least some of it. Didn't travel far. Went across the street to Carmine's Fluff and Fold. I suspect it arrived in shoeboxes. But I was unable to confirm that."

"The boxes off the truck!" Rex explained. "I knew something was dodgy when a well-heeled guy needed to sell sneakers like that. Just didn't add up."

Farrah mused, "A good cover. Who was that again?"

"The crooner, Dean Marcella," Sutton said.

Farah scribbled, then asked, "You say you don't have confirmation of that?"

"Not exactly." Sutton glowered. "But it doesn't take a genius to know he's the one. Plus he owns that private bank across the street from the laundry. He's just transferring the money from the bank to the Fluff and Fold. Another layering move."

"All of the money?"

"Not quite all," Sutton said. "Half of the cash flows to the Desert Tortoise HOA fund. Where Pete Langford makes up another fictitious account. Management and Maintenance, he calls it. Then he takes the money and hands it over to Joey Baker. The gambler in their little gang."

"We found a million stashed at the house where he was hiding." Farrah nodded. "I guess the baby carriage was an excellent cash delivery system."

Rex whistled long and low. Then he asked, "Joey laundered the dough for the organization. But why would he kill Carmine Nelson? That still puzzles me."

"To make the Fluff and Fold available for Dean Marcella. Maybe he wanted to cut out one of the middle men," Sutton suggested.

"Or maybe Carmine annoyed Joey somehow. They got into a squabble about some missing cash, something like that. So he ended up between the sheets," Rex added.

"Boss, you've been watching too many detective movies. Plus I didn't find any evidence of Carmine doing anything unusual. Unless he was scamming his pals and taking a lot of money off the top for himself. But let's get back to Joey. He's key to this operation.

"As you know, Joey plays poker. Nearly every day. He launders the dough by taking large amounts of cash and buying casino chips. He gambles a little and then cashes in the chips. The end result is that he walks in with dirty money and walks out with clean cash disguised as winnings."

"So he isn't there to scam old women." Viv spoke out for the first time. "That's just a cover for a cover."

Rex whistled again. "Talk about fluff and fold. That money's been cleaned and laundered and cleaned again. Layering." He shook his head. When Farrah said nothing, he focused on her. *For a cop she doesn't look too surprised, or what is it? What am I missing...*

He turned to Viv, wondering if she had the answer. The set of her mouth and the calm expression in her eyes convinced him. *She's not telling everything.* He turned his gaze back to Susan Farrah.

She opened a top desk drawer and popped a piece of candy in her mouth. *She's very nervous about something.*

"Very clean," Sutton started again, "the laundering scam."

"So where does the money end up?" Viv asked. "After it leaves the Fluff and Fold, and the church, and the HOA?"

"That's when Joey goes on vacation," Sutton explained. "To the Bahamas or Switzerland. Before he heads to the airport he deposits the cash in the bank under a fictitious name. They transfer the money to an off-shore account. And Joey hops on the plane. When he lands, he walks straight to the bank and makes sure the funds have arrived and are secure."

Farrah kept scribbling. She finally looked up. "So that explains a lot. We have enough to send information to the Financial Action Task Force." Farrah scratched her head. "For years we've been looking down the wrong rabbit hole, hoping to catch them on wire transfer charges. But they've always evaded us. You've got proof, right? Of all of this?" She nodded to Sutton. "You haven't told me where you got all this information."

"I've got proof," Sutton assured her. "I have Google Sheets on a flash drive."

Rex cleared his throat. "Well we found the drive in the hidden locker at the casita. I must have forgotten to tell you, what with the excitement of Joey Baker getting away from your cop."

Farrah glared at Rex. "That was unfortunate. But you interfered with the course of justice by not turning over the evidence."

"And you lost your main suspect. Let's call it even," Rex suggested.

When Farrah didn't disagree, Rex continued. "I know a lot about their motive, how they needed to launder money. But I'm still stuck on why Carmine Nelson? We're still at square one on that."

"Is he taking a fall for the team?" Viv looked carefully at Farrah.

The officer shrugged. She turned to Sutton. "Where's the drive?"

Sutton slipped her hand into her bra and took out the

small object. She wiped it with her sleeve and handed it over to Officer Farrah. "Here you go," she said nonchalantly. "I'm done with it."

Farrah's cell phone on the table began to vibrate. "Yes," she answered crisply. Rex heard a loud voice from where he sat. But he couldn't distinguish the words.

"I know. Got it." Farrah's voice grew more clipped as she ended the call.

She reached for the badge pinned to her shirt. Once unpinned, she held it in her hand to take with her. Her chin trembled. "It seems I've been summoned to the chief's office," she said. "So I'll let all of you go."

"Are you in some kind of trouble?" Rex felt shocked.

"I've been pulled off the case," she admitted. "So like I said, you can all go. We'll be in touch. Or someone will, most likely not me." She glanced longingly toward the badge.

Rex felt Farrah's turmoil. Something was very wrong. What was her connection to the case that she might be hiding?

Though his gut twisted and his mind whirled, he felt unsure how to interpret his response. And then the familiar cylinder of images turned behind his eyes.

The dial whirred around and around and then spun to a halt. A selection of images all in a row. Rex closed his eyes to see an old photograph. It was more distinct than the others. He saw the unmistakable image of Frank Salucci front and center.

Hair longer, touching his collar, Salucci bent toward a little girl wearing a cowboy costume, complete with hat and a toy gun clutched in her chubby fingers. Frank seemed to be speaking to her like a father or an uncle. Rex took longer to focus on the image, his eyes squeezed shut.

The little girl in the photo looked familiar. The tilt of her narrow chin.

Rex opened his eyes. He looked at Susan, who now stood at the open door ready to leave. Then he spoke.

"You're Frank Salucci's daughter. Is that why you're being taken off the case?"

"That's right." Farrah's voice sounded flat. "I'm his only child. So you've figured it out. That's why I've been between a rock and hard place for this entire investigation. For my whole life, if you must know."

61

VIVIENNE ROSE

Inside Viv's front door, Fernando made his way to the kitchen. He checked left, then right before inviting her into her own house. "Have to make sure it's safe," he explained.

"Have a seat." She gestured to the kitchen table. "I'll get a snack. It's been a very long morning." He sat down while she looked into her pantry.

"Looks like I've landed in a good place." Fernando eyed the mound of chocolate chip cookies she held.

"I baked them yesterday." She put the plate of cookies on the table and slid them closer to Fernando, who eyed them appreciatively. "Have a few and tell me, is looking after me a typical assignment for a bodyguard such as yourself?"

"Man, these are good." He smacked his lips appreciatively. "I'm thinking you aren't typical," he said.

Viv blushed. She'd taken an instant liking to Fernando. She felt an immediate connection.

She stifled a yawn. "I'm a bit tired. I was busy being abducted, held at gunpoint, and assisting the cops in arresting a killer." She paused to nod for emphasis. "And don't forget his accomplice," she added. "They got her too."

As he reached for another cookie, she continued, "So I think I'll need a shower and a nap. What about you? Do bodyguards hang out during the day or just show up at night? I don't know the protocol for this, so feel free to explain."

Before he could answer, his phone buzzed. He read the text, his lips forming a straight line. "Officer Farrah wants to know if she can come over and talk to you. Off the record, of course. She's on suspension. No longer assigned to the Joey Baker case."

"I see," Viv said. "Of course she can come over. How about for lunch. Do you want to join us?"

He shook his head. "Nah, that wouldn't be right. I'm on duty and she's on suspension and that would be a boundary issue."

"Okay then." *How refreshing.* Viv was used to Rex butting into her life at the least opportune time. She felt oddly relieved. "I understand about the importance of staying in your own business," she told him kindly.

"What about Rex Redondo?" Fernando slipped his phone into the back pocket of his tight-fitting jeans. "Tell me about him."

"To tell you the truth," Viv said, "my life has been turned upside down ever since I met Rex. He lives right next door. But now that this situation is solved, I think I may be back on track."

A series of meows came from the hallway. Viv stood and then circled back. "I can make up the bed in the catio or you are welcome to sleep on the sofa."

"Meow," Miss Kitty cried, even louder. When he hesitated, Viv said, "You can tell me later. I have a hungry cat to feed.

"I'm coming," she called out. "When you're done with the cookies, I'll introduce you."

Susan Farrah declined the tuna sandwich Viv offered. "I'm not that hungry," she admitted. Her face scrubbed clean of makeup, Farrah looked haggard. *But young,* Viv thought. *The cop uniform ages her.*

"Let's sit outside," Viv suggested.

Wearing aviator sunglasses, Susan sat, her back straight, in the outdoor chair usually occupied by Rex.

Viv sat next to her. She settled her hat on her head, her eyes looking toward the foothills.

"I know you're curious about my suspension," Susan began.

"I did find it odd. So sudden. You'd just gotten good information about a money laundering scam and then boom, you got that call."

"I'd been expecting it." She shrugged. "What you may not know is that I have a personal connection with the case. It's not a secret that I'm the offspring of Frank Salucci. At least my boss and the higher-ups know. They did a background check when I was hired. So they interviewed me and then gave me an extended period of probation to make sure I wasn't going to hand out special favors to my family."

"I saw your photo on Beverly Nelson's piano," Viv explained. "Is Farrah your married name?"

"My mother's name." The woman sighed. "But that's not the worst. There's another connection."

Susan took a deep breath to continue. "I confirmed with my

stepmother before I came over. She said I could tell you. When you wondered why Joey Baker would kill Carmine Nelson, I knew I couldn't dismiss the actual reason. But it's complicated.

"You see, my father hates Joey Baker. Despises him, in fact. It was only a matter of time before he exacted his revenge."

The hair on Viv's neck rose. "That sounds quite ominous."

"Oh, it's real all right. My dad is a very polished gangster, in this area at least. He has been for decades. He's also got a lot of strong feelings about family. Especially about loyalty and all that. He has sayings too. People think he's a regular family man. But that's deliberate on his part. He pretends to be a good guy, which covers up his true personality."

"Won't Frank be put in jail now that you have evidence?" Viv asked.

"Not a chance. He'll slide out from under just like he always does. His attorneys will tie this up in court. You just watch. And if they get close, he'll strike a deal. One where he goes free and gets some other sucker to pay the price."

Susan now sounded quite bitter. She'd obviously been disillusioned by her father for a long time.

"My dad used to tell me, 'I'm not upset that you lied to me. I'm upset that I can no longer believe you.' Now that makes sense, you know, especially when you're a kid. But the consequences when he stops trusting you... That's entirely different. Dangerous.

"For instance, he stopped trusting my first husband. Once I got custody of the kids and he left, my dad started to plot. I knew what he was capable of. I tried to warn my husband, but he insisted that his mother was from an even bigger crime family on the East Coast. And that she would handle my dad."

Viv felt goosebumps rise up her arms. Something was adding up here and she thought she had the answer already. "Joey Baker. He's your ex?"

"That's right," Farrah sighed.

"And his arrest?"

"Was all part of my dad's plan. He told Joey to get rid of Carmine, not because Carmine was skimming or dealing beneath the table. But because he considered him collateral damage. You saw how quickly Dean took over the Fluff and Fold.

"Carmine wasn't a blood relative of ours. He was Beverly's third husband, Joey's mother. Joey came from her first marriage to a guy named Buddy Baker.

"Kinda complicated but it explains the difference in last names. So back to my dad. To Frank, Carmine didn't count. He ordered Joey to kill him so that Joey would get arrested and spend the rest of his life in prison. Payback. For divorcing me."

The very idea of calling another human being collateral damage made Viv's blood run cold. "I find that despicable," she said firmly. "Am I to believe you are no longer part of the family?"

"And now you see why. Things worked out fairly well the past few years. I never saw Joey and I rarely heard from Dad. But now I'll most likely be dismissed."

Farrah looked down at her lap. "It seems I can't get away from Daddy, no matter how hard I try." She began to cry, sobs racking her chest. Viv reached over to put her arm around the woman's shoulders.

Dabbing at her face with the back of her shirt sleeve, Susan hiccupped. "It's just a bit much, you know. I'll have to move away and get another job. I have to find a school for the kids too."

"I wouldn't worry about that quite yet," Viv assured her. "Let me share another motto that doesn't come from a crime boss. It's not what people do, but what you do about it. We can get you through this. You aren't the first woman to be suspended."

Farrah sniffed. "My dad is diabolical."

"He's still the grandfather of your children. If you remember that, you'll make a quicker recovery. Blame, no matter how right you are, never helps. Just put all of your victim thoughts aside and take a deep breath. Starting now." Viv chuckled. "I wish I could have been there when you told your father you wanted to be a cop. That must have made him furious."

A slight smile came to Susan's lips. "He was insulted actually. I'd fraternized with his enemy. Nearly punishable by my own death, but he made an exception since I was his only daughter. I'm blood. You know what he said? 'I'm sorry you want to be a cop. You're wrong, of course. If you were right, I'd agree with you.'"

Viv smirked. "He's good with those sayings. But coming from his lips, they all sound sinister and a bit twisted."

Farrah turned to Viv. "I do feel a bit better. Less overwhelmed. I guess my biggest concern is having to pull the kids out of school."

"Not a certainty as of yet," Viv assured her. "Even if you have to relocate, don't forget children like to make new friends. A chance to reinvent themselves.

"If you start acting like change is bad, then your children will assume they have something to feel bad about. Maybe this cop job isn't what you need right now. Maybe you decided to be a cop just to spite your father. So this suspension can give you time to reconsider. Time to go back to school or talk to a counselor and change course. As for moving, that's up to you. You may want to keep an eye on your father and stay in Palm Desert. What's that saying about enemies..."

"Keep your friends close and your enemies closer. Ironically, it was even said by Michael Corleone in *The Godfather*."

"That's it!" Viv exclaimed.

"I'd like that sandwich now," Susan said.

"I've got lemonade and cookies for dessert," Viv said. "A comfort meal for a woman who requires a bit of tender loving care. Though not the easiest circumstances, you've got this. And I'm here to help."

62

———————————

REX REDONDO

Later that afternoon Rex shifted his glance away from Viv to admire the sparkling surface of the pool. Miss Kitty took the moment to pounce onto his lap. He let his fingers travel through the thick fur on her neck. She began to purr.

And then came the expected tickle in his nose, followed by a distinctive "bork" from the other side of the fence. Rex ignored Kevin's protest, turning his head to sneeze.

He scratched behind Miss Kitty's ears. Another purr rumbled from her chest as she leaned into his fingers. Rex had to admit he enjoyed the connection. She was harder to please than Kevin, so he felt a certain satisfaction that she'd offered him a purr. Plus Miss Kitty has a regal quality that he admired, not unlike Viv.

"Bork!"

Rex looked toward his yard. On the other side of the fence Kevin pawed at the boards. "Jealous much?" he called to the dog. Rex suspected that Kevin might be feeling left out. He glanced toward Viv, whose eyes were closed.

Miss Kitty hopped to the ground. Her tail waved in the

air as she sauntered toward the sound of Kevin's bark. His pawing stopped.

"Meow," she called, rubbing against the fence and then turning to rub her fur the other way.

Kevin yipped excitedly.

I know how he feels, Rex thought.

Viv began to speak. "So you actually see images roll up in your mind? That's how you knew Frank was Susan's father." Her eyes were still closed.

Turning away from watching Miss Kitty, he explained, "When I have, you know, the images, they are usually accompanied by a certain feeling, a sense of things. But I can have the image and the feelings and still not know what it's about. That part isn't always accurate." He thought about how, when he'd first seen the expensive sheets, his conclusion was that he'd be sleeping with Viv. *Look how that turned out.*

"I also saw Susan in an image," Viv said. "She was maybe three or so years old, wearing a cowboy costume. A man bent over as if he was talking to her."

He sat up. "What? You saw it too—in your mind—like a slot machine? Now that's really something." Rex leaned back in his chair, lowering his sunglasses from the top of his head to cover his eyes. Then he cleared his throat.

"Not like that. It was a photo."

"Oh that makes more sense. So let's change the subject. I have an invitation, if you will."

"What do you mean?" she asked.

Rex heard the door behind them slide open. He glanced over his shoulder and then groaned. Fernando Gutierrez stood with his arms folded over his chest. He could have been posing for a muscle man magazine, he looked so perfect and detached.

Rex gulped. "Does he have to hang out so close? He can hear our every word."

"That's his job." Viv smiled. "He's my bodyguard."

Rex did not feel amused. He'd seen the empty plate of cookies on the counter when he'd passed by to the pool. In his opinion, Viv had adjusted to this recent invasion of her privacy all too easily. It was as if Fernando already meant something to her.

"You can't bring him," Rex said stoutly.

"Bring him where?" Viv asked.

"On the cruise. That's what I'm proposing. I booked us a trip to Hawaii. For next week. A quick getaway. As a surprise. We'll sit on the beach and soak up the sun. Doesn't that sound nice? A good way to recuperate from this latest investigation, and I can keep an eye out, just in case people are following you."

When Viv didn't say anything, Rex's agitation grew. "Aren't you excited, you know, to take a trip, get away for a few days?"

"I get seasick," she said calmly.

He'd not thought of that.

"And I don't like buffet food," she added, her voice sounding firm. "Plus what about Miss Kitty; who will take care of her?"

Rex felt defeated. He'd hoped she'd be thrilled that a man, such as himself, had taken charge. He'd offered to escort her on a cruise, playing the role of every woman's dream companion. There were lots of females who would have jumped at the chance.

She could dress up and drink unlimited cocktails and get a manicure.

Viv tipped her bottle of water toward her lips. "Will my stateroom be next to yours?"

It can be, Rex thought. *Once I cancel the one room and book two instead.* He'd not thought that she'd prefer her own accommodations. But if that's what it took to get Vivienne Rose to go on a vacation with him, well then that's what he'd do.

"I've arranged for two deluxe staterooms." Okay, that was a lie, but only by omission. He'd reserve the second room right away, as soon as he could. Turning his lie into a reality.

Viv put her bottle under her chair. She stretched out her legs and rested her arms over her cover-up. He reached to take her hand. Gently touching the red marks on her wrist, he sighed.

"Don't you think you need a rest?"

She drew her sunglasses down to stare at him. "From you?" she teased.

He laughed. "Okay, I am bit much, I admit it."

"Just a bit?" She pushed the glasses back on her nose, leaving him to ponder her meaning.

His cell phone pinged. Followed by a text message on his screen: "Your voyage countdown has begun. Only ten more days until boarding. Sign on to our website to select your preferred dining options."

He lost no time. "I have to answer this," he told her, heading toward the house.

Once he'd finished booking the extra stateroom, he texted Sutton and his on-call doc with the boutique practice. The doc assured him he'd have the prescription delivered, Palm Desert style.

Brimming with goodwill, Rex pushed past Fernando. "Move, would ya?" he said. Then he sat next to Viv. "I've solved everything. You've got a stateroom with a balcony. I've arranged for Sutton to cat sit. My doc has a patch for seasickness. Very chic, worn right behind your ear. And I've booked us a table for dinner every night where waiters bring the food and there's no buffet in sight."

He leaned back in his chair, feeling very pleased with himself. A few texts and a website visit had removed all of Viv's misgivings. He began to hum an old Sinatra song, "The Best Is Yet to Come," under his breath. Until she spoke, making the last note catch in his throat.

"Don't forget Fernando. He'll need his own stateroom for the voyage."

NOTE FROM THE AUTHOR

One of the first reviews for *A Doula to Die For* made my day. The reader said in so many words, "I liked this book because it wasn't about a granny brigade. I'm so tired of those!"

Now don't get me wrong. I love reading about older women who surprise everyone by solving the crime. Just ask Miss Marple. She's on my shelf. And of course there's Jessica Fletcher, the world-traveling detective writer from Cabot Cove. Who happens to write mystery novels and teach a college class in forensics, even though she has no particular degree in criminal justice. But she does rock a business suit and a scarf, and she takes no prisoners to solve the crime.

From the beginning I never intended for Redondo and Rose to be the average sixty-something couple. I wanted to write about a midlife romance that involved people who did not necessarily focus on their family relationships alone. It was my hope to make their relationship sexy and interesting. One where opposites attract.

And to make the stories more intriguing, I put Redondo and Rose in a setting where people go to retire. Palm Desert, right outside Palm Springs, is the perfect place for a seasoned romance between two whip-smart individuals who think their lives are all settled until...they become neighbors.

Thank you so much for all of your feedback this past

year. And for reaching out to tell me your thoughts on the blooming relationship between Viv and her mentalist neighbor.

I can't thank Husband enough for his proof reading expertise and unending support of this writer's process. We do laugh a lot, especially when his character turns up in Rex in all the right ways.

Until then, don't forget, like Frank Sinatra's song, the best is yet to come.

ABOUT THE AUTHOR

Bonnie Hardy, a retired professional turned author, is celebrated for her two enthralling cozy mystery series. The first, set in the picturesque mountain town of Lily Rock, features amateur sleuth Olivia Greer, known for her uncanny ability to draw out confessions from the most unlikely people.

The second series, set in Palm Desert, features the mid-life duo mentalist Rex Redondo and his down to earth next door neighbor doula Vivienne Rose.

Inspired by Agatha Christie, Bonnie's captivating tales

of mystery and community masterfully blend fast-paced whodunits with clever sleuthing.

facebook.com/bonniehardywrites.com

instagram.com/bonniehardywrites

bookbub.com/authors/bonnie-hardy

goodreads.com/bonniehardy

GET A FREE SHORT STORY

Join my VIP newsletter to get the latest news along with contests, discounts, events, and giveaways! I'll also send you *Meadow's Hat*, a Lily Rock Mystery short story.

Sign up on bonniehardywrites.com/newsletter

READ ON FOR A SNEAK PEEK

Sight Unseen

Redondo and Rose Neighbors in Crime Book Three

Chapter One
Vivienne Rose

The cruise ship's horn blast made talking impossible. Viv turned to Rex. "Too loud," she mouthed. When the blast stopped assaulting her ears she yelled, "I hope that doesn't happen very often." She patted both hands over her ears as if to give them encouragement.

A slight smile came to his lips. "Not exactly the peaceful sail I promised," he admitted. Instantly his charm worked its magic, settling over her frayed nerves.

Rex kept speaking in his warm, soothing voice. "I know it wasn't your idea, but I hope you enjoy our cruise. Honolulu is low-key and exotic. The perfect destination port. Why don't we sign in?"

He pointed to a woman wearing a navy-blue blazer over a white shirt who sat behind the table, tapping her pen.

"I think she wants to have a look at your driver's license," Rex said.

Viv handed over her identification with a smile, her ears still ringing.

"Welcome to Aloha Cruise Lines. Is this your first excursion with us?" the brown-haired woman asked. Her bright blue eyes focused on Rex and then turned away.

Viv noted the stylized cruise pin with the wave logo on her jacket's lapel. *Allison Thompson, Information Technology Senior Manager* was printed on the badge.

When neither Viv nor Rex answered, Allison piped up. "*The Legend of the Sea* is our newest ship. We've heard nothing but rave reviews. Let me get you checked in right away." She glanced at her laptop and then frowned. "Unfortunately your luggage has been delayed, not yet transferred to your room."

Viv frowned at the news.

Undaunted, Allison stretched her smile over perfectly aligned white teeth. "Nothing to worry about though," she assured them. "It takes time to get all the luggage in the right hands when we have nearly two thousand passengers. Once we've brought the bags up to your stateroom, we'll send a text and provide a personal escort to take you to your rooms.

"In the meanwhile, you can sit on the well-appointed outdoor lido deck with a view of the sea and look over the Welcome Aboard packet from our captain. Familiarize yourself with all of our amenities. I see you've purchased the unlimited drinks package."

Finally Allison took a breath. Viv cast a glare in Rex's direction. "Unlimited drinks?" She leaned closer to whisper, "Planning on getting me tipsy and having your way with me?"

"The drinks were a part of the deal I got online. Kind of an all-inclusive thing." He kept his pleasant smile, but his eyes twinkled in Viv's direction.

For the first time, Allison paid attention. First to Viv, then to Rex. Her blue eyes widened and remained on Rex. Her cheeks flushed pink. "I wouldn't mind an all-drinks package with my boyfriend." Allison blinked seductively.

"I see," Viv said primly. *And I do see. Rex is irresistible. Women of all ages can't keep their eyes off of him. Must be such a burden*, she chuckled to herself.

As she slid her driver's license back into her purse, a man dressed in navy slacks and a crisp white shirt approached. His badge read *Customer Service Coordinator*. Underneath was his name: Robert Redford.

Viv pointed. "Any relation to the movie star?"

"No, ma'am," he said. "I'm asked that all the time. My parents thought the name would turn me into a Sundance Kid kind of guy. Didn't work of course. We lived in a high-rise apartment in West Manhattan." He smiled sheepishly. "I majored in hotel management at Cornell and I've never ridden a horse, let alone jumped off a mountain."

His lack of pretense made Viv feel better about her luggage.

Redford leaned closer to Allison. She didn't acknowledge his presence, staring at her computer.

"Allison, take the next guest, would you? I need to speak to Mr. Redondo." This time he poked her shoulder with his index finger, making sure she gave him eye contact.

Rex brushed his hand over his hair, looking slightly amused. "You know my name already? I guess I'm known far and wide." He sounded quite pleased with himself.

Skepticism came over Viv at first, followed by curiosity.

She'd agreed to Rex's cruise invitation recently. It was all his idea. For both of them to get away and get to know each other better. But now she wondered if Rex hadn't told her everything about the spontaneous trip.

She knew this wasn't his first cruise. He'd traveled all over the world with his mentalist act, aboard some very exotic ships. Her mind whirled. *What does Robert Redford want with Rex...* She began to speculate.

Maybe Rex is in trouble. A parking ticket in a foreign port; some indiscretion that caused alarm with the police...

"It's a pleasure to meet you." Redford moved around the table to shake Rex's hand. Viv stepped back to give them room. But not so much that she couldn't overhear their conversation.

"How can I be of help?" Rex asked.

Redford gave Viv a quick glance and then gestured with a sweep of his hand. "Ms. Rose may stand over here. She's fully checked in. This shouldn't take a minute."

Viv moved aside as directed, giving Rex a slight wave of her fingers.

Standing at the edge of the pier, she looked toward the cruise ship. *The Legend of the Sea* flag waved from a pole high above the top deck. She felt a shiver of excitement. *My first cruise. At my age. Will wonders never cease.*

Workers bustled onto the pier, loading bags on wheeled platforms. Passengers straggled toward the ramp as staff greeted them. To Viv's eyes the ship seemed enormous. *Like a floating apartment building, with all the windows and levels.*

One open-air deck caught her attention. *I bet that's the swimming pool and fancy spa and gym that Rex told me about.*

"Excuse me, Ms. Rose." Allison Thompson stood at her elbow. "I've been asked to escort you to the lido deck while you wait. Apparently Mr. Redondo is still talking to Mr. Redford. It will take a bit longer."

"Of course." Viv stepped back, following Allison to the ramp. The smell of salt air tinged with diesel fuel clung to her nose. A seagull squawked overhead. The hint of anticipation brought on a giddy excitement. *It's been a long time since I've felt this way.*

Allison left Viv sitting in a chair on the lido deck. "It won't be long," she assured her.

"I don't mind waiting," Viv said. "I love people watching." Once Allison left, Viv realized how lame that must have sounded. *No one's here to watch right now.*

The pool water shimmered aqua blue, smelling slightly of bromine. A filter in the pool gurgled. She was familiar with the stories of people catching illnesses on cruise ships. She felt relieved that everything looked and smelled so clean.

Sitting back to make herself more comfortable, Viv watched as the glass door slid open and a staff member stepped onto the deck. They began work behind an expansive bar. Polished glasses were set in rows, and napkins fanned out over the bar's surface.

Another employee arrived. He released a large cloth and began to wipe down the chairs and stools. Within moments the area was alive with more workers, leaving small vases of flowers and cutlery wrapped in cloth napkins.

Viv's gaze took in the steaming spa on the far end of the pool. Behind that there were more doors with signs that read *Massage, Nail Treatments,* and *Steam Bath.* Lifting her eyes toward the sky, she saw that the lido deck included three levels.

She blinked at the brightness of the sun. Her gaze drifted downward again to stifle a sneeze. She blinked and then looked back toward a long line of elliptical machines. On the upper level they could be seen through expansive glass windows. *The gym reminds me of New York. People exercising, looking down on the streets of Manhattan.* Only in this case the machines faced the pool area.

Only one man exercised on the elliptical. His hands braced on both handles of the machine as he pushed and pulled, bending his head down. Legs pumping, arms moving, he raised his head to look through the window. She felt as if he caught her staring.

She averted her eyes, but then something made her look back again. The man's arms began to flail, as if he'd suddenly lost his balance. Tumbling forward, his head bounced on the arm of the elliptical, his left temple heading straight toward the handle of the machine right next to him. *Bam*, it made contact with the metal, making Viv wince.

"Oh no!" she cried, jumping to her feet. She waited, watching as his body slumped to the floor. She waited another minute. When he didn't move, she felt the rise of panic. One glance told her that the staff had left. And there was no other passenger in view.

Reaching for her cell phone, she heard the glass doors swish open.

Two stewards pushed a cart filled with food through the doorway. "Help," Viv called. "A man has fallen."

The men didn't seem to understand what she was saying. One shook his head and said, "No English."

She pointed to the window and to the bank of ellipticals.

Then her arm dropped, embarrassment flushing her cheeks.

Without thinking, she started to explain about the man but abruptly stopped. In the brief moment it had taken to turn and ask for help, the body had vanished. Sight unseen.

ALSO BY BONNIE HARDY

Welcome to Lily Rock Holiday Mystery Series

'Tis the Season

All Aboard for Murder

Wrap it Up!

Lily Rock Mystery Series

Getaway Death *

Influenced to Death *

Deadly Admission *

A Thymely Death *

Deadbeat Dad *

A Very Tidy Death *

Redondo and Rose Neighbors in Crime

A Doula to Die For *

Between the Sheets *

Sight Unseen *

* Listen on Audible